Lightning Strike

Sherryl D. Hancock

VULPINE
PRESS

Copyright © Sherryl D. Hancock 2018

All rights reserved. No part of this publication may be reproduced, stored in or introduced into a retrieval system or transmitted in any form or by any means, electronic, mechanical, photocopying, recording or otherwise without prior written permission from the publisher.

This is a work of fiction. Names, characters, places and incidents are either the product of the author's imagination or are used fictitiously, and any resemblance to any person or persons, living or dead, events or locales is entirely coincidental.

Published by Vulpine Press in the United Kingdom in 2018

ISBN: 978-1-910780-90-9

Cover by Claire Wood

Cover photo credit: Tirzah D. Hancock

www.vulpine-press.com

To anyone, anywhere, who's looking for love and not finding it…
Let it find you. Lightning does strike when you least expect it!

Chapter 1

"I'm sorry, who wants what?" Remington said in a querulous voice.

John Machiavelli smiled wryly. "I know, I'm sure you've heard all about Wynter Kincade."

"I've *dealt* with Wynter Kincade," Remington said.

"Okay, so I'm sure you know how challenging she is then, but she specifically requested you."

"And what are my options for saying no?" Remington asked with a dour expression.

John grimaced dramatically. "Well, you can say no, but I can tell you that won't go over too well with BJ, and he's a pretty big client for us…"

"BJ Sparks," Remington clarified. "He's the one asking?"

"He's asking for Wynter, but she told him it was you or nobody, so…" John said, his voice trailing off as he gave her a pointed look.

"So, if I say no, you lose the contract," Remington stated.

"Pretty much," John said, nodding. "It does come with a fairly nice paycheck though."

"What are we talking?" Remington asked.

John scrawled out a figure and pushed the pad toward her. Remington's eyes widened at the large sum of money. She drew in a deep breath and blew it out slowly, nodding.

"So how long is the contract?" she asked then.

"Well, she's starting to wrap up her current album with BJ and then she's on tour for probably about eight to nine months and it's a 24/7 gig. But, Remi, this," John said, pointing to the figure he'd written down, "is per month."

Remington's mouth dropped open in shock. "Ou serye?" she asked, unintentionally switching to her native language of Haitian Creole.

"Sorry?" John asked looking confused.

Remington looked back at him for a long moment then rolled her eyes heavenward. "Sorry, that was Creole, I was asking if you were serious."

John chuckled, nodding. "Yes, I'm serious. Creole huh?" he asked then.

"Yeah, my family is part Haitian and they originally settled in Louisiana."

John nodded. "I see, and you speak Creole fluently?"

"Since I was a bebe," she said, smiling, her hazel eyes crinkling at the corners.

"Interesting," John said, "and you joined the marines?"

"Needed some time away from the farm, yes," Remington said.

"Farm?" John asked, leaning back in his chair, looking back at Remington.

"Horse farm," Remington said, "my family breeds them."

John nodded, ever shocked by this woman. He knew that she'd been in the marines, and that alone would qualify her for bodyguard work in his head, but she'd also been a world class Mixed Martial Arts fighter of some notoriety. Kashena Windwalker-Marshal, former bodyguard to the California Attorney General Midnight Chevalier, had recommended Remington highly to him and Joe Sinclair, his business partner. Joe was aware of Kashena's skills and background and felt that if she'd recommended Remington that was good enough for him. They'd hired the woman and put her through intensive classes for bodyguard work, including tactical training she hadn't really needed, evasive and defensive driving, as well as unarmed defense. Joe himself had put her through her paces on the weapons tactical portion and she'd impressed him with her abilities and speed. They both thought that Remington LaRoché was a great addition to their bodyguard detail.

"So, are you going to take this assignment?" John asked after a few long moments, holding his breath without realizing it.

Remington looked pensive, her eyes going back to the figure on the paper and then back up at John.

"How much will it cost me if I kill her myself?" Remington asked mildly, so mildly in fact that it took John a long moment to realize what she'd said.

John burst out laughing, shaking his head. "Just some jail time," he said, grinning.

Remington grinned, her hazel eyes sparkling wickedly.

"So you're the bodyguard?"

"I am," Remington responded, glancing at the slight bleach-blond young woman leaning indolently against the doorjamb of the bedroom Remington was unpacking in. She was watching with an appraising eye but Remington just continued to put away her things.

"So you're gonna be here like all the time?" the woman asked then.

Remington looked over at the woman, her look expressionless. "That's the contract," she replied simply.

"And you gotta be right next door here?" the woman asked then, gesturing behind her to the master suite.

Remington's eyes narrowed slightly, she was getting annoyed with this boi/child. She knew that this was Lauren Samms, Wynter's longtime girlfriend. Lauren had an androgynous look to her, part homeless waif, part baby butch with her spikey blond hair, pierced lip, and forearms covered in tattoos. Remington could see that she was trying to play the part of someone tough, but it didn't quite track with her rail thin body type and baby face. So far, she'd been nothing but annoying to Remington and the bodyguard was doing her best not to be rude, but it was becoming difficult.

She nodded in answer to the last question and turned her back to put things in the closet, hoping that Lauren would get the hint. She didn't.

"I'm not sure I like this whole set up," Lauren said authoritatively.

"Ede m ' bondye…" Remington muttered quietly. *Help me God.*

"What?" Lauren queried sharply.

"I am not the one to discuss your displeasure with," Remington told Lauren.

"What's that supposed to mean?" Lauren asked, becoming increasingly belligerent.

Remington turned from the closet, her look very calm. "It means go talk to your girlfriend."

With that Remington turned back to the closet effectively dismissing Lauren completely. Remington felt rather than saw Lauren debate pursuing the matter further. She waited, thinking that no amount of money was worth putting up with this child for. Finally, she heard Lauren walk away.

Not too much later Remington heard raised voices in the living room. She stepped over to the doorway and listened to ensure that things weren't going to escalate. Wynter and Lauren's fights were legendary in West Hollywood. Things had reportedly gotten physical on a couple of occasions. Remington didn't approve of a woman ever being hit, regardless if it was a man or another woman doing the hitting. She had no intention of allowing that in her presence whether she was Wynter's bodyguard or not.

She heard Wynter yell, "Just drop it, Lauren!"

Then there was a crash of glass. Remington strode into the living room to see Lauren standing with her back to her, facing Wynter, and a glass bottle on the floor between them. Wynter's blue eyes went immediately to Remington standing a foot from Lauren. She held up her hand in a halting gesture, even as Lauren whirled around to look at Remington challengingly.

"What the fuck?" Lauren snapped, looking up at Remington, her brown eyes flashing in annoyance.

Remington looked over at Wynter, her eyes obviously scanning for any damage to her charge.

"I'm fine, Remi," Wynter said, her tone placating.

Remington nodded, then let her eyes fall on Lauren, her look assessing.

"What?" Lauren snapped. "You got something to say?"

Remington just continued to look at the girl, her look unreadable. She saw the fleeting thought Lauren had of attempting to hit her and it caused a slight grin to curl one side of her lips and a gleam to come into her hazel eyes. Lauren saw the look and sucked in her breath, her hand curling into a fist. Remington's eyes flicked to it and then back up to Lauren's eyes, but still she said nothing.

Wynter moved to stop the confrontation she could see about to happen. She had no doubt that Remington could take Lauren apart with her pinky. Lauren just wasn't smart enough to get that yet. Lauren had no idea who Remington was and how dangerous the woman really was in a fight. Wynter had done her research on Remington LaRoché and she knew full well what Remington was capable of; she'd seen her in the fighting ring.

"Lauren, just stop, please?" Wynter said as she inserted herself between them, pointedly facing Lauren and putting her hands on her shoulders.

Wynter felt Lauren tense under her hands, and she narrowed her eyes at the other girl. "Trust me, you don't want to mess with her," Wynter told Lauren.

"She needs to remember whose house she's in," Lauren snapped, moving her head to look around Wynter over at Remington.

"She's here because I need her here," Wynter said. "I requested it, Lauren. This latest round of threats is getting nasty and I want to know that we're safe here. Okay?"

"I can keep you safe," Lauren said petulantly.

"Well, BJ wants me to have a professional, so…" Wynter said.

"Yeah, see?" Lauren said. "I don't get why you broke with your last label, they were good to you…"

"They wouldn't let me grow as an artist, Lauren, we already talked about this. BJ will."

"BJ this, BJ that, fuckin' A!" Lauren snapped again. "It's like you want to fuck him or something."

"He's an amazing musician, Lauren, and you know better than that, with me, come on…" Wynter said her tone cajoling.

"I don't like it," Lauren said, her tone accusatory.

"But it's my career," Wynter said, her tone stronger.

"But it's our lives!" Lauren exclaimed. "I don't get how you just make these decisions without me. Its total bullshit, Wynnie."

"I told you what I was doing," Wynter sighed. "Just because you didn't agree with it, doesn't mean you didn't know."

Remington turned and left the room, sensing that she was hearing more than she needed to.

Later, Wynter knocked softly on the doorjamb of Remington's room. She looked over to where Remington sat in a chair with her feet up on the ottoman reading a book. Remington looked up and stood as Wynter entered the room and set the book aside. Wynter moved to sit on the ottoman, and once she was seated, Remington sat back down.

"You always do that," Wynter commented.

"Do what?" Remington asked.

"Stand when I walk into the room," Wynter pointed out.

Remington nodded her head. "That's what I was raised to do," she said simply.

"Where were you raised?" Wynter asked. She couldn't believe there was such a place that raised people that way.

"Lexington, Kentucky," Remington said.

"Wow, and they raise kids there with these kinds of manners?" Wynter asked.

"My parents did. I can't speak for the entire state," Remington responded.

"Okay, so explain this to me, you were raised to stand when anyone walks into a room?" Wynter asked.

"When a lady enters the room," Remington corrected gently.

"And only ladies?" Wynter asked.

"And respected elders," Remington replied.

"What about Lauren?" Wynter asked her blue eyes sparkling with a challenge.

Remington didn't answer, merely pressing her lips together.

"No answer to that?" Wynter asked, grinning. "Is it because she's so androgynous? Or because you don't like her?"

"I was also taught that if you didn't have anything nice to say…" Remington said.

Wynter laughed at that. "Okay, so you don't like her."

"It's not imperative that I like her," Remington said.

"No, it's not," Wynter said, shaking her head. "I think she's threatened by you, and it's making her act worse than normal."

Remington merely nodded.

Wynter narrowed her eyes. "And you don't want to know why she's threatened by you?"

Once again, Remington didn't answer, her hazel eyes simply looking back into Wynter's evenly.

"Well, I'll tell you anyway," Wynter said, smiling. "She doesn't like anything about my new direction, and you're just part of that."

Remington nodded again.

Wynter looked back at her, shaking her head. "Man, you really don't talk much, do you?"

"I speak when there's something that needs to be said," Remington replied.

"Wow…" Wynter said, her ice blue eyes widening. "How old are you again?"

"I'm thirty-four."

Wynter shook her head. "Way too young to be so controlled and philosophical."

"With power comes responsibility," Remington said.

Wynter looked back at her for a long moment, and then nodded. "Meaning your strength?"

"Among other things," Remington said.

"Such as?" Wynter asked.

"Other abilities," Remington said.

Wynter rolled her eyes. "Not much for bragging, are you?"

Remington shook her head.

"You weren't even when you were fighting," Wynter said. "I mean the MMA stuff. I saw so many interviews with you before and after fights and you are always humble and modest."

If Remington was surprised that Wynter had researched her, it didn't show. She simply inclined her head in recognition of Wynter's comments.

"I have no idea what to make of you," Wynter said, her look a mixture of amusement and wonder. "In any case," she said, shaking her head, "I came to apologize for Lauren's behavior earlier."

Remington once again simply looked back at her, and finally inclined her head accepting the apology.

"I'll try to keep her in check, okay?" Wynter said. "I know you're not getting paid to deal with her antics."

"As long as her antics don't include physical violence, there shouldn't be a problem," Remington said placidly.

Wynter looked back at her bodyguard. "You mean that, don't you?"

"I do," Remington said, her face serious.

Wynter nodded, having thought that was likely the case. Someone like Remington LaRoché with her old-world manners wouldn't accept a woman being hit. She knew that many butches in the lesbian community were gallant, but Remington was different even from them. She had a whole other vibe. Wynter knew it was what had captured her attention, that and Remington's look. She had an extremely attractive, exotic look about her, with her beautiful face and high cheekbones, and her golden skin and light-colored eyes. Remington's hair was always in cornrows. The neat tight braids starting at the center of her head and dangled a foot down her back. They gave her a tough look. Add to that the physicality of her body, with well-muscled arms and trapezius muscles regularly on display in tank tops. From what she'd seen from videos of fights, the woman had some serious muscles, without being overly bulky.

Wynter knew that the lack of bulk was what led Lauren to foolishly think to challenge the former bantamweight fighter. She seriously needed to make sure Lauren watched one of Remington's fights where she moved like lightning, and the poor girl she was fighting couldn't begin to keep up. Remington was not one to be messed with physically. She had no idea what would happen if Lauren ever struck her in front of Remington. It wouldn't be a good situation. Then again, if Lauren was dumb enough to do that again, it might be good for her to get taken to task by someone as dangerous as Remington LaRoché.

Two weeks later Wynter stormed out of the studio, after throwing down her headphones and screaming at her backup band. A stoic Remington followed her out of the studio and through the double doors of the back area. Wynter lit a cigarette the minute she was out the doors. Remington followed suit and stood until Wynter finally sat down on the stairs. Remington took one step down and sat on the stair just below.

"Is it me, am I crazy?" Wynter asked sharply.

Remington looked back at her calmly and after a long moment she shook her head. "I don't know anything about making music."

"Okay, but you listen to music, right?" Wynter asked.

Remington inclined her head in confirmation.

"Okay, so what I'm trying to tell them about the sound I'm looking for… is that making any sense to you?" Wynter asked, her tone strident.

Remington shook her head, slowly, looking apologetic.

"Ugh!" Wynter exclaimed raising her chin in frustration.

Remington just sat, extending her long legs to the step below her, crossing her legs at the ankles, her eyes scanning the area. Wynter looked her over. She was wearing black slacks, a black tank top with a dark denim long sleeved shirt over it, and black leather zipper-style high tops. She spotted a silver ring with a very intricate design. She reached out and touched it, looking at it in fascination.

Remington looked up at her surprised, and then saw what Wynter was looking at.

"I love this ring," Wynter said, smiling, "but it's not a regular ring, is it?"

Remington shook her head. "It's made from an antique teaspoon, one of my great grandmother's."

"It's really cool," Wynter said touching the delicate design on the wide silver ring.

"Thank you," Remington said quietly.

"So back to this music thing," Wynter said, grinning. "What do you think of the song we're working on?"

Remington looked hesitant, then shook her head. "I'm no judge of music."

"Why not? You listen to music, I've heard it in the truck all the time."

Remington looked considering for a long moment, then shrugged. "I am no judge when at times I prefer the purr of an engine to music."

Wynter canted her head at Remington's statement. "That gives me an idea…" she said, and she pulled out her phone, clenching her cigarette between her teeth. "Okay… tell me… do you like this sound…" she said, playing a sound file on her phone. "Or this one?" she said, playing another sound. Both sounds were engine sounds, but very different from each other.

Remington nodded. "The second one," she said with certainty.

Wynter nodded excitedly. "Okay, okay, now… what about this one?"

Remington blinked a couple of times as her eyes narrowed in thought. "Can you play that one again?"

Wynter nodded, hitting play again on her phone.

"That one," Remington said.

Wynter smiled brightly. "Look at that, you just helped make some music," she said with a wink.

Remington pressed her lips together, the corners of her mouth turning up slightly.

"Careful, that was almost a smile," Wynter told her.

Remington blew her breath out through her nose. "I do smile."

"Really? When?" Wynter asked playfully. "Do you smile for the women you date?"

Remington gave her a slightly chiding look, but didn't respond to her.

"Oh, right," Wynter said, nodding, "you wouldn't dare talk about that would you? A gentleman never kisses and tells, right?"

Remington's look flickered, but she inclined her head in affirmation.

"So, who taught you these manners? Your mom or your dad?" Wynter asked.

"My father for the most part," Remington said. "My mother certainly had a hand in it, but my father was a bigger influence."

Wynter nodded. "Well, you can tell them for me that they did an excellent job."

Remington smiled slightly, lowering her eyes.

"You won't do that either, will you?" Wynter asked. "Because that would be bragging and you don't do that."

Remington didn't answer, she just looked back at Wynter.

"So, did you have brothers and sisters growing up?" Wynter asked.

"Two sisters," Remington replied.

"Older or younger? Or one of each?"

"Both younger," Remington replied.

"So you're the oldest… Hmm…" Wynter said, grinning.

Remington didn't respond, she merely nodded.

"Oh my fucking God, Remi, you are going to have to loosen up if we're going to become friends!" Wynter told her.

She caught the flicker in Remington's eyes when she said 'fucking' and canted her head.

"You don't like women to cuss do you?" she asked then.

Remington didn't answer. She just looked down at her lighter, her lips pursing and then flattening, and then going back to normal.

"Women shouldn't cuss, right?" Wynter asked. "Is that how you were raised?"

"Ladies shouldn't cuss," Remington said simply.

"Right so no woman should cuss," Wynter said.

"I said ladies," Remington stated gently.

"What's the difference?" Wynter asked.

Once again, Remington didn't answer, keeping her eyes on her lighter.

"You can't answer?" Wynter asked, narrowing her eyes. "Wait… you can't be insulting either, can you? To a lady?"

"Correct," Remington said.

"So you can't tell me that you don't like it when I cuss, because that would be insulting, but you can tell me that ladies shouldn't cuss," Wynter said.

"Correct," Remington said again.

"So what's the difference between a woman and a lady?" Wynter asked again.

Remington drew in a deep breath, then looked up at Wynter. "A lady is a station; a woman is a gender."

Wynter narrowed her eyes, a grin playing at her lips. "So you mean like a good old-fashioned lady?"

"I don't believe it to be old-fashioned to behave like a lady."

"You don't huh?" Wynter asked her look narrowed. "Should we all stay in the kitchen barefoot and pregnant too?" she asked snidely.

Remington looked back at her for a long moment, her chin raised slightly. It was obvious to Wynter that she'd just insulted her.

"Remi, I'm sorry," Wynter said, reaching out to touch Remington's hand. "I shouldn't have said that, I just… I'm sorry," she said again, shaking her head.

"I believe there's a vast difference between having respect for oneself and being a slave to a man," Remington said, her tone reflecting the tension in her face. "I would never suggest that a woman be beholden to a man, any man, ever."

"I know, I'm sorry, Remi, I really am…" Wynter said, her blue eyes begging Remington to forgive her.

Remington inclined her head but the tension was still palpable.

Wynter knew that any progress she'd just made with Remington had just been lost. She blew her breath out and stood up, and Remington did the same. As she looked up at the woman who was a full five inches taller than her, Wynter wondered if she'd ever stop making an ass out of herself in front of her. She walked back into the studio and Remington followed her as usual.

A week later, Wynter really got to see a different side of Remington. It was a Friday night and Remington had taken the night off. She was going to The Club to meet up with the rest of the group. Wynter was doing the same, dragging John Machiavelli along with her.

Remington looked especially good in black jeans, black leather boots with buckles and zippers as accents. She wore a white denim button up vest with a black tweed and leather sleeved jacket with a leather hood on it. Around her neck, she wore a gunmetal cable chain with a Hollywood Tribal pendent from the MMA collection called the

Phoenix that represented the "indestructible spirit." She also wore a watch that looked extremely expensive, so much so that Wynter had had to ask her about it and take a closer look.

"I got it from a promoter of one of my fights," Remington said offhandedly.

"Remi, this is a Patek Philippe…" Wynter said, looking at the intricately carved rectangular face and sides of the watch. "A very expensive looking Patek Philippe… I think this is incredibly rare, Remi."

"I like it," Remington said simply.

"Uh-huh," Wynter said, shaking her head.

She was looking on her phone. "Remi, you can't even get this anymore and it's worth like at least a half a million, if not more…" Her voice trailed off as she looked up at Remington, shaking her head again as she saw Remington's unimpressed look. "I know, I know, you like it," she said with a grin.

Remington left a few minutes later. Wynter watched as she drove away, still impressed by the 1967 black Pontiac GTO with a supercharged hood scoop and side exhaust. It was one of the most incredible cars she'd seen. Even when she herself drove a sapphire-blue 1967 Shelby Cobra.

Remington sat outside on the patio at The Club. She was smoking and drinking a beer, sitting in a back corner. Many women looked in her direction, though none of them approached her. She was an imposing sight to most. One woman who didn't have a problem approaching the former MMA fighter was Quinn Kavanaugh. Quinn walked out onto the patio looking left and right to locate Remington. She nodded when she saw her and walked over to where she sat. Remington held up her hand to Quinn who clasped her hand companionably as she moved to sit down next.

"How's it goin'?" Quinn asked.

Remington nodded. "Alright, you?"

"Good, good," Quinn said, nodding. "Xandy just got word about the tour BJ is putting together with your girl, mine, Jordan Tate, and Billy and the Kid."

Remington looked surprised. "Haven't heard anything like that."

"Maybe he hasn't approached Wynter yet," Quinn said, shrugging.

"Billy Montague?" Remington queried.

You didn't have to be around the music industry long to have heard about Billy Montague; the woman was legendary for her tantrums and hissy fits. She was a bodyguard's nightmare and, no one knew how her husband, Skyler, put up with her. Most had him pegged for a saint. It didn't bode well that Billy would be on the tour.

As Quinn and Remington talked, a woman ventured toward the two bodyguards. She was small, standing only about five four, with long golden-brown hair and green eyes. She wore a black dress that stopped high on her thighs, with colorful embroidery at the neck, and a lace up V-neck, with knee-high caramel suede boots. Standing with her hands clasped together uncertainly, she glanced repeatedly at the two women sitting in the corner.

Remington's eyes connected with the other woman's and she grinned, her eyes softening as she did. It seemed to be the encouragement the girl needed, and she walked toward them then. As she approached, Remington stood up, so Quinn did as well.

"Got me doin' it now, damnit!" Quinn muttered.

"Hi," the young woman said, looking directly at Remington as she did.

"Hello," Remington said, inclining her head respectfully.

"I'm Katrina," the young woman said with a soft smile.

"Nice to meet you, Katrina. I'm Remington, this is Quinn," she said, gesturing to the Irishwoman at her side.

"Hi," Katrina said to Quinn, then her eyes went back to Remington.

"I'm gonna go work on calming Xan down," Quinn said, winking at Remington. "I'll be back." She smiled at Katrina again. "Good to meet you," she told the girl as she touched her arm and walked back toward the patio door.

The girl glanced over her shoulder as Quinn went back inside, then looked back at Remington.

"I hope I didn't interrupt," she said, her look concerned.

"Not at all," Remington said. "Please…" she said gesturing to the chair Quinn had just vacated. She remained standing until Katrina had taken a seat.

"That's very gallant of you," Katrina said smiling.

"What is?" Remington asked.

"Standing until I sat down," Katrina said. "Where are you from?"

"Lexington, Kentucky," Remington said, smiling at the girl.

"So sort of the south…" Katrina said.

Remington smiled, inclining her head. "Yes, it's a much-contended location when it comes to the war of north and south."

"I guess you've heard all of that, huh?" Katrina said.

"For many years," Remington said, smiling, glancing up as the patio door opened again. Wynter stepped outside with John Machiavelli not far behind.

"Is that Wynter Kincade?" Katrina asked, sounding surprised.

"Yes," Remington said, her lips twitching as Wynter looked in her direction, her eyes widening noticeably.

Remington looked back at Katrina then. "Can I get you a drink?" she asked, as she held up her empty bottle.

"Sure," Katrina said, "white wine, please?"

"I'll be back shortly," she said, moving to stand and walking toward the outside bar.

She stopped to shake John's hand. "Sorry about this," she told him, glancing at Wynter, who grinned unrepentantly.

"Yeah, you owe me," John told her, clapping her on the shoulder. "Cassie assures me that hanging around lesbians doesn't make me one though," he said with a wink.

Remington laughed out loud. "She's right about that," she assured him.

She looked over at Wynter then, pointing at her. "You behave."

"Or what?" Wynter said, batting her ice blue eyes.

Remington narrowed her eyes and pursed her lips but didn't answer. Wynter only smiled widely at her. Remington shook her head and looked at John again.

"I apologize in advance for any trouble she causes you. I'll be here to back you up if she gets out of hand," she said, giving Wynter another narrowed look.

Then she headed for the bar and ordered another beer, a shot of bourbon, and a glass of white wine. As she walked back, she heard Wynter whistle lowly. She simply shook her head and kept walking. As she got back to where Katrina sat, she handed the girl the glass of wine and sat down.

"Thank you," Katrina said, smiling up at Remington. "Okay, what is that a shot of?"

"Bourbon," Remington told her. "It's actually from my hometown; it's called Town Branch."

"I see," Katrina said, smiling and nodding. "I've never had bourbon."

"I can get you one, if you'd like to try it," Remington said, smiling.

Katrina pressed her lips together pensively, looking like she wanted to say something, but wasn't sure she should.

"Did you want to taste it?" Remington asked, holding out the shot.

Katrina bit her lip, taking the shot glass. She took a sip and made a face.

Remington laughed softly. "It's not for everyone," she said as she took the shot back and drank it.

"I think I'll stick to my wimpy wine," Katrina said.

"Not a thing wrong with wine," Remington told her.

"So do you know Wynter Kincade?" Katrina asked then.

Remington considered her answer then nodded.

"And that man with her?" Katrina said.

"He's my boss," Remington said.

"Oh!" Katrina said, looking surprised. "Is this awkward?" She gestured to the bar in general.

"Not at all, he knows I'm gay, it's not a problem," Remington said.

"Okay, good," Katrina said. "Did I hear right that you're a famous fighter?"

"I don't know about famous, but the fighter part is accurate," Remington said modestly.

"I heard someone say you're like a batman weight champion?" Katrina said, stumbling over the last three terms.

Remington chuckled. "Bantamweight," she corrected gently. "It's the weight class I fought in."

"Oh," Katrina said, grimacing, "sorry."

"It's alright, it isn't exactly a normal term," Remington said amicably.

"Were you a champion though?" Katrina asked.

Remington hesitated then inclined her head. "Yes," she answered simply.

Katrina gave her a measured look. "Most women here would have been announcing that on the way into the bar, but I had to pry it out of you."

Remington didn't know what to say to that.

"If I Googled you right now, what would I see?" Katrina asked.

"I have no idea," Remington answered.

"Will you tell me your last name?" Katrina asked.

Remington gave her a closed mouth smile, looking a bit abashed. "LaRoché," she said.

Katrina nodded, picking up her phone and tapping out Remington's name. Her eyes widened at the results.

"Five-time bantamweight champion, not just a fighter, but an MMA fighter… overall the highest paid fighter of her time… You met the president?" Katrina asked, looking awed.

Remington smiled, nodding her head.

"Are these pictures… accurate?" Katrina asked, her eyes widening as she looked up at Remington.

"Which?" Remington asked.

Katrina turned her phone around showing Remington a picture of her from before her last fight. She wore a red and black sports bra, and black shorts.

"That was before my last fight," Remington said, nodding.

"Which was how long ago?" Katrina asked, her look pointed.

"About eight months ago," Remington said.

"So fairly accurate pictures," Katrina said, smiling as she bit her lip.

Remington looked quizzically back at Katrina.

Katrina laughed softly at Remington's look. "I'm just saying that you're hiding a fairly spectacular physique over there."

"Oh," Remington said, pressing her lips together, her eyes sparkling in embarrassment.

"That embarrasses you?" Katrina asked.

Remington shrugged. "It was my job to be in shape," she said simply.

"And what a shape it is…" Katrina murmured, her smile bemused. She looked at Remington. "Do you dance?"

"I…" Remington stammered, "not usually, no."

"Not even a slow song?" Katrina asked.

Remington looked back at Katrina, drawing a breath and blowing out slowly. "A lady asks you to dance, you dance…" she said, smiling at Katrina.

Fortunately for Remington, the song that came on was a slow one and she rose and took Katrina's hand to lead her to the dance floor. The song "Send My Love (To Your New Lover)" by Adele played. Remington took Katrina in her arms, putting one hand at her waist, and taking one of Katrina's hands into hers. Katrina put her other hand up on Remington's shoulder, smiling shyly up at her. Remington lowered her head, putting her cheek against Katrina's head. Katrina closed her eyes, enjoying the feeling of this extremely strong woman holding her so gently.

Wynter watched from where she sat. She'd been watching Remington the entire time, always curious about the ever-silent bodyguard. She'd been shocked when she'd seen Remington smile a number of times, even laughing a rich sound. Now, watching her dancing with the brunette, she felt a tug of jealousy. She knew it was stupid, but she felt like Remington never opened up to her the way she seemed to have with who Wynter assumed was a complete stranger. Knowing she was being completely ridiculous didn't make the feelings go away. Wynter ordered a double shot, drank it and then ordered another.

John Machiavelli sat behind and to the left of where Wynter sat, doing his best to be invisible. He could sense Wynter's tension and he could see that she was staring at Remington constantly. It hadn't been a surprise to him that she'd wanted to come to The Club. On the way in she'd been greeted by Xandy, Quinn, and a couple other members of the group. She'd made a beeline for the patio after looking around the bar, and once there she'd quickly located Remington and had made a dismissive comment about 'a groupie.' John wasn't sure what was going on, but he was sure that Wynter Kincade had a thing for her bodyguard and he wasn't sure how that was going to go.

Jet and Quinn walked out onto the patio, and Quinn walked directly over to the DJ. She smiled up at the girl, who promptly leaned down to talk to the red-haired Irishwoman. There was a quick conversation, ending with Quinn leaning up to kiss the woman on the cheek and giving her a wink. She glanced over at Jet then, nodding with a sly grin.

After the first slow song, surprisingly another played, another Adele song, "The River Lea." Quinn walked by Remington, patting her on the back companionably as she walked back over to Jet. Remington raised her head to glance suspiciously over at Quinn and Jet. She then glanced over at the DJ and got a wink. She knew then, that Quinn had arranged for a second slow song; it was Quinn's way of 'helping.' She shook her head, grinning, as she looked back down at Katrina.

"What?" Katrina asked.

"My friends are scheming," Remington said.

"Against you?" Katrina asked, smiling.

"They're just trying to help," Remington responded.

"Hmm," Katrina murmured, sliding her hand inside Remington's jacket and caressing her neck softly.

Remington looked back at her with a soft smile. She lowered her head, putting her lips against Katrina's temple, closing her eyes at the feel of Katrina's hand on her neck. When the song ended, their eyes met and Remington smiled, her hazel eyes almost gold at that point.

Katrina bit her lip. "Do you think you'll kiss me any time soon?" she asked shyly.

Remington pressed her lips together as her eyes sparkled with humor. She lowered her head and put her lips right next to Katrina's.

"I do believe I might…" she whispered, her lips brushing against Katrina's as she did. Then she kissed the girl softly, her lips strong but extremely gentle.

Katrina sighed against her lips, her hand at Remington's neck brushing back and forth across Remington's skin. When their lips parted, Remington stepped back and led her back to where they'd been sitting. She didn't see Wynter watching her. Katrina, however, caught the narrowed look in her ice blue eyes. She blinked a couple of times, shocked by it.

In the end, Remington and Katrina stayed outside talking until the bar closed. Remington offered to drive Katrina home and she accepted happily. She'd come with friends who'd long since left the bar. Katrina was surprised, but appreciative of Remington's car.

"It seems to fit you, pretty well," she told Remington.

"I think so," Remington agreed, smiling.

At Katrina's apartment, Remington got out of the car and walked around to the passenger's side, opening the door for Katrina and taking her hand to help her out. She then walked Katrina to her door. Katrina wanted more than anything to invite her inside but she sensed easily that Remington not only wouldn't accept, like most other women would, but it would likely put her off. That was the last thing she wanted to do.

"I had a really great time tonight," Katrina said, smiling up at Remington.

"I did as well," Remington said warmly. "Thank you for that."

"You have my number… I really hope you call me," she said, her voice slightly tremulous.

"I will call you," Remington said, "but you need to know that the work I do is pretty much twenty-four hours a day, seven days a week. This was a rare night off for me. So I can't promise how much time I will have like this."

"I understand," Katrina said, nodding. Remington had explained that she was a bodyguard and that her 'detail' was 24/7. "I'd be happy to spend any time with you that I can."

Remington lowered her eyes, smiling almost shyly.

"You are nothing like any woman I've ever met," Katrina said, looking up at Remington, her eyes softening as she noted Remington's look. The woman was far from egotistical and it was astounding.

"And that's a good thing?" Remington asked.

"It's a very good thing," Katrina assured her.

"Okay," Remington said. "Well, I better let you get inside."

"Okay," Katrina said, her eyes staring up into Remington's.

Remington lowered her head to kiss Katrina's lips softly, her hand reaching up to touch her gently under the chin. When their lips parted, Remington stepped back and waited while Katrina put the key in the door and unlocked it.

"Good night," Katrina said, as she stepped inside.

"Good night," Remington answered.

Later back at Wynter's house, Remington was stood in the kitchen eating a handful of almonds when Wynter walked in. She was still wearing what she'd been wearing at The Club: a low cut black halter top, faded hip hugger jeans, a leather biker style jacket, and high-heeled boots.

"Late night snack?" Wynter asked as she entered the kitchen.

Remington turned to look at her, nodding. "Yep," she said.

"Did you have fun?" Wynter asked. Her tone held an edge, and Remington could tell she'd been drinking.

"I did," Remington said simply.

"You're home awfully quickly to have slept with her, or are you that fast?" Wynter asked, her tone almost malicious.

"Fè jalouzi…" Remington muttered under her breath. *Jealous.*

"What?" Wynter snapped, knowing that Remington hadn't just spoken in English.

Remington looked back at her giving nothing away as she shook her head. "Nothing."

"You said something," Wynter said, narrowing her eyes.

"I did," Remington replied, her look derisive, but she said no more.

"That's a really irritating habit you've got," Wynter said. She knew she was acting like a bitch, but she was unable to stop herself at that moment.

"What is that?" Remington asked. She leaned her elbows on the vast granite island between them looking directly at Wynter.

"Saying shit behind my back," Wynter said.

"I was facing you," Remington replied calmly.

"You know what I mean!" Wynter snapped. "Talking in that… whatever it is."

Remington's face remained a calm mask, telling Wynter she was being inane.

"It's called Haitian Creole," Remington said evenly.

"What did you say?" Wynter snapped.

Again, Remington simply looked back at her, unaffected by her tone. She straightened up from the counter and inclined her head to Wynter. "Good night," she said, then walked out of the kitchen, leaving Wynter staring openmouthed after her.

Remington had just hung up her coat when Wynter walked into her room.

"Who do you think you are?" Wynter asked sharply.

Remington stood where she was, looking mildly surprised that Wynter was pushing this so hard.

"I believe the question should be who do you think I am?" Remington said.

"What's that mean?" Wynter asked, forever confused by the way Remington handled things.

"It means that if you think I am some kind of servant to be spoken down to, you are very mistaken."

"You work for me!" Wynter snapped.

"I work for John Machiavelli," Remington replied. "I'm assigned to you, *currently*."

"Is that your way of threatening to quit?" Wynter asked.

"It's my way of reminding you that you are more than welcome to change that status if you don't feel your interests are being served."

"My interests?" Wynter asked, seizing on the one thing that stuck out to her.

Remington looked back at her calmly, inclining her head.

"Now," Remington said, moving to sit on her bed and remove her shoes. "If you'll excuse me, I'd like to go to bed."

Wynter stood staring down at Remington, taken aback by her calm reception to her anger and assertions. After a long moment, she finally decided she was making a fool out of herself, and turned and left the room. Remington watched shaking her head, and continued to get ready for bed.

Chapter 2

The next morning an extremely hungover Wynter sat huddled in a chair on the back patio, with the built-in fireplace going due to the chill in the winter air. She smoked and sipped her coffee. Lauren had come home after a night of drinking and doing god only knew what drugs and they'd had a fight. Fortunately, it had been a very quiet fight, so Remington hadn't become involved. It had, however, resulted in some nasty bruises on her arms from where Lauren had grabbed her. Wynter was still smarting from the argument she'd had with Remington the night before as well. She knew she'd been a complete bitch, but she just hadn't been able to shut up or let it go. She wanted to push Remington to react to her. She wasn't sure why exactly, but she did.

She saw Remington walk through the dining room, turning her head and locating her out on the patio. Wynter half-expected Remington to come out and tell her she was quitting and she was willing to beg Remington to stay.

Remington stepped out onto the patio, her eyes taking in Wynter's disheveled appearance and suspected that she was hungover. Remington lit a cigarette and sat in a chair across from where Wynter was huddled. She looked around the rustic patio and at the arbor above their heads that would bloom with wisteria in the Spring. There was also a built-in barbecue and counter as well as the built in fireplace. It was just the beginning of the beautifully landscaped backyard, with lush trees and a built-in spa.

"Remi," Wynter began softly. "I'm sorry about last night."

Remington nodded slowly, her look closed.

"I was drunk, and in a bad mood and I took it out on you, and I'm really sorry."

"Is it that you truly have no respect for me?" Remington asked. She wasn't accusing her in the slightest, it was an honest question.

"No, it isn't that," Wynter said shaking her head vehemently. "I just get used to fighting all the time and I forget sometimes that not everyone is like me."

"Fighting all the time," Remington repeated. "Like last night with Lauren?"

"You heard that?" Wynter asked, shocked.

Remington nodded her head.

"God, you must have like super hearing or something, because I thought we were really quiet."

"Perhaps compared to other arguments you were quiet," Remington said, a slight grin on her lips, but then her eyes narrowed. "She hurt you, didn't she?"

Wynter's eyes widened at Remington's question. She started to shake her head, but Remington pinned her with a look. Taking a deep breath, she nodded slowly. Remington's lips flattened in displeasure.

"She was high," Wynter said, shaking her head, "she didn't realize how hard she grabbed me."

Remington looked back at her for a long moment. "Does it happen often?"

"No," Wynter said, shaking her head, "no, just when she's really high, and feeling really insecure."

Remington wondered if that was fairly often, but didn't say anything. They were both silent for a few minutes, each smoking and lost in their own thoughts.

"Can you forgive me for last night?" Wynter asked.

Remington thought about the question for a moment. "As long as you can respect that my position isn't beneath you, it's in front of you."

Wynter's eyes widened and her chin came up as she understood Remington's meaning. It was true, Remington was the person standing between Wynter and danger, and that position deserved her respect. She nodded with that new understanding evident on her face.

"I really am sorry, and I do respect you, Remi. I just need to be better about showing you that."

"Then we can forget what happened last night." Remington said simply.

Wynter smiled almost sadly, wondering how many times Remington would forgive her impulsivity.

"So…" Wynter said hesitantly, unsure if she wanted to approach this particular subject.

Remington waited, lighting another cigarette.

"If you're planning on seeing the girl from The Club last night," Wynter said. "I just wanted to tell you that you're more than welcome to invite her over here."

Remington's lips twitched slightly. "And you'd be okay with that?"

"Yes, I mean, since you kind of work all the time on account of me, I know you're not likely be able to see her as much as you'd normally be able to."

Remington nodded slowly, her look considering.

"Are you planning to see her again?" Wynter asked then, her tone gentle, not wanting to irritate Remington by being nosey.

Remington didn't answer at first, then grinned, inclining her head. "Yes."

"She's really cute," Wynter said, smiling slyly now.

"Yes," Remington said, nodding, "she is."

"So, call the girl," Wynter told her.

"I plan to," Remington said.

"And don't do that whole wait like a week game, it's really annoying," Wynter said.

"I don't play games," Remington said simply.

"I should have known that, huh?" Wynter said. "No true gentleman would do that."

"Indeed," Remington said, winking at her.

"You certainly smiled a lot last night. And even laughed a couple of times. Out loud."

Remington chuckled. "I told you, I do smile."

"Just not around me," Wynter said rolling her eyes, her tone self-effacing.

Remington contemplated her words for a minute, then said, "This is a serious job."

"I know, but it doesn't mean we can't get along and be friends, does it?" Wynter asked.

Again, Remington didn't answer right away. Her eyes narrowed slightly, but then she nodded. "I suppose it doesn't have to mean that, no."

"Good," Wynter said, smiling.

Remington looked at her watch. "We have that meeting at the studio at noon," she said, looking over at Wynter. "Are you going to be alive?"

"Ugh, I hope," Wynter said.

"We can pick up some Yaka Mein on the way, that'll help."

"Yaka what?" Wynter asked.

Remington grinned. "It's an old Creole hangover cure."

"It doesn't include anything really creepy does it?" Wynter asked making a face.

"Well, the chicken sacrifice is usually the worst part," Remington said seriously.

"What?" Wynter breathed, going pale.

Remington burst out laughing, a rich infectious sound. "I'm only kidding. It's a soup, nothing weird in it, I promise."

"You suck!" Wynter exclaimed, then held her head for the shot of pain that went through her head.

"We need to leave early," Remington said, nodding. "Let's try for eleven and we can stop on the way."

"Okay," Wynter said, her voice softer this time.

Wynter and Remington arrived at Wild Irish Silence studios twenty minutes early. Wynter sat down in the conference room sipping the Yaka Mein. For the most part it was beef soup with spaghetti noodles and various spices. But it was working to make her hangover better.

"You are a god," Wynter told Remington, to which Remington only nodded with a knowing grin.

Quinn and Xandy arrived shortly after. Remington and Quinn shook hands and both stood by the wall, while Xandy sat down next to Wynter.

"What is that?" Xandy asked Wynter.

"It's called Yaka Mein," Wynter said, holding it out to Xandy. "It's actually pretty good, but it's some Creole hangover cure."

"Is it working?" Xandy asked as she saw Billy Montague arrive and start walking toward the conference room.

"So far," Wynter said, looking up and grimacing. "It needs to work faster... I'm not ready for this..."

Billy Montague, tiny, long jet-black hair, blue eyes, and a wicked smile, swept into the room. Behind her was her husband Skylar Kristiani, a handsome man with dark hair, shot through with just a few gray hairs. No doubt put there by his ever-dramatic wife.

Billy walked straight over to Quinn and Remington and looked them both up and down. Both bodyguards did their best not to ogle. Billy Montague was a damned hot looking woman, it was nearly impossible not to be impressed.

"Wow..." Billy said, her tone a sexy drawl. "If this is what butch lesbians look like, sign me up!" She said the last with a wink at both

Quinn and Remington. "Oh, hi girls!" she said, turning to Wynter and Xandy and sitting down.

Skylar walked over to Quinn and Remington and extended his hand to each of them.

"My sincerest condolences," he said with a crooked grin.

Quinn and Remington chuckled, nodding their heads. They could only imagine what it was like to actually have to live with Billy Montague. If there was a Hall of Fame for dramatic flair and tantrums, Billy Montague would be its very first inductee.

"Sky?" Billy said, glancing back at her husband. "Where's Kid? He's coming to this isn't he? I'm damned if I'm going to remember half of what BJ tells us…" she said, shaking her head.

Wynter and Xandy exchanged a look.

"He'll be here, Billy, don't worry," Skylar said, moving to lean against the wall next to the bois.

"Good thing," Billy said, throwing herself back in the high-backed conference room chair. "Can't remember a damned thing these days…" She looked over at Wynter and Xandy and made a face. "I guess you kids don't have that problem, huh?"

"Nope," Wynter said simply.

"Uh-uh," Xandy murmured.

Billy looked back at both women and raised an eyebrow. "Okay you two are way too fucking hot to be lesbians," she said with a wicked grin. "And you're with that one back there aren't you?" she asked Xandy, her thumb indicating Quinn.

"Yes ma'am," Xandy said, her tone tremulous.

"Ma'am?" Billy snapped. "Did you just call me ma'am?"

"Um, yes?" Xandy said, looking terrified suddenly.

"Ah Jesus…" Skylar breathed, pushing off the wall. "She was being respectful, Billy. Take it easy."

"How fucking old do you think I am!" Billy exclaimed, vaulting to her feet and turning to Xandy.

In a flash Quinn was there putting her arm out to block Billy from getting any closer to Xandy.

"You need to relax," Quinn told Billy, in the suddenly quiet room.

"Or what?" Billy asked, looking up at Quinn. "I'm betting you won't hit a girl."

"Touch one hair on my girl's head and you'll find out," Quinn said with a menacing smile.

Billy's blue eyes widened at the look on Quinn's face. Then she craned her neck around to look at Xandy.

"That's pretty hot, right?" she asked Xandy.

Xandy had no idea how to answer. Billy just laughed and sat back down.

"Relax Braveheart, I'm cool," Billy said.

"He was Scottish, I'm from Northern Ireland," Quinn said wryly as she turned and walked back over to the wall.

"Same difference," Billy said.

"Two different islands, babe," Skylar said, grinning at Quinn.

"Shut up, Sky," Billy said, even as she smiled, not looking back at her husband.

Jerith Michaels, also known as "the Kid" of Billy and the Kid walked in. He walked over and shook hands with Skylar immediately, then looked at Quinn and Remington.

"Hi," he said, smiling, his eyes sparkling. "I'm Jerith."

"Quinn," she said, nodding and shaking Jerith's hand.

Jerith looked at Remington. "Holy shit, you're Remington LaRoché."

Remington nodded her head. "It's good to meet you."

"It's great to meet you. I've seen you fight, you're like lighting."

Remington inclined her head. "Thank you," she said humbly.

"She's who?" Billy asked, leaning around to look at Wynter.

"She's a former MMA fighter," Wynter told Billy.

"Seriously?" Billy asked.

"Yes," Wynter said, "like five-time champion."

"I don't know squat about that stuff," Billy said, shaking her head, "but that definitely explains the build."

"You haven't seen anything," Wynter said, grinning, as she pulled out her phone and showed her a pre-fight picture of Remington.

"Holy fucking shit!" Billy exclaimed loudly.

"And how do I know Billy's here?" asked BJ from the door to the conference room, his grin wide.

Jordan Tate and her husband Dylan Silver walked in with BJ. Dylan made a beeline for Remington, apparently a fan of hers as well. Wynter glanced back at Remington and could see that her bodyguard was distinctly uncomfortable with so much attention. It was only made worse when before he got down to business, BJ informed Remington that he too thought she was an amazing athlete.

"I've watched fights for years," BJ said, "male and female, and I've never seen anyone as fast as you." He shook his head. "It's a damned shame you retired."

"Gonna have to check this chick out…" Billy muttered.

Jerith handed Billy his phone a moment later, grinning. Billy spent the next few minutes occupied with watching highlights from Remington LaRoché's fights. BJ looked over at Jerith and grinned, knowing he was helping by distracting Billy, keeping her from causing trouble momentarily. Jerith gave BJ a completely innocent look. Wynter glanced back at Skylar Kristiani and saw that he was nodding with a grin on his lips as well. These men apparently knew how to handle the dynamic singer quite well.

"So, a couple of you know," BJ said, glancing at Xandy and Quinn, "but I've been working on putting this together for a bit. I've finally got four power house women under my label." His eyes touched on each of the women, then he grinned, his light green eyes widening. "And I want to show them off…"

"Wait, what?" Billy asked, looking up.

"The four of you, on tour, together," BJ said, his look pointed, telling Billy that he wasn't going to argue with her on this one.

"You want to put me out there with these kids?" Billy asked.

"I want one of my top acts to go out with two of my newest artists, Wynter and Xandy, yes," BJ said.

Billy narrowed her eyes at BJ. she wasn't fooled by his stroking. "Who's the headliner?"

"There is no headliner," BJ said. "Just like our last major label tour."

BJ's band Sparks had toured with Billy and the Kid, Jordan, and Fast Lane.

"Why isn't Cassie here? Fast Lane's not one of your top acts anymore?" Billy asked sharply.

"Cassie is pregnant, and Mackie would kill me if I even breathed in her direction right now," BJ said, his look serious.

Billy snapped her mouth shut then, glancing back at Skylar who nodded at her. BJ saw the confused look on both Wynter and Xandy's faces.

"Cassie Roads is the lead singer of Fast Lane, as you may already know. Cassie had a couple of miscarriages a couple of years back… one almost cost her life. The fact that she's pregnant at all is a miracle, but Mackie isn't taking any chances with her health. He's not letting her out of his sight for much. And he definitely wouldn't let her tour right now."

Both Xandy and Wynter nodded, understanding now what had shut Billy up about Fast Lane. In the back of the room, Remington glanced at Quinn, who nodded, having known about John Machiavelli's wife being pregnant with a risky pregnancy. Remington's opinion of John Machiavelli raised a few more points at that moment.

The meeting continued with BJ laying out the tour schedule. When they got to the point of discussing travel arrangements things got a little sticky again.

"Jordan and her band will have their own bus," BJ said, holding his hand up as Billy sat forward, looking over at Jordan, who'd yet to say anything in the meeting. "She's pregnant again, Billy, and their daughter will be traveling with them too."

Billy's mouth dropped open as she looked over at Jordan. Jordan's gold eyes sparkled as she glanced over at her husband Dylan. As Skylar was for Billy, Dylan was Jordan's 'calm mate.'

"So that's what it takes?" Billy said snidely. "Skylar, get me pregnant again, will ya?" she called over her shoulder.

"Not if my life depended on it, babe," Skylar replied rolling his eyes.

Quinn and Remington looked over at him with varied degrees of amusement on their faces. Skylar gave a dramatic shudder, grinning all the while.

"Don't be a bitch, Billy," Jordan said, keeping her tone perfectly calm.

"Kiss my ass, Jordan," Billy replied with a sweet smile.

"Not on your life, honey," Jordan replied, narrowing her eyes slightly.

Dylan reached his hand over to lay it over Jordan's hand on the table, and leaned over to say something in her ear. Jordan nodded, and said nothing else.

BJ was ever pleased by the match he'd accidentally made in putting Dylan and Jordan together to write songs when Jordan was blocked. Dylan had been the one man that not only had a way of calming Jordan down, but also wouldn't take her crap when she tried to dish it at him. He was perfect for her. Jordan was BJ's best friend in the world, and he loved her dearly, but she could be impossible at times.

"Now, back to what I was saying," BJ said, looking pointedly over at Billy. "I was about to say that Billy and the Kid will have a bus as well."

"Why didn't you just say that!" Billy snapped.

"Because you interrupted him, Billy," Jerith told her calmly.

Billy shot Jerith a vile look, but didn't say anything. BJ knew that Billy wouldn't blow up at Jerith. She needed him and she knew it. Jerith Michaels had proven to be a force to be reckoned with when Billy had temporarily left Billy and the Kid. Jerith had put out a solo album, aptly titled "Solo" and it had gone platinum quickly. Jerith Michaels didn't need Billy Montague, but she definitely needed him, and everyone knew it now.

"Wynter and Xandy, you girls okay in a bus together?" BJ asked.

Xandy nodded, looking over at Wynter who also nodded.

"Good," BJ said, looking relieved. "I don't need a bloody convoy goin' down the road, I'll get fined!" he said, with a grin. "Now, you two," BJ said, looking to the back of the room at Quinn and Remington.

"Wot?" Quinn said, looking instantly wary.

BJ grinned knowing her well at this point, and appreciating her concern, considering the personalities already clashing in this pre-tour meeting.

"I'm counting on you two to be my point people on security for this tour." He held up his hands as Quinn came off the wall ready to protest mightily. Remington merely pursed her lips, narrowing her eyes slightly. "There will be other security hired for the tour, but you two girls are my aces, okay? And I assure you, you will be highly compensated for the…" His eyes touched on Billy and Jordan. "Trouble."

"Did I just lose my bodyguard?" Wynter asked Xandy under her breath.

"It sounds like it," Xandy said, grimacing, "and I lost my girlfriend."

"Guess you two will have to learn to share," Billy said, smiling blithely at them.

"I've never been good at sharing…" Wynter said pointedly.

"Might want to work on that one, sweetie," Billy said, giving Wynter a knowing wink.

Wynter started to stand, and Billy was already grinning wickedly, happy to have riled the younger singer.

"Knock it off, Billy," Jerith warned.

Wynter felt a hand at her back and glanced back to see Remington standing by her chair, her hazel eyes narrowed slightly as she shook her head slowly. Blowing her breath out, Wynter sat back down.

Billy grinned gleefully, knowing now what would get to Wynter Kincade.

Remington stepped back to the wall then, glancing at Quinn.

"Máthair Dia…" Quinn muttered under her breath, saying "mother of God" in Gaelic.

"Pwoblèm p ap fini…" Remington muttered at the same time. It was a Haitian Creole saying that translated to 'problems will not end', or more aptly, 'when it rains it pours.'

On the way back to the house, Wynter was fit to be tied.

"What the fuck is he thinking?" Wynter exclaimed, not for the first time. "I can't be on tour with that woman, I'll fucking kill her!"

Remington didn't reply, knowing that Wynter was beyond hearing anything she would say.

"And what the fuck is up with her coming at you like that?" Wynter said then, staring over at Remington as if she herself had done something wrong. Remington looked warily over at Wynter.

Billy had walked over to Remington at the end of the meeting, and slid a fingernail down the side of Remington's cheek. "Looks like you'll have time to give me some lessons, huh?" she'd said, glancing back at Wynter.

"What did she mean by lessons?' Wynter asked, still storming.

"I have no idea," Remington answered simply.

"Her husband was standing right there! Is she fucking crazy?" Wynter asked.

"Maybe," Remington offered.

"You're not helping right now," Wynter said, her look narrowed.

Remington pressed her lips together, doing her best to subdue a grin.

"Stop it," Wynter said.

"Why are you letting her get to you?" Remington asked. "You know she's just playing a game, and you're letting her win."

"How is she winning?" Wynter asked.

"Do you think she's still raging about you right now?" Remington asked.

That pulled Wynter up short and she screwed up her lips in consternation. "Probably not."

"Li te voye flè," Remington said then.

"I'm sorry, what?" Wynter asked, looking confused. "That's Creole right?"

"Haitian Creole, yes," Remington said. "It translates to she's throwing flowers, but it's an old saying that basically means that she's talking nonsense and you shouldn't listen."

"Tell me again," Wynter said, her look serious.

"Li te voye flè," Remington repeated.

"Li te voye flè," Wynter said, doing her best to get the accent right.

"Got it," Remington told her, grinning.

A few days later, Remington had the unfortunate luck of having to drive both Wynter and Lauren into the city. When they all went to leave, using the Escalade from Mach 3's fleet, Wynter started to get in on the passenger's side.

"Wynter, get in back with me," Lauren told her.

Wynter looked over at Remington as she got in on the driver's side. Remington simply shrugged.

"Wynter," Lauren said again, her tone sharper this time.

Wynter caught the narrowing of Remington's eyes.

"Okay, okay," Wynter said, holding up her hand at Lauren to keep her from saying something else.

Lauren did not like Remington at all. She told Wynter that she needed to get rid of the woman and get a normal bodyguard. Wynter refused, not wanting to even discuss the matter anymore with Lauren. She claimed that BJ had requested Remington and that she had no say in the matter. The last thing she wanted was for Lauren to hear that she'd personally requested Remington. Lauren was insecure enough without adding more fuel to the fire.

In the back seat, Lauren made a point of putting her arm around Wynter, pulling her close, and kissing her lips deeply to the point that it made Wynter uncomfortable. When she dragged her lips away from Lauren, Wynter glanced toward the front and caught Remington's eyes in the rearview mirror. She grimaced apologetically.

There was music playing; rock music that Remington tended to listen to. When one song ended, Lauren made a rude noise, and said snidely, "We're really rocking out this morning, huh?"

Once again, Wynter saw Remington's eyes in the rearview mirror. They were more green than gold and from what Wynter had seen so far, which usually indicated irritation. Still, Remington didn't say anything. She just switched the speakers to the front so they wouldn't have to listen.

"You could just put on some good music," Lauren said, her tone nasty.

I could just throw you off a bridge too, enèvan bra, but... Remington thought maliciously.

After they'd stopped to let Lauren out at her "appointment" which to Remington had become code for 'drug deal,' Wynter got into the front seat. As she did, she heard Remington mutter something she'd heard from her before.

"What was that?" Wynter asked, recognizing the Haitian Creole that Remington used often.

Remington curled her lips in a sardonic grin. "I said 'bon Deberá enèvan bra,' " Remington she said smiling pleasantly.

"Which translates to…" Wynter said, her voice trailing off as she gave Remington a sidelong look.

"I forget," Remington said her look far from honest.

"You've never forgotten a word of Creole in your life, Remington LaRoché," Wynter said, narrowing her blue eyes. "What does it mean?"

Remington had the temerity to look embarrassed for a moment, embarrassed and somewhat ashamed.

'It's unkind," she told Wynter.

"Which is rare for you, isn't it?" Wynter asked.

"Not when it comes to her, no," Remington answered honestly.

"You two really don't like each other," Wynter said.

"At least it's mutual," Remington said mildly.

"So what did you say?" Wynter asked again.

"It means, 'good riddance irritating brat,' " Remington said.

Wynter looked back at her for a long moment and then started to laugh, shaking her head.

"You really need help when it comes to being insulting," Wynter told Remington.

"Oh, believe me, I can be very insulting when the need arises," Remington told her.

"Oh, my…" Wynter said, widening her eyes. "So is Katrina still coming over tonight?"

"As far as I know," Remington said, glancing over at Wynter. "And you're sure you're okay with this?"

"I am sure I'm okay with this," Wynter said, nodding. "If Lauren is home, I'll make sure to keep her bound and gagged upstairs with me, okay?"

Remington made a noise in the back of her throat.

"We won't mess up your date, I promise," Wynter said, holding up her hands.

That evening Katrina arrived at the house and Remington opened the door, smiling down at her. Katrina walked inside, looking a bit awestruck. Remington couldn't blame her for that, the house was impressive. Starting with the stone path that led to the front door, looking like a lush garden and the entry of natural stone and exposed timber and natural wood crown molding. There was a solid wood coffered ceiling that opened into an impressive dining room with one wall covered with a colorful and beautiful mural.

"This is amazing," Katrina said, as she admired her surroundings.

Remington nodded. "It is definitely that," she said, smiling.

Remington led Katrina into the massive kitchen. Katrina noted the pot simmering on the stove and could smell fresh bread.

"You cook too?" Katrina asked, her tone shocked.

"A few things," Remington said, smiling. "Since it's cold, I figured soup would be good. This is an old recipe, it's called Squah Soup."

"It is Haitian?" Katrina asked.

"Creole, yes," Remington said. "Is that okay?"

"Of course!" Katrina said. "I've never had Haitian food before."

"Well, it's Haitian Creole, so it's different from both Haitian food and Creole. When people came from Haiti to America, settling in Louisiana, they used what they could get, so it changed the way people made the old recipes."

"I guess that makes sense," Katrina said, nodding.

Remington pulled out a chair for Katrina and served the food. Katrina was still astounded and enchanted by Remington's old-world manners. During dinner they talked and drank wine.

"This soup is amazing," Katrina told Remington. "So's this bread. You have very good taste," she said, smiling.

"Thank you, I'm glad you like it," Remington said, inclining her head.

They talked about other things for a while.

"I'm sorry this is a bit weird date-wise," Remington said at one point, looking somewhat embarrassed. "I mean, having to be in someone else's house and all."

"It's okay. With what you do I understand that it's not easy to get away. It's not like a normal job," Katrina said, smiling. "I really am glad you called me, and I'll take whatever time I can get with you at this point. It was really nice of Ms. Kincade to say I could come here."

"I promise I'll have another night off again at some point," Remington said, but then grimaced slightly.

"What?" Katrina asked, seeing the look.

"We just got told about a tour that starts in about three weeks, so I'll be lucky to get a day or two off between now and then," she said, looking apologetic.

"That's what I get for getting involved with someone so important," Katrina said, grinning.

"Hardly important," Remington said, "just protecting someone who is."

"And protecting someone is very important, Remi," Katrina said.

Remington looked circumspect, but nodded.

Later they took their wine and moved to the large living room with the huge flat screen TV hanging on one wall. They watched movies for a few hours, with Remington's arm on the back of the couch behind Katrina. At one point during the movie Katrina jumped, moving closer to Remington. She glanced up at Remington and bit her lip, smiling shyly as she did.

Remington caught the look and smiled softly too, leaning down to kiss Katrina's lips gently, her arm moving to encircle the other woman's shoulders. They kissed for a few minutes, but Remington kept the kisses sweet, not pushing for anything else. To her it would be completely inappropriate for anything else to happen between them in Wynter's home. When their lips parted again, Remington looked down at Katrina, her look searching. Katrina wasn't sure what Remington was looking for, but she could tell that this was not going to be the night they made love for the first time.

She'd figured that would be the case. Remington didn't strike her as the type to do something like that in her employer's home. This was definitely a very different kind of relationship. Not that she minded at all, it was nice to have a woman treat her gently for a change. To keep

Remington from feeling like she needed to explain herself, Katrina simply leaned her head against Remington's shoulder and turned back to watch the movie.

After two movies and a few glasses of wine, Katrina was getting sleepy. The rain outside had picked up and the wind was starting to howl.

"I think maybe you should stay here tonight," Remington said, her tone concerned.

"I don't want to be a bother," Katrina said, shaking her head.

"It's not a bother," Remington said, touching her cheek. "I don't want you driving in that rain, especially not tired and after a couple glasses of wine…"

"I'm fine, really," Katrina said, though her tone indicated she was less sure of that, even as she said it.

"Please stay here tonight," Remington said softly.

Katrina couldn't help but be moved by Remington's tone of voice combined with the look of concern in her hazel eyes.

"Are you sure it will be okay?" she asked Remington.

"I'm sure," Remington answered, nodding.

"Okay," Katrina said, "thank you for offering. It's very sweet of you."

"Come on," Remington said, taking her hand as she turned off the TV. "I need to do a final check on Wynter anyway."

"Okay," Katrina said, getting up to follow Remington.

Remington led her up the stairs to the bedroom almost at the end of the hall, and gestured for her to enter. Katrina walked into the room. It was nice, spacious, and it even had a door out onto a balcony of its own.

"Make yourself comfortable." She opened a drawer in her dresser. "If you want something to sleep in, see if anything in here will work. I'll be right back," Remington told her.

Remington knocked lightly on Wynter's door. Lauren had not come home yet. She heard Wynter say, "Come" and opened the door.

"Everything okay?" Remington asked, seeing Wynter sitting on her bed, using her iPad.

Wynter looked up, her face completely free of makeup, her long dark hair falling around her shoulders. She wore a lavender tank top and matching bikini underwear and nothing else, it was what she usually wore to bed. Remington made a point of keeping her eyes slightly averted, which made Wynter grin.

"Everything's fine," Wynter said, her tone reflecting her amusement at Remington's discomfit. "Is everything okay over there?" she asked, a wry grin on her lips.

Remington gave her a narrowed look, and then quickly looked away again, making Wynter chuckle softly.

"I hope it's okay, I told Katrina she could stay the night. It's getting ugly out there," Remington told her.

"Of course it's fine," Wynter said, nodding. "I'm hoping Lauren passes out wherever she is so she doesn't try to get home in this."

Remington raised an eyebrow at the term 'passes out,' but nodded.

"If you need anything, let me know," Remington told her.

"I'll be fine," Wynter said. "You can close your door tonight if you… aw… need to," she said, with a wink.

Remington once again gave her a narrowed look. "That wouldn't be appropriate."

"Which part?" Wynter countered.

"Either," Remington said.

"I see," Wynter said, nodding and grinning at the same time.

"Do not start," Remington said seriously.

"I didn't start anything…" Wynter said, stretching with her arms above her head, her tank top rising to expose a fair amount of tanned and very toned skin.

Remington closed her eyes, shaking her head; the woman was just too much sometimes. She heard Wynter chuckle again.

"Good night," Remington said pointedly.

"Good night…" Wynter said suggestively.

Remington glowered at her for a moment, then turned and walked out the door, closing it softly. Wynter sat on her bed, her look contemplative. She found herself feeling a bit jealous that Katrina was sleeping in bed with Remington that night, and part of her was relieved that apparently, they wouldn't be having sex at all that night. She knew it was silly, but it didn't matter, she was glad.

"Everything okay?" Katrina asked when Remington walked back into the room.

"Everything's fine," Remington said, smiling. "That looks pretty good on you," she said, grinning and indicating the shirt Katrina wore.

It was a black and purple Venum tank top with the snake head and name "Venum" on it in white. It was a little bit big on Katrina, because she was small, but Remington thought it looked pretty good.

"Is this from your fighting days?" Katrina asked.

"Yes," Remington said, nodding, "I wore a lot of Venum's stuff. I liked it."

Remington pulled clothes out of a drawer and told Katrina she'd be right back. She went into the bathroom and came out wearing a dark gray tank top that said, "Rowdy Women" with the letters MMA under it in white, and black boy shorts.

"Is that what you normally sleep in?" Katrina asked as Remington put her clothes in the hamper in her closet.

"For the most part," Remington said, nodding.

Katrina was sitting on the end of Remington's bed. She got up when Remington walked back over to her. Remington looked down at her, reaching to touch her cheek gently, then leaned down to kiss her softly on the lips.

"Ready for bed?" Remington asked. "Or did you want to watch some TV up here?"

"We could watch some TV," Katrina said. "Maybe the news has some information on this storm."

Remington nodded, picking up the remote on the nightstand, and turned on the TV. They both settled on the bed, sliding under the covers and leaning against the headboard. Remington found some news and turned it up. There were the usual stories about robberies, murders, etc. They promised weather after the commercial break, so they waited. When the news came back on, however, they did the sports stories next. There was a story about a football player involved in a scandal, and then the sportscaster said, "Speaking of scandal, Akasha Salt is doing her best to stir a scandal in the world of MMA fighting. Check out this clip of Ms. Salt in New York earlier today."

Katrina glanced over at Remington and saw her roll her eyes, then she looked back at the TV. They were showing a black woman, her hair a mass of wild curls, who was making wild gestures and talking to the camera.

"Yeah, Remington LaRoché is nothing but a coward. She quit this sport because she didn't want to face me. She retired, because she knew I was coming after her title!"

Katrina looked over at Remington again, and saw that she was grinning sardonically as she shook her head.

"Who is that?" Katrina asked, her tone a bit appalled.

"She's another MMA fighter," Remington said.

"She talks like she doesn't like you very much…" Katrina said, shaking her head.

"She talks a lot," Remington said, nodding, her look unaffected by Akasha's harsh words.

"And what she's saying doesn't bother you?" Katrina asked.

Remington grinned, shrugging. "Like I said, she talks a lot."

Katrina shook her head. She couldn't believe that having someone talk about her that way didn't bother Remington, but she really didn't look the least bit concerned.

"There you have it," the sportscaster was saying. "Did Remi LaRoché really retire to avoid a bout with Akasha Salt? We'll be working on getting a comment from Ms. LaRoché shortly."

"Bon chans…" Remington muttered, saying 'good luck' even as the sportscaster continued.

"But the former Women's UFC Champion isn't one for speeches or comments."

They then showed a clip of Remington; it was a pre-fight interview. She was asked how she thought she'd fair against the other fighter.

"I think if she's better than me, she'll win," Remington had said simply, then walked away.

The interview looked back at the camera then, a grin in place. "And there you have it."

"Of course, Remi LaRoché went on to win that fight," the sportscaster said. "She was an undefeated champion of the sport, and that's got to rub other fighters the wrong way. Perhaps that's what's happening to Ms. Salt. We'll just have to see if Remi LaRoché will have anything to say about the matter."

Again, Katrina looked over at Remington who simply quirked her lips in a grin.

"Undefeated?" Katrina asked as the news went to another commercial break.

Remington nodded, her look completely lacking any sort of ego.

"That sounds like it's pretty impressive."

Remington only shrugged.

"You really don't show off at all, do you?" Katrina asked, mirroring the observation that Wynter had made of Remington earlier on.

"I was raised better than that," Remington answered.

Katrina nodded, grinning. "I guess you were, but isn't that like part of that kind of sport? The crap talking?"

Remington considered for a long moment. "I guess for some it is, but it never was for me. I don't talk about it, I just do it."

"I guess that does seem like you," Katrina said.

They watched TV for another half hour. When both of them grew tired, Remington turned off the TV, and settled down. Katrina lay down too, facing Remington, unsure again suddenly. Remington made it easy, holding her left arm out so Katrina could move closer to her, then Remington put her right hand at Katrina's waist. They fell asleep facing each other, with Katrina snuggled close to Remington.

Wynter got up in the middle of the night, going down to the kitchen for water. On her way back to her room she couldn't stop herself from looking into Remington's room. She saw the two women sleeping close together and felt that same odd stab of jealousy, but shook her head at herself.

As if she sensed her there, Remington stirred and looked over her shoulder.

"Everything okay?" Remington whispered.

Wynter smiled slightly, nodding. "Yeah," she said softly. "Sorry to wake you, go back to sleep."

Remington looked back at her, like she was trying to discern if Wynter was telling her the truth. Finally, she nodded, turning her head back toward Katrina again. Wynter left the room as quietly as she could.

The next morning, Katrina awoke to find Remington wasn't in bed. She looked around, then noted that the door to the balcony was slightly ajar. She got up and looked out onto the balcony. Remington was on her phone. She could hear her speaking to someone, but couldn't understand what she said.

"Oken li se fin," Remington was saying. "No… no… wi… li se konsekans… no, manman… li se fin…" She sat back in her chair, taking a drag off her cigarette, blowing out a stream of smoke a few long moments later. "Dakò… wi… Mwen renmenw tou. Bon babay." She hung up a moment later, tossing her phone on the coffee table in front of her. She sat back and lit another cigarette, taking a deep drag and blowing the smoke out slowly. She knew she was smoking more lately due to the stress of the current situation, it was becoming a nasty habit.

Katrina opened the door to the balcony. Remington glanced over her shoulder, as she stood up, smiling at Katrina.

"Bonjou," Remington said, her accent very clear at that moment. "I'm sorry, good morning," she said then, realizing she was still speaking Creole.

"How do you say it?" Katrina asked.

"Bonjou," Remington repeated slowly.

"Bonjou," Katrina repeated, her accent not quite right, but Remington smiled anyway.

Remington gestured to another chair on the balcony. Katrina sat then Remington followed.

"So, you stay standing until I sit down?" Katrina asked.

"Yes," Remington said, nodding.

Katrina nodded too. "It's really nice. It makes a woman feel special."

"As all women should," Remington said, inclining her head.

Katrina bit her lip, looking back at Remington, still so surprised by her ways, but finding them very endearing, especially when paired with someone whose appearance was so contrary to the ideal of a "gentleman." People would expect Remington to be very street sounding and acting, more like a hood than the fine gentlewoman that she actually was.

"Did you sleep well?" Remington asked.

"I slept great," Katrina said, "really great, thank you."

Remington nodded, looking pleased. "And the storm seems to have given way to a beautiful day."

Katrina looked out to the sky and took a deep breath of fresh clean air.

"Yes, it does," she said, smiling.

"Who the fuck is Akasha Salt?" Wynter practically yelled from the balcony door.

Remington shook her head ruefully even as she stood.

"Stand down, Remi," Wynter said, motioning for Remington to sit.

Remington remained standing until Wynter glanced up from her phone again and rolled her eyes. She sat down so Remington would sit too.

"So?" she asked when Remington didn't answer her original question. "Who the hell is this bitch?"

"Good morning," Remington said pointedly.

Winter gave her a quelling look then glanced over at Katrina, having just noticed her sitting there.

"Oh, hi, sorry," Wynter said then, and she reached across the coffee table to extend her hand to Katrina. "I'm Wynter."

"Hi, I'm Katrina," Katrina said, smiling and shaking Wynter's hand.

Wynter leaned back, throwing Remington a look. "So?" she asked again.

Remington shook her head. "She's another MMA fighter," she said simply.

"Well, I guessed that from the story, Rem. I meant why is she going after you so nastily?"

Remington shrugged. "She's always been a talker."

"Talk?" Wynter repeated. "You mean talking shit. Did you hear what she said about you?"

"Yes, I heard," Remington said.

"And you're going to go hand her her ass, when?" Wynter asked, her tone deceptively sweet.

Remington shook her head. "I'm not, I'm retired."

Wynter looked back at Remington thinking she had to be joking. When she realized she wasn't she made a noise in the back of her throat.

"You can't let her get away with that bullshit!" she raged. "I mean," she said, her look suddenly hesitant, "unless you really are afraid of her."

Remington's hazel eyes stared back at her for a long moment, her face very serious.

"I'm not afraid of her," she said simply.

"Have you fought her before?" Wynter asked.

"Twice," Remington said.

"And you're undefeated," Katrina added.

"So that means you've beaten the bitch twice?" Wynter asked.

Remington inclined her head.

"Then what the fuck!" Wynter exclaimed. "Who the hell does she think she is?"

"It's safer to mock the Devil while in Heaven," Remington said.

Wynter narrowed her eyes. "She thinks she can talk shit because you're retired."

Remington didn't answer, merely looking back at Wynter.

Wynter looked over at Katrina. "Have you seen any of her fights?"

"No," Katrina said, shaking her head. "I did look up her record though."

"Oh, you need to see her fight," Wynter said, glancing at Remington who was already rolling her eyes and shaking her head. "Bullshit, Remi, she needs to see that," she said, looking up one of Remington's fights on YouTube on her iPad.

After a few moments, she found what she was looking for.

"This, you need to see this," she said, looking over at Katrina, as she leaned forward to hand Katrina the iPad. "It's like Remi's greatest hits… literally!"

Remington reached for another cigarette, giving Wynter a narrowed look. Wynter simply smiled back at her as she moved to kneel next to where Katrina sat.

"Now look at this… she's so damned fast! Quinn was telling me that no one is as fast as Remi is… See that! She totally avoided that kick, and look… see? She punches so fast that they don't even have time to react… look, right there! She smacks the girl and just kind of dances away… I don't think that chick even got one hit..."

Remington sat back in her chair, leaning her head back, staring up at the sky as she smoked her cigarette, wishing she was somewhere else at that moment.

Wynter glanced over at Remington and could see her discomfit. She grinned knowing that Remington would never have shown Katrina any of this. Remington did not brag, she did not blow her own horn, even if it was an amazing one. Wynter couldn't think of one famous person she knew that wouldn't grab the chance to impress someone with their work, but that wasn't Remington, not at all. If Wynter hadn't figured out all on her own how amazing a fighter her bodyguard was, she'd never have known.

Katrina looked over at Remington as well, seeing that she was embarrassed by the lavish compliments coming from Wynter. She couldn't disagree with Wynter in the slightest, however. Remington was an amazing fighter. It was easy to see why she'd been a five-time UFC Women's Champion, and Akasha Salt's outrageous claims seemed all the more inflammatory now. Everyone who knew anything about Remington's fighting abilities would be appalled by Akasha's claims and derision. And that was definitely the case.

Remington's phone pinged with multiple messages. She read them then put her phone down without answering any.

"Who's that?" Wynter asked, moving to sit in her chair again.

"Quinn," Remington said, her grin embarrassed. "Jericho… Cody… Lyric… Mackie."

Wynter chuckled, shaking her head. "They're all probably hearing the news at this point."

"Or they heard it last night, like we did," Katrina said.

"You heard this last night?" Wynter asked, looking from Katrina to Remington.

"On the news," Remington said nodding.

Wynter's phone started ringing and she picked it up, looking at the display, laughing. "It's Xandy," she said answering the call. "Yeah… she's right here… I know, she's gotten texts from lots of people already… She what? Oh"—Wynter looked over at Remington—"Quinn says you need to 'beat the piss out of that skank.' "

Remington rolled her eyes and shook her head, looking over at Katrina.

Katrina laughed softly. "I guess your friends don't like Akasha talking about you like that."

"I guess not," Remington said.

Remington's phone pinged and she picked it up, groaning out loud this time.

"Wait, hold on," Wynter said, her eyes on Remington. "Who is it?"

Remington gave her a deadpan look, and turned the phone around to show her the name.

"Oh, crap, Billy just texted Remi, I'll call you back," Wynter said, hanging up a moment later. "What did she say?"

Remington shook her head. "I can't repeat it."

Wynter grinned, glancing over at a confused-looking Katrina. "She won't cuss in front of ladies."

"Let me see it," Wynter said holding out her hand for Remington's phone.

Remington hesitated.

"Oh for God's sake, I'm not going to answer her!" Wynter said, rolling her eyes.

Remington handed her the phone.

Wynter read it and her eyes widened. "Wow…" she said simply.

"Who's Billy?" Katrina asked.

"Billy Montague," Wynter said, handing Remington back her phone.

"You mean… Billy and the Kid, Billy Montague?" Katrina asked, looking shocked.

"Yeah," Wynter said, nodding, "she seems to have a thing for Remi."

"But…" Katrina stammered. "She's straight isn't she?"

"And married," Remington added.

"Maybe she wouldn't consider sex with another woman cheating," Wynter said, winking at Remington.

"That's not funny," Remington said, her tone serious.

"What did she say?" Katrina asked curiously.

"Don't," Remington said, as she saw Wynter start to tell Katrina. "Don't even think about it."

"Why?" Katrina asked, looking over at Remington. "Was it that bad?"

"She used the word 'cunt' more than once," Wynter said, grinning.

"Wynter!" Remington exclaimed, giving her a pointed glare.

"What! You said I couldn't tell her, you didn't say I couldn't use a word…" Wynter said, laughing at Remington's obvious outrage.

"I've heard that word before, Remi, it's okay," Katrina said, winking at Remington.

"It isn't that I think you haven't heard it…" Remington started to say, but let her voice trail off as she realized she was outnumbered.

"Has she told you about her military service?" Wynter said then, her eyes sparkling mischievously.

"Bondye ede m '…" Remington muttered.

"What does that mean?" Wynter asked, before Katrina could. Then she looked at Katrina and said in a conspiring tone, "She says it a lot." Katrina nodded, grinning.

Remington pursed her lips, the desire to keep the phrase to herself warring with her manners. When a woman asked you question, it was imperative that you answer it. That was what she'd been taught. She narrowed her eyes at Wynter, who grinned gleefully, guessing easily what was going on in Remington's head by the look on her face.

Finally, Remington sighed loudly. "It means 'god help me,' " she said, her tone telling Wynter she was not happy with her at that moment.

"I see. That explains a few things," she said, winking.

"You know…" Remington said her voice trailing off ominously.

Wynter looked shocked. "Remington LaRoché that sounded like it was almost a threat! Did you just almost threaten me?"

"That would be wrong," Remington replied, her tone far from convincing. "And it's LaRoché, row-shay, not row-sh."

Wynter's eyes widened further, as she pressed her lips together in an effort not to smile. She saw Remington's eyes narrow immediately and started to laugh.

"I'm sorry," Wynter said, still laughing, "but you've never corrected me before…"

Remington tilted her head to the side, and a resounding pop could be heard as she stretched her neck. Wynter immediately pressed her lips together again, this time looking circumspect. She knew she was pushing too hard now, and she didn't really want to piss Remington off. She'd been truly surprised by not only the almost threat, but the correction as well.

"LaRoché," Wynter said, pronouncing it perfectly this time. "Got it, won't get it wrong again, I promise," she said her with wide eyes.

Remington closed her eyes, shaking her head slightly as she grinned.

"So," Wynter said, looking over at Katrina, "you should see the uniform in her closet, it's got an amazing number of medals and ribbons on it."

"Wynter," Remington said, her tone aghast.

"What?" Wynter queried with a cheeky smile. "She knows you were a marine, right?" she asked, glancing between Remington and Katrina.

Katrina looked surprised, and Wynter gave Remington a quelling look. "You served your country, that's not the first thing you tell the girl? What is wrong with you?" she asked, shaking her head, like she couldn't imagine.

"You were a marine?" Katrina asked Remington.

"Yes," Remington said.

"She was in Iraq," Wynter told Katrina.

Katrina looked at Remington for confirmation and she nodded.

"For how long?" Katrina asked.

"Four years," Remington said.

"That's a long time," Katrina replied.

"Three tours," Remington said simply.

"And she has the medals to prove it," Wynter added, winking at Remington. "You should check it out. Her uniform is in her closet."

Katrina looked hesitantly at Remington. "I don't want to invade your privacy," she said.

Remington gave her a soft smile. "If you'd like to see it, you're welcome to look," she said.

Katrina smiled, biting her lip. "Is it okay if I go look now?"

Remington smiled, nodding, and stood up as Katrina did. As soon as Katrina stepped inside, Remington turned to look at Wynter.

"What are you doing?" she asked, her tone bewildered.

"Telling her stuff about you, that you never will," Wynter countered mildly.

"Why?" Remington asked, still looking puzzled.

Wynter looked back at Remington for a long moment, not sure how to answer her question, since she herself wasn't sure why she was doing it. It was as if she needed to prove to someone else who Remington was, as if someone else believing Remington LaRoché was someone amazingly special would mean that she wasn't crazy. And maybe, just maybe, it would mean that Wynter wasn't crazy for wanting to know so much more about her and she wasn't risking a seven-year relationship for something insane.

"Wynter?" Remington queried, seeing that Wynter was considering her answer carefully.

Wynter finally shook her head. "I just think she should know how awesome you are."

Remington looked surprised by that answer, but she didn't have time to question Wynter further, because Katrina walked back out onto the balcony then. Remington turned to look at her, she'd never sat down after Katrina had left the balcony.

"That looks impressive," Katrina said, moving to sit down again, her eyes on Remington as she did the same. "Why do you still have your uniform? You aren't still in, are you?"

"Technically, I'm a reservist," Remington said, surprising even Wynter this time.

"You are?" Wynter queried.

Remington gave Wynter a rueful grin. "Yes, and the marine birthday is coming up, which is the only reason it's in my closet here. It looks like I'm going to miss it, however," she said, shrugging.

"Because of the tour?" Wynter asked.

Remington nodded.

"When is it?" Katrina asked.

"November eleventh," Remington said.

Wynter grimaced. It was right about the time the tour would start. "That sucks, I'm sorry."

"The marines aren't going anywhere," Remington said with a confident grin.

Remington's phone pinged again. She glanced down at it, and dropped her head, shaking it.

"What?" Wynter asked.

"Billy said she's going to make a statement to the press," Remington said.

"And that's bad?" Katrina asked.

"Billy isn't really the diplomatic type," Wynter said. "And I'm betting whatever she says won't be okay with Remi…"

"Her responding to Akasha at all is not okay with me," Remington said seriously.

She texted Billy and asked her to please refrain from saying anything. A moment later, the reply came back and Remington grimaced as she read it.

"What did you say?" Wynter asked.

"I asked her not to say anything," Remington said.

"And what did she say?" Wynter asked, her look darkening significantly.

"She asked what I'll do for her," Remington said, her tone wry.

"Oh hell no!" Wynter snapped, seeing that Remington was already responding. "What did you tell her?"

Remington tossed her phone on the coffee table again, leaning back, ignoring Wynter's glower. Wynter picked up the phone to look at the message she'd sent.

"Are you fucking nuts?" Wynter asked Remington. "You know how she's going to take that."

Remington didn't answer. Katrina looked between Remington and Wynter, sensing some serious tension, and she thought it was of a sexual nature, but wasn't sure. She also wanted to know what Remington had said to Billy Montague, but she wasn't brave enough to do what Wynter had just done. She simply looked over at Wynter, who looked supremely unhappy with her bodyguard.

"She told Billy she'd give her whatever she wants," Wynter practically spat. "Mark my words, that's going to come back to bite you square in the ass, Remi," she said as she stood up.

Remington stood as well, clearly not worried about Billy Montague. Wynter looked up at Remington for a long moment, then shook her head and walked back into the house. Remington looked over at Katrina, seeing that Katrina didn't understand exactly what was going on. In truth, Remington was surprised by Wynter's obvious ire, but had no idea what it was about, so she couldn't comment.

"How about some coffee?" Remington asked Katrina to break the tension.

Katrina laughed softly, nodding.

Chapter 3

"Look, I'm sorry," Wynter said, feeling like she was forever apologizing to Remington.

The fact was she couldn't stand the silence in the car. Remington had seen Katrina off that morning, then showered and dressed, then had waited patiently for Wynter to get dressed for Natalia's class. Waited patiently, but with a kind of tension that Wynter could tangibly sense and she hated it.

As she looked over at Remington, she could see that her look had not changed. "Remi, I'm sorry, okay? I just hate that Billy pulled that on you, and that you had to basically beg her to keep her trap shut. It's not cool."

Remington turned her head to look over at Wynter.

"Why does it matter to you?" she asked, her tone not accusing, simply questioning.

Wynter looked back at Remington. She'd known she was going to ask that and still didn't having an adequate answer.

"Everyone knows how Billy is," she said, shrugging. "I just don't think you'd want to get caught up in her drama, especially not with the tour coming up."

Wynter could see that Remington didn't believe her attempt at an explanation for a moment. Fortunately, she let it go anyway. Her phone pinged then and she looked at the message. It was Lauren saying she was sorry she hadn't made it home the night before. Wynter texted back and just said she was glad she hadn't been out in the storm. She and Remington continued the drive in silence.

At Natalia's class, however, Remington was set upon the moment she walked in the door.

"You are going to respond, right?" Jericho said.

"She's gonna hand her her teeth," Quinn practically growled.

Wynter sighed, shaking her head as she glanced back at Remington. "Have fun," she told her bodyguard as she went off toward the dance floor to get ready for class.

Remington narrowed her eyes at Wynter's retreating back but then looked at the other women giving her varied degrees of glowering looks.

"Who's working with me this morning?" Remington said, ignoring the comments and heading toward the room that had recently been set aside for weight training and footwork.

Quinn, Jericho, and Rayden exchanged looks, each grinning or shaking their head, and followed Remington. Eventually, Jet, Sebastian, Tyler, Raine, Skyler, and Cody joined the group doing the MMA-style workout. As the music started for Natalia's cardio dance class, the bois started their workout, shutting the door to the room and putting on bands like Disturbed, Linkin Park, and Breaking Benjamin.

Remington went through her paces, doing bag work with high kicks, knee strikes, spinning back kicks, and various punches and elbow strikes. The others did their best to keep up. Most successful was

Quinn, who'd been doing MMA fighting for years. Raine also did surprisingly well, always able to pick up new moves quickly.

By the time Natalia's class was over, the bois were sparring, but it was quickly suggested that Quinn and Remington spar in the main area so everyone could watch. To Wynter's surprise, Remington agreed. Mats were dragged out and then Quinn and Remington stood facing each other on the mats. Both women wore gloves and had already agreed to keep contact to a minimum. Wynter and Xandy stood off to the side watching, both nervous.

Jericho stepped in to act as referee. She had them touch gloves, backed them up, then gave them the signal to start. Quinn moved toward Remington, who stood her ground watching every move Quinn made. Faking to the right, Quinn brought in a left hook, and Remington shifted her feet quickly, shifting back at the last minute, grabbing Quinn's arm as she extended, twisting it down, sweeping her feet with right food and taking her down to the mat. Remington jumped back up and extended her hand to Quinn to help her up. Quinn nodded, grinning. She knew she was out-matched, but she also enjoyed the challenge. They faced each other again and took fighter's stances. Quinn bounced on her feet, whereas Remington remained perfectly still, her body tense, but her eyes taking in Quinn's movements. Quinn surprised everyone in doing a series of kicks, advancing on Remington quickly. Remington backed up, putting her hands up to block any kick that got too close. When she was near the end of the mat, Remington ducked a high kick, coming up with lightning speed she was known for to grab Quinn's ankle, shoving her back. Quinn managed to keep her balance, going for a spinning back kick, which came dangerously close to Remington's head. Remington shifted just in time to keep from being caught.

"Nice," Remington said, smiling and nodding to Quinn.

Remington stilled for a long moment, and Quinn stood at the ready. Suddenly Remington advanced quickly and Quinn attempted to throw a jab, but Remington shifted quickly and, seeing an opening, she threw a punch at Quinn's face, stopping right when her fist would have connected. Quinn yanked her head back, but knew that had Remington not stopped, she'd have taken a pretty hard blow. She grinned widely, nodding in admiration.

They sparred for another ten minutes. Quinn grew tired, not having quite the stamina that a seasoned fighter like Remington did. At five eight, Quinn was only an inch shorter than Remington was, so they were well matched that way, but Remington had about fifteen pounds on her, and it was all muscle. As they faced each other, Remington could see Quinn was tired and breathing heavily.

"Trase?" Remington said, her eyes sparkling with admiration for the other woman. "Call it a draw?"

Quinn shook her head, bouncing on the balls of her feet. Remington nodded, respecting that Quinn wanted to finish the fight. She brought her hands up, showing Quinn that she was ready again. Quinn shifted forward, moving quickly, and throwing a quick jab. Remington side stepped the fist, and grabbed her arm, spinning with admirable speed, putting her hip to Quinn's midsection and quickly flipping Quinn over her shoulder. Her arm came down and locked around Quinn's shoulders, raising her fist and doing a quick movement to indicate where she would have punched Quinn in a real fight. Quinn put her right arm out, hitting the mat in a tap out movement. Remington immediately released Quinn, getting to her feet and extending her hand.

"Damned good…" Quinn said, shaking her head. "Guess that's why you're the champ, huh?"

Remington merely inclined her head, quirking her lips.

"I know I feel safer already," Wynter said, grinning at Remington as she walked over to pick up her water and take a drink.

"Now, when are you going to do that to Akasha Salt?" Jericho asked.

Remington shook her head. "I'm retired," she said simply. "Veruca is on her own."

"Veruca?" Quinn queried. "I thought her name was Akasha?"

"Veruca is what her fellow MMA fighters called her," Remington said, smiling slightly.

"As in Veruca Salt from Willy Wonka?" Xandy asked.

Remington pursed her lips, nodding. "As in 'I want it now, daddy!' " she said in a fair imitation of the spoiled character from the classic movie. "She always wanted everything right now, including my title."

"But you beat her twice," Wynter added.

"Three times actually, but only twice officially," Remington said, in a very rare show of ego.

"Wait, what?" Quinn asked.

Suddenly everyone was on their phones looking it up. Remington stood by, shaking her head, wishing she'd kept her mouth shut.

"Wait, who's Sage Baker?" Wynter asked having looked up Akasha Salt and Remington LaRoché battles and seeing that name associated with the results.

Remington didn't answer her look wary.

"She's Akasha Salt's girlfriend," Jet said. "Holy fuck, she's hot…" She glanced up at Remington. "You tap that?"

Remington looked shocked by the question.

"She won't answer that in mixed company," Wynter told Jet.

Jet wiggled her eyebrows, grinning unapologetically.

"This says that Akasha accused you of hitting on Sage…" Devin said, looking over at Remington.

"She wouldn't do that," Wynter said.

"No, she wouldn't," Kashena agreed, glancing at her friend.

"She hit on you?" Jericho asked, seeing the look in Remington's eyes.

Everyone looked at Remington for the answer. Remington didn't answer for a long moment, but finally inclined her head, because she knew she wasn't going to get out of it without some kind of answer.

"Ah-ha!" Quinn exclaimed. "That's why Akasha is after you, she knows she can't even keep her girl happy."

"And with a girl that looks like that… that would be a full-time job…" Jet said, her tone low.

"Well, you can't let her keep talking shit about you," Tyler said. "It'll never stop."

"She'll get bored, eventually," Remington said.

"I wouldn't count on it," Quinn said. "She wants your title, and she's not going to give up till she gets it."

"I retired, it's no longer my title," Remington said.

"But you were the one that held it last, and this is personal for her," Jericho pointed out.

Remington didn't respond. She shrugged at the group as she picked up her bag.

"I'm going to go shower," she told Wynter, and then walked away.

The group watched her go.

"She needs to put the beat down on that Salt person," Sebastian said.

"Yeah, she does," Rayden agreed.

Wynter shook her head. "She's pretty adamant about it," she said.

"Akasha Salt's gonna talk herself into some serious trouble," Quinn said with a mutinous look.

"I can't believe anyone would take her seriously," Zoey said.

"People tend to listen to whoever is talking," Jericho said, making a face to indicate her poor opinion of that kind of person.

"Well, maybe we need to come out and say something…" Jet said.

"Oh, she won't like that at all," Wynter said, shaking her head. "Billy Montague was going to say something to the press about the whole matter, and Remi promised her anything she wanted not to do that, so…"

"She wot?" Quinn said, looking stunned.

Wynter rolled her eyes. "Yeah, don't get me started on that…" she said, her voice trailing off ominously.

"Billy Montague? As in Billy and the Kid, Montague?" Jet asked.

"The very same," Wynter said.

"She's straight," Jovina said.

"They're all straight," Cat said, grinning. "Till they're not."

"She's married!" Zoey exclaimed.

"And her husband was right there when she was flirting with Quinn and Remi," Xandy said, glancing at Quinn.

"She was just screwing with you," Quinn said, shaking her head.

"I'm not totally sure about that," Wynter said, her tone annoyed.

A few eyebrows went up at Wynter's tone.

"Guess we're gonna find out," Quinn said looking at Xandy.

Back at the house, Wynter went upstairs to take a shower. Remington sat out on the patio smoking and letting her mind wander over the morning. The last thing she wanted was to talk about all the garbage in the past. No, she hadn't gone after Sage Baker, she didn't go after other women's girlfriends. Sage had shown up at her apartment in New York, claiming she wanted to talk to her about Akasha. Remington had let her in, and offered to take her coat. When Sage had dropped her coat, she was wearing nothing underneath and had locked her arms around Remington's neck and kissed her. It had been a surreal moment, and the sheer sensuality of it had temporarily kept her morals from kicking in. Sage Baker was beyond beautiful. She was exquisite. With skin the color of polished mahogany and light green eyes that matched her name, high cheekbones, perfect pouty lips, and the body of a model. There wasn't a flaw on the woman.

It had taken Sage's loud moan to make Remington realize what she was doing, her hands having been grasping at the woman's skin, her own body a riot of sensations. Breaking the kiss, Remington had carefully set Sage away from her, handing her coat to her while she averted her eyes and had done her best to compose herself.

"You know you want me, Remi…" Sage had said in a heavy Jamaican accent.

"Sage, you're Akasha's girlfriend," Remington had said simply.

"But I can be your girlfriend instead," Sage had replied.

Remington had blown her breath out, shaking her head. "I don't take what does not belong to me."

"Let me belong to you then," Sage said, moving to wind her arms around Remington again.

Remington had pulled her head back, reaching up to take Sage's arms gently in her hands to remove them from her neck.

"Please go," she'd said politely, her eyes still averted because while Sage had put on the coat, she hadn't bothered to close it.

Sage had apparently been shocked to be turned down, and she'd turned nasty immediately.

"You'll be sorry, Remi!" she had told her, striding to the front door and slamming out of it.

The next day the story had been printed that Akasha was challenging Remington to a fight. "I want her title, and she knows it," had been Akasha's statement.

Behind the scenes, Remington had been assailed with texts from Akasha calling her every kind of nasty name for trying to attack Sage. Remington had simply cancelled her number and changed it. It had been a nightmare for a while. Whenever she'd run into the couple, Akasha had made a show of 'owning' Sage. Remington would look at

Sage, her look indicating disappointment for what she was letting Akasha believe. Sage would only sneer back at her.

Remington was so deep in her thoughts, she hadn't heard Laruen come in and go upstairs. What she did hear was a crash. She was up and out of her chair instantly, and vaulting the stairs two at a time. She could hear yelling coming from the master bedroom, and she threw open the door to see Lauren standing over Wynter screaming at her.

Remington took two long strides and put her arm around Lauren's throat, pulling her back away from Wynter. She then extended her hand to Wynter to help her up. Lauren struggled furiously against Remington's grip, but to no avail. When Remington tightened her arm at Lauren's throat, Lauren stopped struggling immediately and started struggling to breathe. Remington had just seen the bruise already starting at Wynter's mouth.

"You're done," Remington growled into Lauren's ear.

With that she marched Lauren out of the room, down the stairs, and out the front door. She walked her all the way to the curb, then let go of her, giving her slight shove. She then turned and walked back into the house shutting the door and locking it, putting the chain on this time.

She walked back into the master bedroom to find Wynter sitting on the bed. She went to sit on the bed facing her. Wynter's head was down, and Remington could see that she was trying to hold it together emotionally. Remington reached out, touching her under the chin to tilt her head up, so she could see what damage Lauren had done. She grimaced at the trickle of blood from Wynter's mouth and brushed it away with her thumb.

Wynter gave an anguished sob then and started to cry, leaning the top of her head against Remington's chest. Remington put her arms around the smaller woman, holding her while she cried. Wynter cried in earnest, her hands grasping at Remington's shirt in her desolation. Remington could hear Lauren pounding on the door downstairs. She seriously considered going back down there and beating the crap out of the woman but knew that Wynter needed her there at that moment.

After twenty minutes, Wynter leaned against Remington, her cheek against Remington's shirt, now wet from her tears. She felt exhausted suddenly. She let Remington's warmth envelop her, lulling and calming her. She felt Remington's hands at her back, moving back and forth soothingly and she closed her eyes, unable to think about what had just happened. It was too much to deal with.

Remington felt Wynter's breath become even, and she also felt her lean more heavily against her. She knew she was asleep. She carefully lay Wynter down and covered her up. As she stood and looked down at the dark-haired vixen, suddenly she looked very small, and Remington felt a stab of guilt for having not been there to stop Lauren before she'd struck her.

She walked out of the bedroom and down the stairs, checking the front door to see if Lauren had been foolish enough to hang around. She hadn't. Remington picked up her phone and called John Machiavelli to let him know what had happened. John was expectedly angry about the danger to Wynter having come from her own girlfriend, but he also stated that he wasn't surprised. He thought Wynter and Lauren had a strained relationship these days. Apparently, Wynter had made a few statements the night at The Club when John had been with her that had led him to believe that Laruen had changed significantly over the years.

"She got into drugs a few years back," John told Remington. "Wynter said she did too, but quickly figured out that it was a dangerous path. She quit, Lauren didn't, and that seems to be where the problem is."

Remington nodded. "I'm pretty sure she was high this morning."

"Try to get her to take out a restraining order," John said. "I think Lauren's name is on that house, so she has a legal right to be there. Wynter needs to take legal action if she wants to keep her away."

"Think she's going to do that?" Remington asked.

"I don't know," John said sounding unhappy at the situation.

Remington checked on Wynter a few times, seeing that she was still sleeping. It had been three hours since the incident when Remington walked in to see that Wynter's eyes were now open. She moved to squat next to the bed, putting her eyes on the same level with Wynter's.

"How are you?" Remington asked her.

Wynter blinked a couple of times, still looking tired. "Okay," she whispered, her voice barely audible.

Remington nodded.

"Lauren?" Wynter asked, her voice still a whisper.

Remington narrowed her eyes at the mention of the other woman's name. "She left," she said simply.

"Did you hurt her?" Wynter asked worriedly.

Remington flinched at the concern in Wynter's voice. "No, I escorted her to the curb."

Wynter nodded. "She was high, Remi," she said then.

Remington didn't respond to that. Instead she said, "She hit you."

"I know," Wynter said, "but I got in her face."

"That doesn't make it okay, Wynter."

"I know, but…" Wynter began, shaking her head, knowing she sounded like so many other women who refused to see an abusive relationship.

"You need to take out a restraining order against her." Remington told her.

"No," Wynter answered instantly, shaking her head. "I won't do that."

Remington looked back at her, her chin rising slightly with the desire to argue. Her eyes looked up at a spot on the wall as she fought for control of her anger.

"Why?" she asked when she finally had her emotions under control.

"Because it'll ruin her and me… and… I just can't, Remi, okay?"

Instead of answering her, Remington put her hand to Wynter's mouth, her thumb touching the bruise, and looked into Wynter's eyes.

"And when she kills you?" she asked in a low, serious tone.

"She won't do that, Remi," Wynter said, moving to sit up in an effort to get away from Remington's worried look.

Remington stood up, looking down at Wynter. "You think that, you don't know it," she said, her tone saying that she was a fool to do so.

"I know her, Remi, okay? She's not normally violent. It sounds like she got ahold of some really bad shit last night and it's messing with her head."

Remington nodded, her look telling Wynter that she knew she was doing her best to cover for Lauren. Finally, she shrugged, shaking her head.

"It's your house and your life," she said simply.

With that, she turned and walked out of the room. Wynter sat staring at where Remington had stood. She knew that she just needed to make it to the tour and then it would give Lauren some time to think about things. She loved Lauren but her drug use was getting out of hand. That's what she'd been telling her that morning when Lauren had shocked her by hitting her and knocking her to the ground. She knew that she needed to use this incident to get Lauren to quit. Maybe she could get her into rehab somewhere. That was the thought that kept her occupied for the next few hours. The apology emails, texts, and voicemail messages started coming in from Lauren by mid-afternoon. By that evening she was begging to come home. By eight she was at the front door and Wynter was letting her in. Remington stood at the top of the stairs watching. Wynter walked Lauren into the living room where they sat and talked. Remington shook her head and went into her room, closing the door quietly.

She texted John to tell him what was going on. She also asked for another night off before the tour, two if she could get it. John responded that he'd make arrangements for two days, knowing that Remington probably needed to get her head together. He knew how she felt, having to guard someone who was in danger but refused to take it seriously. It was difficult. He'd had the same problem with his wife, Cassie.

Remington also texted Katrina asking her how she was doing. They spent the evening texting back and forth and finally on the phone talking about whatever came to mind.

John came through with two days off for Remington, five days after the incident with Lauren. Remington immediately called Katrina asking her to spend those days with her. Katrina happily accepted.

John showed up on Friday morning and Remington briefed him on things in the house. Lauren had been avoiding Remington purposefully and that was just fine with her. Wynter had been pointedly quiet as well, speaking to Remington only when she had to and not talking about the incident with Lauren.

Remington picked Katrina up at her apartment. They went and had a late breakfast and walked around West Hollywood for a little while, walking along Santa Monica Boulevard and into whatever shops caught their eye. It was relaxing. Remington was dressed casually in faded jeans, black combat boots, a black tank top, and a denim camouflage jacket with the Affliction brand name on it. Katrina had dressed up a little, having been excited to see Remington again. She wore black pants, a black off the shoulder blouse with belled sleeves, intricately embroidered with flowers. Over that she wore a soft black cardigan, and heeled suede boots. Her makeup was soft and her long hair flowed in long waves. She looked distinctly feminine and it was a look that appealed to Remington very much.

They made an interesting couple walking down the street, especially when Remington reached over and took Katrina's hand. Katrina glanced over and Remington smiling and squeezed Remington's hand gently. At the Beverly Center they walked through stores. Katrina was particularly interested in taking Remington into Diesel, a very cool clothing store that just screamed "Remington" to Katrina. She quickly found out that Remington's weakness tended to be shoes. She immediately picked up a pair of men's high tops that were made out of blue denim and black leather. They looked at other things, but in the end that's what Remington bought. In fact, she bought a few pairs of shoes. They walked into a store called Traffic and Katrina found it interesting that Remington never even glanced at the women's clothing. She always went to the men's side. Remington noted the grin on Katrina's face, knowing what she was likely thinking.

"I don't bother with women's clothes," Remington told her. "They don't make clothes that fit me very well."

Katrina nodded. 'I figured it was something like that."

Remington picked up a black hoodie that had red and greenish blue wings over the shoulders.

She glanced at Katrina. "Go and look at the women's stuff if you want," she said, smiling, having noted that Katrina hadn't really looked.

"Okay," Katrina said, and went over to the other side of the store.

To Katrina's complete dismay, she loved almost everything on that side of the store. She was just looking at a price tag when Remington walked up.

"Did you find anything you like?" Remington asked.

Katrina had to choke back a cough when she saw the price of the jacket she'd been admiring. Remington quirked a grin, her hazel eyes sparkling.

"You like that one?" she asked.

"No," Katrina said shaking her head. But her eyes told a different story.

"Yes, you do," Remington said, smiling.

"What did you pick up?" Katrina asked, in an effort to distract her.

Remington reached over and picked up the jacket Katrina had been looking at, adding it to the things in her hand.

"What else do you like?" Remington asked, smiling.

"Remi…" Katrina said, shaking her head. "I don't need it. It's okay, really."

Remington looked back at her with a small smile on her face. "I don't need any of this," she said, holding up the clothes she had picked, "but there's no fun in that."

Remington walked around, looking at various things. She picked up a lace hem skirt. "This looks like you, to me."

Katrina pressed her lips together, thinking that it did, but she couldn't even begin to imagine how much it cost. The jacket Remington had picked up so blithely was almost $1,600!

"What about this…" Remington said, picking up a gold and black sheer blouse with a plunging embroidered neckline.

When Katrina didn't answer, Remington waggled her eyebrows at Katrina, making her laugh.

"Remi, you don't have to get me anything, it's totally okay," Katrina said gently.

"I know I don't have to get you anything," Remington said, "but I'd like to, if you'll permit me."

Katrina bit her lip in consternation. "Can we go somewhere… not so…" she began hesitantly.

"Expensive?" Remington supplied.

Katrina blew her breath out, nodding. "Yes!" she said, chuckling.

Remington considered for a moment. Finally, she nodded and set the top back on the rack.

"But I am getting you this," Remington said, holding up the jacket.

"Remi…" Katrina said her look fretful.

"Please?" Remington asked. Her look was so sweet that Katrina couldn't even begin to think of a way to say no.

Katrina closed her eyes, grimacing as she nodded to Remington.

"Good," Remington said, "now try it on so we can make sure it fits."

Katrina went to take off her sweater.

"Wait, wait," Remington said, glancing around for a spot to set her purchase down.

She turned to Katrina to help her remove her sweater and laid it over her arm. Then she helped her put the jacket on. It was a black lambskin motorcycle-style jacket with a sweatshirt-style hood. It looked very cute on Katrina.

"Pafè," Remington said. "Perfect," she then translated.

Katrina looked in the mirror across from her, loving the way the jacket looked, but still worried about Remington spending so much money on her. The last thing she wanted Remington to think was that she wanted her to spend money on her. It had nothing to do with why she was with her.

"You like it," Remington said from behind her, her head down next to Katrina's ear. "I can see it. Please let me get it for you."

"I love it," Katrina agreed, turning to look up at Remington. "I just don't want you to feel like you have to do things like this…"

Remington looked down at the other woman, smiling softly. "I want to do this," she said softly. "I know I don't have to, onètman."

Katrina smiled, wondering if Remington even realized how often she used Creole.

"What does onètman mean?" Katrina asked.

"It means honestly," Remington told her.

Katrina nodded. "Okay, yes, it would be wonderful if you want to buy this for me," she said, doing her best to sound grateful. She had no idea how to be grateful enough to justify a purchase at this level.

Remington smiled brilliantly, nodding her head. "Se bon," she said. "This is good."

A few minutes later, they walked out of the store, and Remington promptly took her hand and led her to the escalator and to the store Forever 21.

"Remi!" Katrina gasped. "No…" she said sincerely, even as her eyes darted all over the store.

"And I say, yes," Remington said, smiling. "I can shop for you or with you, ou chwazi, your choice. I will admit I have a lot less self-control when buying for someone else though…"

"Meaning?" Katrina asked, her tone pointed.

Remington grinned. "Meaning I'll spend a lot more on my own…" she said, shaking her head mournfully.

Katrina blew her breath out, shaking her head. "That's just blackmail Remington LaRoché."

"You say blackmail, I say incentive," she said, grinning unapologetically.

In the end, Remington picked out so many things that she thought she'd like to see Katrina in, they spent the next three hours with Katrina trying on outfits, dresses, and shoes. Remington sat in a chair outside of the dressing room, thoroughly enjoying the impromptu fashion show she was getting. Katrina was a beautiful girl, and she had a very specific style. She looked beautiful in flowery prints, and peasant-style blouses. She had hippie, flower child look, and Remington enjoyed seeing her smile as she stepped out of the dressing room in different outfits. The smile on Katrina's face was the first way Remington knew whether or not she liked whatever she had on. Remington used that to make her decision on whether or not to say she liked it. Fortunately, her true opinion and Katrina's rarely differed.

After an exhaustive day of shopping, and a lot of mileage put on Remington's credit card, much to Katrina's dismay, they decided to have dinner at Remington's apartment. They went to the grocery store to shop for food.

"I have very few things there, since I'm not living there right now," Remington explained as they strolled through the market.

"Well, that does make sense though," Katrina said, "since you're staying at Wynter's. It must be strange though."

"Why do you say that?" Remington asked as she picked up a bottle of wine, and a bottle of Town Branch Bourbon.

"How do you buy food? Things like that?" Katrina asked.

"I buy what I like. It goes in with theirs, but it works out okay, usually," Remington said but there was something in her voice that made Katrina think it wasn't always that simple.

Katrina heard it. "Usually?" she asked. "Did something happen?"

Remington sighed. "Things are a little weird right now."

"Weird how?" Katrina asked, glancing around to make sure no one was paying attention to them, knowing that Remington wouldn't talk too plainly about Wynter.

Remington shook her head. "I'll tell you about it later," she said, thinking the same thing.

You never knew who was listening, especially in Hollywood. The last thing Remington wanted was to cause Wynter more headaches. They finished their shopping trip and went back to Remington's car. It was a short drive to her apartment, since she lived in West Hollywood.

Katrina was not completely surprised by Remington's apartment. It was a nice place, with great views of the Hollywood area. Her furniture was very modern, black and low slung. Even the end tables and coffee tables were black. The accent colors were gray and white. The large flat-screen TV hung on the wall above a low black and chrome console.

Remington noted Katrina's eyes widen at her furniture.

"I guess it's a bit stark," Remington said, shrugging.

"It's fine, it's nice actually," Katrina said. "I'm just not used to modern furniture," she said shrugging. "My apartment is made of odd ball pieces I've been able to beg, borrow, or steal. Not something this cohesive."

"Cohesive," Remington repeated with a wide smile. "Interesting word."

"Well, it does all go together," Katrina said, smiling widely.

"It lacks imagination," Remington said, shrugging. "I know."

"It doesn't," Katrina said, "it says a lot about you, though."

"What does it say?" Remington asked, as she started to unload the shopping.

Katrina looked around, noticing that even the kitchen had little color, other than the light earth tones of the granite countertops.

"It says you're not really fussy when it comes to your space," Katrina said.

"Well, that's true," Remington agreed. "You're probably really going to hate the bed," she said looking amused.

"Why?" Katrina asked.

"It's really modern," Remington said. "I found it in Japan and liked it."

Katrina smiled. "To be perfectly clear here, Remington, I don't hate your living room furniture at all. I like it. I think it fits you very well."

"Well, let's see what you think about the bedroom then," Remington said holding her hand out to Katrina.

In the bedroom, Katrina was indeed surprised, but also fascinated by the bed. It was on a low platform, the mattress was offset on the platform, and there to the right of the mattress were lit blue squares set in a black lacquered frame that ran the length of the mattress. It was very modern indeed.

"Wow," Katrina said, smiling as she did, "you're right, it's really different, but again, so much you, I think."

Remington gave her a sidelong look. "You think?"

"Well, what I know of you," Katrina said, suddenly feeling shy.

They were standing in Remington's bedroom, and Katrina had been wondering all day, in fact all week, if tonight was going to be the first time they would finally make love. Suddenly they were in a bedroom, and Katrina couldn't help but wonder again.

"We need to start dinner," Katrina said then, knowing she needed to get out of the room before she did something really stupid like throw herself at Remington and make a fool of herself.

Remington nodded, turning to leave the room. Katrina followed.

They made dinner, and ate talking and drinking wine. Afterwards, Remington cleared the dishes, but Katrina insisted on washing them. Remington acquiesced after a lengthy discussion.

"Go relax," Katrina said, "it's one of your few days off."

Remington nodded. "Alright. Do you want another glass of wine?"

"Yes, please," Katrina said, smiling.

Remington poured the remainder of the bottle into Katrina's glass. She then got a glass out of one of the cabinets, put ice in it and poured herself bourbon.

Katrina found Remington sitting in the living room a little while later. She had her feet up on the coffee table, looking very comfortable, having long since taken off her jacket and kicked off her shoes.

Remington stood when she saw Katrina walk into the room.

"Oh…" Katrina said, grimacing. "I didn't want to disturb you."

"You didn't," Remington said, smiling as she stood looking at Katrina.

Katrina walked over, holding her glass of wine, and sat down. Remington sat down next to her, facing her. Remington drained her glass, and then surprised Katrina by taking the glass of wine out of her hand and setting it on the coffee table.

Turning back, Remington leaned in, and kissed Katrina's lips softly. Katrina put her hands to Remington's waist, her thumbs moving back and forth on the material of the tank top Remington wore as Remington continued a slow exploration of her lips. Remington's lips on hers were soft, gentle and Katrina sighed quietly, feeling almost dizzy with the desire that filled her. As if she'd sensed it, Remington slid one hand behind Katrina's neck, pulling her closer, her lips deepening the kiss slightly. Katrina's hands tightened at Remington's waist, then slid around her back. They kissed for what seemed like hours. Eventually, Remington stood up, extending her hand to Katrina.

She led Katrina back to her bedroom, then gently pushed her down to sit on the bed. Her lips took gentle possession of Katrina's again as she pressed her back to lie on the bed. Remington took hours to make love to her, her movements slow and deliberate. No woman had ever taken so much care caressing and making her feel desired.

When Katrina finally lay naked under Remington's hands, she was way beyond logical thought. Her body responded to every touch, and she felt as if she could fly apart at any moment, but Remington lips never became demanding. Katrina pulled at Remington, who still wore an exercise bra and boy shorts.

"Remi… please…" Katrina said softly. "I want to see you…"

Remington smiled down at her, and inclined her head. She removed the rest of her clothes, then went back to kissing Katrina again as she pressed her well-muscled, but still lean body against Katrina's side.

As she kissed Katrina her hand caressed and touched everywhere. Katrina turned to face Remington, wanting to touch her as much as she was being touched. She pressed herself against Remington, who surprised her by moving to her back, and pulling Katrina over her. Remington kissed her again, her hands sliding over Katrina's back, pressing her closer, and moving her body against Katrina's sensually. Within minutes, Katrina was moaning softly, her breathing becoming quick short gasps. She moved faster, wanting Remington closer. When Remington slid her hand between them, touching Katrina, it was all Katrina could take. She came gasping loudly, pressing her body against Remington's hand.

As her shudders subsided, she kissed Remington, her whole body still trembling. After a few minutes, she sat up and straddled Remington's waist and looking down at the ex-fighter, her eyes taking in Remington's incredible physique.

"Oh my god, Remi, you are so incredible…" she breathed, her eyes reflecting her awe, as her hands touched Remington's abs and slid upward.

Remington sat up, pulling Katrina back down with her, her lips on Katrina's again. Katrina started moving her body on Remington's, pressing and grinding. Remington's breath became uneven, and her hands pressed Katrina's body closer.

Katrina became excited again, and in the end, they came together. As they lay together afterwards, Remington lifted her hand to Katrina's face and stroked it as she looked up into Katrina's eyes. Katrina smiled down at her.

****

Wynter was climbing the walls. She'd been sitting out on the patio for two hours, smoking, and drinking Smirnoff Ice. Fortunately, Lauren had left the house a couple of hours before. Lauren was driving her insane! She had been constantly underfoot for the last week and Wynter had been ready to kill her a few times. It was interesting to her that Lauren had chosen to leave the house the same day Remington had left the house as well.

She was pleasantly surprised when Xandy walked out onto the patio.

"Hey, what are you doing here?" Wynter asked smiling.

"I thought I'd come check on you," Xandy said.

"Where's Quinn?" Wynter asked.

"She's in talking to Mackie. Where's Remi?"

"Probably fucking Katrina as we speak," Wynter said, sighing.

Xandy's eyes widened significantly. "Okay…" she said hesitantly.

"Sorry," Wynter said, grimacing, "but you did ask."

"I guess I didn't really expect that level of detail," Xandy said, grinning.

"Yeah, sorry," Wynter said, rolling her eyes. "It's all I've been thinking about all day, so…"

"Why?" Xandy asked.

Wynter looked pensive, blowing her breath out as she shook her head. "Because I'm stupid."

"You're wot?" Quinn asked, as she walked out onto the patio. She leaned down to kiss Wynter on the cheek.

"Stupid," Wynter repeated.

"Why?" Quinn asked, moving to sit down.

"Because she's been thinking about…" Xandy began.

"Because I've been obsessing about sleeping with my bodyguard all day," Wynter said, lighting another cigarette.

Even Quinn was shocked for a moment. She glanced at Xandy who simply shrugged.

"And this started when?" Quinn asked.

"Oh, the same day I met her," Wynter said simply.

"Uh…" Quinn stammered.

"At the benefit concert?" Wynter supplied.

"Didn't she stop you from getting in?" Quinn asked.

"Yeah but she was totally hot about it," Wynter said, grinning.

"Okay…" Quinn said, grinning.

"I know, I'm stupid, I get it," Wynter said.

"Wynter, what about Lauren?" Xandy asked.

Wynter made a face, shaking her head. "She's driving me crazy right now… I just… I don't know."

"Do you still love her?" Xandy asked.

"I don't know," Wynter said. "Things have gotten… bad."

"Bad how?" Quinn asked, her tone all bodyguard all of a sudden.

Wynter didn't answer, but her face said it all.

"How's Remi taking that?" Quinn asked.

"Oh, she was pretty pissed… and then she was mad at me. Still is, I think."

"Why?" Xandy asked.

"Because I wouldn't take out a restraining order against her."

"What happened?" Xandy asked, sensing Quinn's sudden agitation. She had a problem with women being hit as much as Remington did.

"The night of that storm, Lauren didn't come home," Wynter said. "But she came home later that day, after class… and I really kind of laid into her about her drug use… It's getting bad… and well… she…"

"She wot?" Quinn asked her tone ominous.

"She hit me," Wynter said. "She was really high, and I really don't think she meant to do it, but—"

"It doesn't matter," Quinn said, shaking her head. "She had no right and I seriously hope Remi took her apart for it."

"No," Wynter said, "but she did march her out of the house."

"And then you let her back in," Xandy said, grimacing.

"Yeah," Wynter said, nodding.

"Why?" Quinn asked.

"We've been together for seven years, Quinn," Wynter said.

"Yeah, and apparently a week too long if she thinks she can do that and get away with it, which she did," Quinn said, her tone agitated.

"Quinn," Xandy cautioned.

Quinn looked over at Xandy and saw the way she was looking at her. Quinn blew her breath out slowly.

"If you want Remi, why don't you just go for it?" Quinn asked.

"I'm not her type," Wynter said. "She likes the really girlie girls, like Katrina."

"Aw, Wynter," Quinn said, rubbing the bridge of her nose with her forefinger. "I dunno if you've looked in a mirror lately, but you're very much a girlie girl."

"Yes, but not Remi's kind of girlie girl, Quinn," Wynter said. "She hates that I cuss, drink, smoke… pretty much everything I do…"

Quinn looked considering, then nodded. "Yeah she does tend to like them a bit more… aw… innocent."

Wynter gave Quinn a narrowed look. "Thanks," she said wryly.

"Happy to help," Quinn replied, grinning.

"I need to get her out of my brain!" Wynter said, scrubbing at her face. "I'm so totally obsessed with her, it's driving me crazy!"

"Oh, I get that," Xandy said, nodding.

"You do?" Wynter asked.

"Oh yeah," Xandy said, smiling over at Quinn. "I was completely obsessed with Quinn when I first met her too. I thought I was going nuts."

"You weren't even gay then," Quinn said, grinning.

"At least I didn't think so," Xandy said, nodding.

"But when you figured it out… it was it like bam!" Wynter asked.

"No, it took a while to convince her," Xandy said, winking at Quinn.

"And now?" Wynter asked, looking at Quinn.

"Now," Quinn said seriously, "she's not just in my head, she's in my blood."

Wynter sighed. "See? That's what I want! I want someone to say that about me… I want to be in someone's blood… Jesus…"

Xandy and Quinn looked at each other, both of them understanding Wynter's anguish.

"You don't think you have that with Lauren?" Xandy asked.

"What she's got in her blood is drugs and alcohol," Wynter said sadly.

"Well, you need to get rid of her," Quinn said.

"And then what?" Wynter said. "Be alone? No thanks."

"Alone?" Quinn queried. "You could have any woman you want."

"Except the one I actually want," Wynter said.

"You aren't in love with her…" Xandy said, her tone somewhat worried.

Wynter shook her head. "I don't think so, but I know I want her more than any woman I've ever wanted before." She leaned forward conspiratorially then. "Did you know I specifically requested her?"

"No," Xandy said.

"Yes," Quinn said at the same time.

"You did?" Wynter asked, looking at Quinn. "How?"

Quinn grinned. "I offered to take the bullet for Remi, but Mackie told me that you'd specifically requested her."

"Take the bullet?" Wynter repeated.

"Yeah," Quinn said, grinning unrepentantly, "you have kind of a rep, babe."

Wynter sighed, shaking her head.

"If it makes you feel any better, you aren't quite the bitch everyone thought…"

"Oh, gee, thanks," Wynter said, giving Quinn a narrowed look.

Quinn just laughed shaking her head.

"Well, it's worse, 'cause I told Mackie that I want Remi in the room with me while we're on tour."

"You wot!" Quinn exclaimed.

Wynter nodded, grimacing at Quinn's glowering look.

"Wow… that's going to be… aw… fun," Quinn said.

"Not if things stay the way they are between me and Remi they won't be."

"I was being sarcastic, love," Quinn said, winking.

"I know! And thanks for that," Wynter said, sounding anything but grateful.

Xandy and Quinn left the house a little while later. Wynter didn't feel any better when they did. She ended up going to bed early that night, doing her best not to picture Remington and Katrina having sex all night long.

She awoke to Lauren cussing a blue streak.

"What?" Wynter said, starting awake and sitting up. "Lauren, what are you doing?"

"Just tryin' ta get undressed here, thas all…" Lauren slurred.

Wynter shook her head. Lauren was obviously drunk and probably high again as well. So much for all the promises she'd made this last week about getting off the drugs. Laying back down, Wynter turned over facing away from where Lauren was getting undressed.

She felt Lauren get into bed behind her, then she felt her hands slide over her ass.

"C'mere baby…" Lauren murmured, grabbing at her breasts from behind.

"Lauren, stop," Wynter said, her tone sharper than she'd meant it to be. "You're drunk."

"So?" Lauren snapped. "I'm not a dude, I don't gotta get it up er nothing… I can fuck you with this," she said, shoving her finger into Wynter's body making her gasp in pain.

"Jesus!" Wynter exclaimed jumping away from Lauren's hand.

"Come back here, I wanna fuck…" Lauren said. She was attempting sexy, but it came out more like a man than Wynter had ever heard.

Lauren grabbed her arm, pulling her back to her and fastening her mouth on Wynter's, her hands sloppily trying to caress her. Wynter could sense the underlying violence in Lauren's movement, and didn't want to instigate another fight. She did her best to relax and get into it, but Lauren's breath smelled, and she did as well. In a last-ditch effort to keep her revulsion from showing, Wynter imagined that Lauren was actually Remington. That was the only thing that got her through it. Afterwards, Lauren fell into a deep sleep, or maybe she passed out, Wynter wasn't sure which. Either way, she crawled out of bed and took a shower scrubbing Lauren's smell off her. She ended up going into Remington's room to sleep, pressing her face into Remington's pillow and inhaling the scent she always wore.

Two days later, Remington arrived back at the house feeling relaxed, happy, and sated. She and Katrina had spent a good deal of time exploring the new level of their relationship. It had been a nice couple of days. Remington was hoping that things at the house had finally settled down. As she opened the door, she was blasted with music pouring from the Bose speakers in the kitchen. The Evanescence song "When You're Sober" was on and Wynter was singing it with abandon as she cooked.

The line, that talked about how the other person couldn't take responsibility for their actions, but there was no playing the victim this time, obviously struck a chord.

Remington looked around wondering where Lauren was. She watched as Wynter moved to the music and sang the words. Wynter turned and saw Remington standing in the doorway. She picked up the remote to the Bose and turned the music down.

"So, you're back," she said, her tone icy. "Did you have fun?"

Remington noted the tone, and saw how tensely Wynter was now moving.

"Did something happen?" Remington asked sounding worried.

She couldn't see Wynter's lips press together. All she could see was Wynter shaking her head.

"It is what it is, you know?" she said, her tone forcefully cheerful.

"Wynter…" Remington began cautiously. "John was here, right? Because if he wasn't here…"

"Nothing fucking happened Remi, okay!" she yelled.

Remington's chin came up, noting the slightly hysterical ring in Wynter's voice. She watched as Wynter threw meat into a pan and splashed her arm with hot grease, causing her to cry out. Remington was there instantly, as Wynter grabbed a towel to wrap around her arm.

"Let me see it," Remington said.

"It's fine!" Wynter snapped, yanking her arm away from Remington and turning her back to her.

"Wynter, let me see it," Remington said again, keeping her tone calm.

"Just leave it alone, okay?" Wynter said.

"Please, honey… just let me see it," Remington said then.

Wynter closed her eyes at the endearment Remington used. She felt Remington turn her around, and take the towel off the burn. Wynter hissed in pain.

"Okay, put it under cold water…" Remington said, turning on the faucet and moving Wynter's arm under it. "Just hold it there for a minute, okay?" she said gently.

Wynter did what Remington said, refusing to look over at her however. After a few long minutes, Wynter pulled her arm out of the cold water and put the towel around it again, holding her arm up in front of her like a shield as she leaned against the counter.

Remington stood in front of her, looking down at her. She knew she'd missed something. Something else had happened, and not even John had known. The guilt welled up again and Remington felt the stab as she looked down at the woman she was supposed to protect.

Lowering her head, Remington put the side of her chin against Wynter's temple.

"I'm sorry…" she whispered.

"Don't," Wynter whispered harshly, tears in her voice.

"I'm sorry…" Remington repeated her hands on Wynter's shoulders.

Wynter's resolve weakened and she felt tears in her throat. She'd just started to lean into Remington when they both heard Lauren coming down the stairs. Remington stepped back and leaned on the opposite counter, and Wynter turned back to cooking.

"Oh, look who's back," Lauren said, her tone full of venom.

"Yes, look who's back," Remington said, her tone low, her hazel eyes narrowing at Lauren.

"When's dinner, babe?" Lauren asked, grabbing at Wynter's ass.

Remington curled her lip wanting nothing more than to grab Lauren's wrist and snap it in two.

"So," Lauren said, as she hopped up to sit on the counter next to where Wynter stood, "did you get some?"

Remington stared at her with a face that could have been carved out of marble for all the emotion that showed on it. She stepped forward and leaned down to Wynter on her right side.

"I'll be upstairs if you need me," she told Wynter gently.

With that she turned and walked out of the kitchen.

Chapter 4

The day of the beginning of the tour dawned. Wynter couldn't get out of the house fast enough. Remington carried their bags to the waiting Escalade. Lauren lurked around the front door, and Wynter wasn't looking forward to that scene. She tried to make it quick, kissing Lauren on the lips and saying she'd call her when she could. Unfortunately, it wasn't that easy. Lauren grabbed her arm, pulling her roughly to her, smashing her mouth down on hers.

Remington stood leaning against the column a foot from them with a direct look. Lauren could almost feel Remington's eyes boring into her, and she looked up, irritation clear on her face.

"Do you mind?" she snapped. "I'm trying to say goodbye to *my* girlfriend," Lauren said, tightening her grip on Wynter's arm, causing Wynter to wince.

"You put one more bruise on her, and it'll be the last thing you do," Remington said simply, her arms crossed over her chest, her eyes narrowed.

Wynter felt Lauren tense so she quickly kissed her again trying to prevent a huge fight occur on their front stoop. When Lauren insisted on lengthening the kiss, Remington moved to stand up straight, her look bordering on hostile.

"We do have a plane to catch," Remington said evenly.

"I need to go," Wynter said, pulling away and backing up closer to Remington just in case Lauren thought to try and grab her again.

Lauren had the temerity to step forward like she was going to try and stop Wynter from leaving. Remington stepped forward giving her a warning look.

"The lady said she needs to go," Remington said, her tone brooking no argument.

Lauren's lips twitched with the desire to say something, and a slow dangerous grin spread over Remington's lips, her eyes just daring Lauren to say the wrong thing.

Wynter tugged at a handful of the leather jacket Remington wore, trying to get her out of there before things escalated. Remington glanced back at Wynter and saw the pleading look in her blue eyes and she gave in.

They walked to the Escalade, and Remington opened the door for Wynter, before climbing in behind her. Someone else was doing the driving this time. They made it to Long Beach airport where BJ's plane waited to take the group to New York where they were starting the first leg of the tour. Wynter and Remington were the first to arrive, so they were able to choose seats. Wynter headed to the back of the plane and sat down on the couch. Remington followed her, setting Wynter's carry-on bag near her on the couch and moving to set her laptop case down.

By the time the rest of the group showed up, Wynter was already tired. The night before had been long, and she knew they had a show that night, so she needed to rest. She lay down, trying to get comfortable, but found the arms of the couch were too low. She shifted and turned around. Remington watched her with a raised eyebrow. Wynter finally sat up, looking pensive, glancing over at Remington.

"What do you need?" Remington asked her.

"I spot for my head," Wynter said. "The couch arm is too low. I'll end up with a kink in my neck, and pillows are just going to fall over…"

Remington glanced behind her to see a pillow on the nearby seat. Leaning back, she grabbed the pillow and placed in on her lap, patting the pillow. Wynter looked back at her questioningly.

"You have a show tonight, right?" Remington said.

"Yes," Wynter said, nodding.

"You need sleep, right?" Remington asked then.

"Yes," Wynter replied again.

Remington patted the pillow again, her look pointed. Wynter pressed her lips together, nodding as she moved to lie down on the couch again, and put her head on the pillow in Remington's lap. Remington put her arm up on the back of the couch, holding the book she was reading with her other hand. Wynter turned to face Remington's torso, breathing in the crisp clean scent she wore, combined with the leather of her jacket. She shivered slightly as the cool air hit her. Remington reached above her to turn the air off, then shrugged out of her jacket, and laid it over Wynter's upper body. Wynter snuggled under the jacket sighing at the warmth still contained in it from Remington's body heat.

Xandy and Quinn walked to the back of the plane and saw Wynter lying with Remington's leather Affliction jacket over her, and her head in Remington's lap. Remington glanced up at the two as they settled themselves in chairs near her.

"Morning," Remington said.

"Damned early," Quinn grumbled.

"Hi," Xandy said, smiling. "She's already out?"

"Yeah," Remington said, "I don't think she got a lot of sleep last night."

Xandy looked pensive, but nodded.

It was another half hour before Billy made an appearance, and naturally grumbled about the couch being taken. Remington merely looked back at Billy smiling smugly.

"If you weren't so fuckin' hot," Billy said, sliding a nail along Remington's jawline, "you wouldn't get away with that."

Remington's lips curled in a sardonic grin. Billy turned and walked back toward the front of the plane and they took off twenty minutes later.

Wynter awoke three hours into the flight. She sat up and looked around, as she slid her arms into the sleeves of Remington's jacket. She got something to eat from one of the flight attendants and then sat back on the couch, listening to Quinn and Remington debate fight techniques. Wynter noted that even while she was involved in conversation, Remington stood when she'd gotten up and did the same when she'd come back to the couch.

"Yeah, but if you go into that one you better be committed," Remington was saying.

"Nah, you can back out," Quinn said, shaking her head.

"How?" Remington asked, looking doubtful.

"As fast as you are?" Quinn said. "And all that stride length? Two fast steps you're out."

"Yeah, but one good hit and I'm down," Remington countered.

"Right, well, that's the fast part," Quinn said, grinning, "but you get in there, and you can take your opponent down in one quick move."

Remington looked considering, but shook her head slowly. "Not sure I'd risk that one."

"Aw, I'll show you next time we spar," Quinn said. "You could pull it off, I know ya could."

Billy walked by, headed to the bathroom at the back of the plane. She made a point of sliding her hand over Remington's knee as she passed, her blue eyes sparkling mischievously. Wynter narrowed her eyes immediately, glancing over at Xandy who just shook her head.

"Why do you let her get to you?" Remington asked catching Wynter's glare. "You know that's what she's doing."

"She needs to stay on her side of the fence," Wynter said.

Remington chuckled, shaking her head and exchanging a look with Quinn. They both knew that Billy Montague was only harassing Remington because she knew Wynter would react to it, whereas Xandy simply looked on patiently.

When Billy came back through, she went to sit on Remington's lap, throwing her arm around her shoulders.

"So, what are you bois back here talking about?" she asked, smiling down at Remington.

"Fighting techniques, different throws," Remington replied with a mild look.

"Throws?" Billy queried.

"Ways to take someone down to the mat," Quinn provided.

"Ohhh…" Billy said, her tone full of sexual innuendo. "You can do that to me anytime," she said, sliding the back of her index finger down Remington's cheek.

"Her girlfriend might have a problem with that," Wynter said.

"From the way you're acting, you'd think you were her girlfriend," Billy replied mildly, the sparkle in her blue eyes belying that mild tone.

Wynter narrowed her eyes at Billy. "Don't you have a husband to take care of?"

"He's asleep, but thanks for your concern," Billy replied tartly.

Wynter started to stand up, but Remington was faster once again and quickly stood first, easily picking Billy up as she did. She set her on her feet, turning so her back was to Wynter.

"Oh my, so strong…" Billy said, smiling lasciviously.

Wynter sprang to her feet and reached for Billy. Quinn jumped up, taking Billy by the shoulders and pulling her back, as Remington turned to deal with Wynter.

"Stop," Remington told Wynter calmly, seeing that her eyes were blazing.

"She needs to just—" Wynter began.

"Just stop," Remington said, her voice still calm and still soft, her eyes searching Wynter's. "This isn't about her… Don't make it about her."

Wynter looked up at Remington surprised by what she was saying. Her lips parted to say something, but then she shook her head and sat back down. Remington turned to Billy then.

"Ms. Montague," she said, her tone both formal and polite, "please respect my position enough to stop causing trouble for me, Dakò? Okay?"

Billy stared up at Remington, smiling softly, then she lowered her eyes and nodded. "I apologize," she said, not to Wynter, but to Remington.

With that she walked away. Quinn and Remington rolled their eyes at each other, each grinning and sat down again.

Later when Xandy and Quinn went forward to talk to Jordan and Dylan, Wynter took a moment to speak to Remington without the others around.

"What did you mean earlier?" she asked. "When you said that it wasn't about Billy."

Remington looked over at her, her look considering. "I think it's about you and Lauren," she said honestly.

"How?" Wynter asked.

"You can't control how Lauren acts, or what she does, and now you feel out of control with how Billy is acting."

Wynter looked back at Remington, canting her head sideways. "Couldn't be that I'm totally jealous of her attention to you?"

Remington looked surprised by that question but then suddenly cautious.

"Why would you be jealous of that?" Remington asked.

Wynter dropped her eyes, shaking her head. "I'm just saying, you think it's about Lauren, and I think it's because Billy's a bitch."

"Okay, but you know that, so stop helping her out by letting it bother you," Remington pointed out.

"Are you into her?" Wynter asked suddenly.

Remington's mouth dropped open slightly at such a direct question. She closed her mouth, looking toward the ceiling. "Other than teenage fantasies," she said with a sly grin, "no."

Wynter narrowed her eyes, not liking that Remington had any fantasies relating to Billy Montague. "Teenage fantasies?"

Remington looked embarrassed and lowered her head, her lips pursing in consternation.

"Oh my… you're actually embarrassed," Wynter said, her ire increasing. "Jesus, how many of them did you have?"

Remington coughed, shaking her head and looking away. "Not the time or the place," she said simply.

"Name the time and place, I'll be there," Wynter replied seriously.

Remington looked over at her sharply, once again surprised by Wynter's tone.

Wynter knew she was saying too much, and showing too much as well. To deflect whatever questions Remington might ask, Wynter stood and stretched. Remington stood as well, still looking perplexed by Wynter's comments. Wynter walked past Remington and headed for the bathroom. In the bathroom, she put the lid on the toilet down and sat on it, banging her head against the wall for a few minutes.

"Just shut up next time, Wynter, just shut up…" she muttered to herself.

She knew that her obsession with Remington was going to continue to be an issue, but she had no idea what to do about it. She desperately wanted to make a play for Remington to see what would happen, but she was afraid that if she did and Remington turned her down, it would hurt a lot and Remington would leave. Self-control wasn't something Wynter Kincade had in any quantifiable amount. It was one of her biggest flaws.

By the time they landed in Albany, New York, Wynter was climbing the walls wanting out of the plane. It was 4 p.m. local time and their first show was set for 7 p.m. In the meantime, they needed to do a sound check and get ready for the show. A fleet of Escalades picked them up from the airport and drove the twenty-five minutes to the venue, Times Union Center. Remington and Quinn stood by and directed the security team that met them at the venue. Then they each made their way to either side of the stage, waiting while sound checks were done.

The first sound check was with Jordan, who sailed through with minimal drama. Next was Billy who screamed at the sound engineer for twenty minutes because she kept getting feedback.

Wynter stood next to Remington watching Billy rage.

"She just loves to yell, doesn't she?" Wynter said to Remington. "Is that really what people think I'm like too?"

Remington's look said yes because she couldn't.

"Damnit…" Wynter said. "Gotta change that. I don't want to sound like that to people!"

"It's all under your control," Remington told her. "Just be who you really are."

Wynter glanced up at her in surprise and then smiled as she realized that Remington was trying to encourage her.

After Billy's sound check, Wynter walked out onto the stage. She shaded her eyes because the light crew was doing their thing at the same time and it was rather bright.

"Memphis, is it?" Wynter called, having heard the sound engineer's name a few times.

"You got it, sweetie!" came the reply from the brash-blond sound engineer. One of the best.

"For my in-ears, I just want the rhythm line, okay?" Wynter asked.

"Got it," Memphis replied, winking at Wynter. "Go for it."

Wynter started to sing one of her new songs. Her voice started low and soft, and slowly built. When she hit the highest note there was a screech of feedback and she winced at the loud sound.

"Sorry!" Memphis called. "This system is garbage! Can we try it again, Ms. Kincade? Just the last few notes, please."

Wynter nodded, taking a deep breath and beginning to sing again. This time when she hit the note and held it, the sound was perfect. Remington found herself smiling proudly at the incredible beauty of Wynter's singing. She had an incredible voice that went right through a person.

"She's got some serious range on her," Jordan said from beside Remington.

"Range?" Remington asked.

"You know how her voice started out low then built and finally hit that last note?" Jordan said. "That's her range, and I'm betting the longer she works with Beege, the farther he'll push her. She's definitely got a serious future if she doesn't fuck it up."

"How would she do that?" Remington asked.

Jordan was surprised by the question. "Oh, things like drugs, drinking, screwing around, getting arrested…"

Remington's eyes widened. "I thought those kinds of things made you rock stars famous," she said, grinning.

"Only the men, sweetie," Jordan said, her tone sneering.

"Double standard?" Remington said.

"We're in America, right?" Jordan replied, winking.

"Yes we are…" Remington replied.

Wynter walked off stage then and smiled at Jordan.

"Nice job," Jordan said, "short and sweet."

"Well, I figure Billy took care of the bitchfest for all of us," Wynter said, grinning.

"She always does," Jordan replied, grinning as well.

Fortunately, the hotel they were set to stay in that evening within was walking distance from the center, so the group was able to go back to the hotel to get ready for the show. The room Remington and Wynter had was a single queen, much to Remington's dismay. Wynter made a show of asking for a room with two beds, but was told that the hotel was completely booked due to their show that evening.

"I'm really sorry, Ms. Kincade," the girl said. She was a big fan. "When the rooms were booked they didn't tell us anything about who would be staying in them."

Wynter nodded, glancing up at Remington.

"Sorry, Remi," she said.

Remington just nodded, and turned to pick up their bags to take them to the room.

Twenty minutes later Wynter was prowling the room, pacing. Before long, she grabbed her cigarettes and her phone and walked out onto the room's small balcony. Remington stood in the doorway watching Wynter pace back and forth in the span of a ten-foot balcony. Wynter was playing music on her phone and was singing and smoking as she paced.

"You do realize people can see you from here, right?" Remington said at one point, seeing people standing on the street below, only two floors away, looking up at her.

Wynter glanced down at the street, waved to the people below and continued to pace.

"They have cameras," Remington pointed out.

"So?" Wynter said, rolling her eyes. "What am I doing that's interesting?"

"I think people feel whatever you do is interesting," Remington replied.

"Remi, I have cameras pointed at me all day every day, I don't even care anymore. I mean," she said, turning to lean a hip against the railing looking back at Remington, "unless you want to give them something interesting to take pictures of..." Her voice trailed off seductively.

"Not funny," Remington said her eyes narrowed.

"Are ya sure?" Wynter asked, grinning. "'Cause I think it was kinda funny," she said with a wink.

Remington just looked back at her, her face composed in a serious look.

"Oh my God, Remi, lighten up, sheesh!" Wynter exclaimed throwing her hands up.

"Have you had bodyguards that took you up on that offer previously?" Remington asked doubtfully.

Wynter laughed mirthlessly, shaking her hair out. "Oh, sure, all the time, actually," she said derisively. "Problem was they were all men."

Remington looked shocked. "Are you being serious?"

Wynter threw her a disdainful look. "Sadly, yes, I am."

Remington shook her head. "Fout…" she muttered, not liking the feeling of possessive rage that wiggled its way into her heart.

"Is that why you requested me?" Remington asked.

Wynter looked over at her sharply, then she sighed, shrugging. "I guess, partly."

"What does that mean?" Remington asked.

"What's 'fout'?" Wynter countered.

"It's like… damn," Remington said.

"So you're allowed to cuss in front of me if it's in Creole?" Wynter asked, grinning.

Remington drew in a breath and blew it out in obvious frustration as she shook her head. "No, that was inappropriate of me."

"Remi, I didn't even know what it meant," Wynter said, wondering if the woman ever gave herself a break.

"What did you mean by partly?" Remington asked again.

Wynter's lips twitched, she had hoped Remington wouldn't ask the question again. She lit another cigarette and continued to pace. Finally, she shrugged noncommittally.

"I don't know, I guess that I liked you right off the bat, and I felt like you could really protect me."

Remington's look reflected shock.

"You liked me right off?" Remington asked.

"Yeah," Wynter said, grinning, "you didn't take my shit."

"I also manhandled you," Remington said.

"Is that what that was?" Wynter said, smiling with her tongue between her teeth. Her eyes shone mischievously which should have warned Remington. "I've been handled rougher during sex, Remi."

Remington closed her eyes, feeling the words go right to her core. What was it about this woman that had a way of making her body stir in ways it never had, even when she was being outrageous?

Wynter saw the look on Remington's face, and knew she'd nailed her with that one. She did her best not to look triumphant.

"What I mean to say is that you hardly 'manhandled' me," Wynter explained, her tone perfectly innocent this time.

Remington didn't fall for it. She knew that Wynter liked her effect on people; she knew she was just the target for the moment.

"Why do you do that?" Remington asked her, trying to turn the tables.

"Do what?" Wynter asked innocently enough, but the look in her eyes told Remington she knew exactly what she meant.

Remington lowered her chin, looking directly into Wynter's eyes. "Say things like that."

Wynter was about to say, 'like what?' but the words died on her lips as she stared back up at Remington, getting tangled in the sudden desire to push her luck.

"Because I want to," Wynter said her answer completely honest.

"Because you want to or because you want people to react?" Remington asked, her tone softening.

"Because I want you to react," Wynter said, feeling her pulse race and her breathing becoming heavier as she waited for Remington's response.

"Me?" Remington asked.

"You," Wynter said, her eyes staring up into Remington's, her look completely open.

Remington contemplated Wynter's words as she looked for signs of deception on Wynter's face. She couldn't detect any sign of deceit, or any sign that Wynter was kidding. It scared the hell out of her. That fear manifested itself physically as Remington took a step back, keeping her eyes on Wynter.

Wynter didn't say a word, she didn't move for a long moment. She felt the stab in her heart at Remington's rejection. She'd known it would hurt if she rejected her, but she'd pushed anyway. Fortunately, she hadn't gone too far yet.

She tossed aside her cigarette and stripped off the tank top she wore, exposing a black lace bra and a lot of perfectly smooth, toned and tanned skin. She walked past Remington into the room and headed for the bathroom.

"I'm going to take a shower," she said over her shoulder.

Remington stood where she was, putting an arm out to brace herself on the doorjamb. She knew the picture of Wynter in the black lace bra was going to be burned into her brain for many nights to come. The woman had an illegally sexy body and it was going to be living hell to live with that for the next eight to nine months. Blowing her breath out, Remington looked up at the ceiling, hearing the shower start.

"E koulye a, mwen bezwen yon douch frèt…" Remington muttered under her breath. *And now I need a cold shower.*

The first show went off with a few minor glitches though fortunately, nothing horrendous. There was resounding applause and each of the acts did at least two encores. It was a triumphant night and Wynter returned to her room feeling her soul restored a bit. Remington LaRoché might not adore her but her fans sure did. She was thrilled at their reception of her new songs. They were an extreme departure from her previous music, and she was very connected to it. Having her fans seem to really love the new stuff made her feel incredible.

"They loved it!" Wynter said to Xandy not for the first time. She was so thrilled she knew she was repeating herself.

"I know that feeling," Xandy said, nodding. "When I first changed over to BJ's label I was worried that people would miss the bubblegum stuff…"

"Exactly!" Wynter said. "Fucking Lauren keeps going on about how I should stick with the formula, the formula, the formula! Ugh I fucking hate that term!"

Quinn and Remington were behind the two singers and Quinn had sensed Remington's tension all night.

"What's goin' on?" Quinn asked as the girls continued to talk excitedly.

Remington glanced at Quinn, grimacing slightly, then shook her head. "Nothing I can't handle."

Quinn nodded, accepting that answer for the moment. "Well, you let me know if I can help at some point, clear?"

"Clear," Remington said, nodding with a smile of appreciation.

In the hotel room, Wynter went to take another shower. Remington sat down in the chair and started doing research on her laptop on their next stop in Wantagh, New York. She was still doing calculations when Wynter walked out of the bathroom wearing a skimpy tank top and bikini underwear.

"That isn't what you're wearing to bed…" Remington said, her voice trailing off short of saying 'are you' because she was hoping Wynter would take the hint.

"Yep," Wynter said, as she climbed onto the bed, grabbing her iPad off the nightstand.

Remington looked over at the woman for a long moment. Her long dark hair was pulled back into a messy ponytail and her face was devoid of all makeup. She looked far too damned good for Remington to be stuck in a room with for the entire night. What's worse, she was hardly wearing anything! And apparently, she expected to sleep that way next to Remington.

"You need to put on more clothing," Remington said seriously.

Wynter grinned rebelliously. "Try and make me," she said, without looking at Remington.

"Wynter…" Remington tried to reason.

"I can't sleep in a bunch of material, Remi!" Wynter snapped. "You're fucking lucky I'm even wearing this; I usually sleep naked. So give it up already."

Remington's lips twitched, feeling like a rat caught in a trap. She shifted her head, stretching her neck and heard it pop. It was going to be a long night.

In the end, Remington ended up sleeping in the chair she sat in. She woke up with a major crick in her neck, but at least had avoided more issues.

The group joined the buses that morning at ten. It was getting cold in New York at that point. Wynter continued to use Remington's leather Affliction jacket, so she pulled out another jacket she'd brought. It was a brown leather bomber-style jacket with a US Marines patch on one side, and the patch that identified her as an Iraq War Veteran and a patch that said "LaRoché". Wynter couldn't help but admire the jacket and the woman wearing it.

The three-hour bus ride went smooth enough. There was press work to be done for the show, and then there were contest winners to meet so it was a long day. Wynter was exhausted before they even did their sound check that afternoon. Remington made a point of getting her something to eat in the afternoon and handed it to her as they walked to the next press conference.

"What's this?" Wynter queried.

"Food," Remington told her. "You didn't eat any breakfast, and it's almost two, you're running on fumes."

"What have you had to eat?" Wynter asked.

"I don't have a show to do tonight," Remington answered immediately.

"Meaning nothing," Wynter said, handing Remington half of the sandwich back. "You're working tonight too."

Remington smiled, nodding her head. "Alright, thank you," she said and leaned in to kiss Wynter on the temple.

The cameras didn't miss the nice gesture. They'd also caught the discussion between them on the balcony, including Wynter taking off her shirt and walking into the room. Wynter had already had numerous texts from Lauren about the story. She hadn't taken the time to address them yet. There were already questions about a burgeoning of a love affair between the wild child, sexy singer and the gentlemanly retired MMA fighter. The press was watching them carefully.

After the sound check, they had two hours before they needed to leave for the show. Wynter crawled into one of the bunks on the bus to attempt to sleep. It was cold so she once again pulled Remington's jacket over her to help keep her warm. Remington woke her an hour and a half later.

"You have a half an hour," Remington told her gently.

Wynter nodded, rubbing her eyes. "Okay."

She sat back and picked up her phone. There were so many messages from Lauren she shook her head. She just couldn't deal with Lauren's insecurities at that point, so she deleted the messages and set her phone aside. The fact was, she did want Remington so telling Lauren that she didn't was outright lying, and she wasn't up for doing that before the show.

There were more technical issues at the show that night, and they had Billy screaming and throwing things backstage. Jerith Michaels sat back watching his lead singer lose her mind. Everyone noticed that Jerith never lost his temper; it was why he was the head of the band.

As everyone climbed onto the buses that night, they noticed the temperatures had dropped significantly. Their next show was in Columbia, South Carolina, which was a twelve-hour drive. The buses were going to drive through the night to get there.

Wynter had chosen the bunk on the top, with Remington in the bunk below her. She was freezing, her teeth chattering. She did everything she could think of to get warm, even putting on more clothing and socks, but she couldn't. Finally, she did what she promised herself she wasn't going to do again so soon.

"Remi?" she queried softly.

"Hmm?" Remington responded tiredly.

"I'm freezing," Wynter whispered.

"Put on more clothes," was Remington's response.

"I did! It's freezing in here," Wynter whispered.

Remington was silent for a long few moments then Wynter heard her sigh.

"Come down here," Remington resigned.

Wynter climbed out of her bunk and crawled into the lower one. Remington held the blankets aside for her and Wynter snuggled under them, and right next to Remington.

"Oh my God, you're so warm!" Wynter said, still shivering.

"Jesus, you're freezing!" Remington exclaimed, having touched Wynter's arm. She immediately wrapped the blanket tighter around Wynter, pulling her closer.

Wynter snuggled against Remington, doing her best to ignore the fact that Remington smelled so damned good it wasn't even funny. Remington wore a white thermal long sleeved shirt and black yoga pants. Wynter had on her sweatpants and a short-sleeved flannel shirt.

"Didn't you bring any cold weather stuff?" Remington asked.

"Some, but I usually can't stand to have too much on me when I sleep… Plus I figured the damned bus would be heated."

"Well, I'm sure it is, but it's really getting cold out there, so it probably can't keep up all the way back here," Remington said.

Wynter shivered again and Remington tightened her arms around the smaller girl.

"Try to get some sleep, Wynter, tomorrow is going to be another long day."

"I know," Wynter said, nodding, closing her eyes.

She lay in Remington's arms and tried not to imagine what it would be like if they were actually lovers. Since she was facing Remington, she could smell her skin. Her lips were so close to her neck. Wynter wondered if Remington had any weaknesses, or if she was impervious to everything.

Remington lay telling herself over and over not to think. She could feel Wynter breathing against her neck and Wynter's hand curled around the button-down lapel of her thermal shirt. She could also feel Wynter's body pressed against her in various places. She couldn't keep the picture of Wynter in her lace bra from flashing through her head. She gritted her teeth, and found that inhaling through her nose only made her painfully aware of how good the girl smelled. Her hair, her skin… *Jesus…* was all she could think.

It took both of them a long time to get to sleep. During the night, Quinn got up to go to the bathroom and walked by their bunk. She noted how close they were. She couldn't help but think that they looked good together. When she got back to the larger bed that she and Xandy had claimed, she climbed in behind her girlfriend, sliding her arms around her. Xandy immediately snuggled back against her and Quinn smiled fondly, unable to imagine her life without this beautiful creature.

The next morning, Quinn told Xandy about seeing Wynter and Remington sleeping in the same bunk.

"Do you think there was anything to that story yesterday?" Xandy asked.

Quinn shrugged. "Maybe not, but Remi was definitely agitated after that first show, so… I dunno… I'll see if I can get anything out of her. I just hope Wynter isn't pushing too hard."

"What do you mean?" Xandy asked, knowing that Quinn understood Remington better than she did.

"If she pushes Remi too hard to get to her, Remi will push back, and I doubt Wynter's ever been in a situation like that."

"What would Remi pushing back look like?" Xandy asked.

Quinn looked pensive. "If I had to say, I'd bet she'd go ice cold and there won't be any thawing her out after that. I could be wrong though," Quinn said. "Remi's a whole other mystery sometimes."

Xandy smiled. "Well, I get that…" She reached up to touch Quinn's lips.

"I wasn't mysterious," Quinn said, her grin engaging. "I was just not what you were used to."

"Oh my God, you were the farthest from anything I'd ever known," Xandy said, laughing softly.

"And sometimes that's a really good thing," Quinn said.

"Well, it definitely was for us," Xandy agreed.

She looked pensive then.

"What is it, love?" Quinn asked.

Xandy blew her breath out. "I really don't like Lauren," she said. "I just want Wynter away from her. She's not good for her."

Quinn smiled. "I know, babe, I know."

"Remi would be good for her," Xandy said.

"But would she be good for Remi?" Quinn asked.

Xandy pressed her lips together. "I don't know," she said, shaking her head. "She's so wild and independent, and Remi really seems to prefer women who aren't so… outlandish."

Quinn chuckled. "Outlandish, huh?"

"You know what I mean," Xandy said. "Wynter is this totally free spirit and independent as all get out. Remi seems like she's like you, she needs to be needed."

"Is that what I need?" Quinn asked, grinning.

"You know it is," Xandy said, smiling. "That whole white knight complex you have."

"Uh-huh," Quinn said, grinning.

"You know it's one of the things I love most about you," Xandy said, sliding her hand through Quinn's red hair. "And your wild side too," she said, sliding her hand up Quinn's tattooed arm.

Quinn and Xandy made a very different couple. Xandy with her honey-blond hair and almost lavender eyes and her farm girl innocent look, and Quinn with her short red hair, tattoos and piercings, and her tendency to wear Harley Davidson gear and leather. But it was obvious to anyone who was around them for long that they were very much in love.

Wynter woke first. She lay in Remington's arms enjoying the feeling of such strong arms holding her close. The glaring difference between how it felt to be held by Remington and to be held by Lauren was just one more thing to put in the "lose" column for Lauren. Taking a chance, Wynter put her hand up on Remington's shoulder and slid it down over her arm. The muscle there bulged and felt firm and unyielding. Remington shifted in her sleep, the muscle under Wynter's hand flexed and Wynter had to clamp down on the thrill that went through her. This woman was so incredibly attractive to her at that moment, she was sure she was going to go crazy.

Wynter tilted her head up, looking up at Remington's face. She had a strong jawline, whereas Lauren's was somewhat weak. Remington had so much character in her face with the high cheekbones and sensuous lips. Lauren had always had the look of a boy, an effeminate boy. Wynter has realized that it no longer attracted her.

She knew that it was more than just looks though. Remington had a history, a past, experiences, she had morals and standards and ways of being that she stuck to no matter what. Lauren didn't seem to know what her opinions were or what she stood for ever. She just existed and lately she existed by using Wynter's money to buy drugs and booze and stay out with her friends. Lauren was immature and Wynter was tired of it.

Wynter felt Remington stir and she glanced up to see hazel eyes, more gold than green in the morning light, looking down at her.

"Bonjou," Remington said, grinning tiredly.

"Good morning," Wynter replied. Remington's accent was more pronounced at that moment, Wynter assumed because she was tired.

"How did you sleep?" Remington asked politely.

"I slept great… once I wasn't freezing to death," she said, grinning.

"I'm glad," Remington said, smiling.

"Thanks to you," Wynter said, levering herself up to kiss Remington on the cheek.

Remington smiled fondly. "You're welcome."

Wynter shifted to open curtains and looked out the window, unintentionally pressing closer to Remington as she did. Remington rolled from her side to her back so she could allow Wynter better access to the window. Unfortunately, it also put Wynter lying more on top of her.

"I wonder where we are," Wynter said, watching for freeway signs.

Remington levered up on her elbows to look out the window as well. It put their faces close together at that moment and created an intimate moment between them.

Wynter suddenly realized that not only were their faces close, she was practically lying on top of Remington. She knew she should move but her body said, *Oh hell no!* Instead, she flexed her fingers that were resting on Remington's chest, still looking out the window.

Remington felt Wynter's nails graze her chest through the thermal shirt. She had to clamp down on the shudder that went through her. Dropping back onto the bed, she looked at her watch and did a quick calculation.

"We should be about an hour or two out by now," she told Wynter keeping her tone perfectly normal, despite the sensations Wynter's slight weight over her was causing.

Wynter turned her head, looking down at Remington, her blue eyes searching.

"I'm sorry if I'm a pain in the ass, Remi," she said softly.

A grin tugged at Remington's lips. "You aren't so bad," she replied, her voice equally soft.

Wynter chuckled. "Well, that's good to know," she said, reaching out to touch one of Remington's braids. "Do you ever wear your hair down?" she asked curiously.

Remington thought about her answer.

"I haven't in a long time, this is just easier," she said indicating to the braids.

"How often do you have to have them redone though?" Wynter asked.

"About every six weeks or so, depending on how fast my hair decides to grow," Remington answered, grinning.

"So they have to take your hair out of the braids to do that, right?" Wynter asked.

Remington nodded. "Yeah, of course, why?"

"'Cause I want to see what you look like with your hair down," Wynter said simply.

"Why?" Remington asked again.

Wynter looked back at her for a long moment. "Because I'm betting not many people have seen that," she said smiling then.

Remington wet her lips, almost nervously looking bemused.

"And, I'm betting you look really, really hot," she added with a reckless wink.

Remington shook her head. There was the Wynter she was used to again. Stretching, Remington could feel her joints pop and groan from the position she'd laid in all night holding Wynter. She noted that Wynter was watching her with amusement.

"Do your muscles always do that?" Wynter asked, grinning.

"When I lay in the same position all night, yes, and it's my joints, not my muscles," Remington said nodding with a grin.

"Oh, that's my fault," Wynter said, grimacing.

"It's the cold's fault," Remington told her.

Wynter reached out, sliding her hand over Remington's shoulder and under the neck of her shirt. She leaned over and felt for the bunched-up muscles where her neck and shoulder met.

"Wow, Remi, you're really tight right here," she said, rubbing gently at the knots she felt. "Sit up," she told her bodyguard.

Remington raised an eyebrow at her commanding tone and received a sweet smile and batting eyelashes in return.

"Please sit up?" Wynter said in an overly sweet voice.

Remington chuckled and did as she was. Wynter moved behind her and used both hands to do her best to loosen up the muscles that were in knots. Remington LaRoché was pure muscle and it was sexy as hell. Wynter was used to Lauren's slight build and complete lack of muscle of any sort. *I've got more muscle than Lauren!* she thought, rolling her eyes.

She felt Remington jump slightly when she touched a spot near the trapezius muscle on her right side. She pulled back the material of the shirt Remington wore and saw a one-inch scar that was still red.

"What's this?" Wynter asked, touching the scar gently.

"It's from a surgery," Remington said.

"What happened?"

"It was an injury," Remington said, shrugging slightly. "My last fight, I ripped a tendon."

"Ouch," Wynter said.

She felt and heard Remington chuckle. "Yeah, it hurt."

"I'll bet," Wynter said, sliding her hand around the scar to continue trying to smooth out the knots. "How exactly did it happen?"

"I did a throw and she grabbed my arm at the last minute and it gave," Remington said.

"And you still won?" Wynter said astounded.

Remington nodded.

"Wow…" Wynter said. "I'd have been curled up in a corner crying."

Remington didn't answer. Wynter's hands were still on her bare skin and she was having a hard time concentrating on the conversation. She did, however, stretch her neck, something she did when she was agitated or nervous, or in this case both. Once again joints popped.

"Ugh, quit doing that!" Wynter said, smiling even as she winced.

"It bothers you?" Remington asked.

"It's a terrible sound; it sounds like bones breaking or something."

Remington laughed. "It's actually just gas bubbles from your joints and completely normal."

"And you know that how?" Wynter asked, always surprised by Remington.

"You do what I did for long enough, you learn a thing or two about physiology," Remington answered, grinning.

Wynter nodded. "I guess it's probably helpful."

"Yes, it is," Remington said nodding.

Wynter slid her hands down Remington's back, not wanting to stop touching her bodyguard, but knowing that if she didn't stop soon she'd do something to put Remington off again, and she really didn't want to do that.

"Is that better?" she asked when she forced herself to sit back.

Wynter was rewarded with the sight of Remington rolling her shoulders, her muscles rippling, even visible through the shirt she wore. It was a lovely sight to behold, Wynter had to force herself not to sigh out loud.

"Yes, much better," Remington said, glancing back at her and smiling. "Thanks."

"Only fair, since I'm the one that caused them to get that way," Wynter said with an embarrassed smile.

"It was the cold," Remington told her again.

"And being stuck holding me all night so my teeth wouldn't chatter and keep you awake," Wynter added, winking at Remington.

Remington laughed softly. "Okay," she said as she got out of the bunk.

"Wait," Wynter said, putting her hand out to stop her. "Did I just finally win an argument with you?" she asked, her looked awed.

Remington looked amusedly back at her. "If that's the way you'd like to see it," she said, inclining her head.

Wynter stared back at Remington openmouthed, and saw the grin curling Remington's lips and the mischievous light in her eyes.

"Oh my God, you suck!" Wynter said, reaching out to smack Remington's arm playfully.

Remington laughed and once again, Wynter realized how much she liked the sound of her laugh. She didn't do it very often, so it was to be savored when she did.

Wynter and Remington joined Quinn and Xandy at the table in the front of the bus, grabbing coffee from the kitchen on their way. Quinn and Remington talked about their upcoming day and the security issues they might have.

"The auditorium actually looks pretty decent in terms of security," Remington was saying, showing Quinn layout on her laptop. "Mostly, we'll need people at the sides to ensure no one goes behind the curtains here and here."

Quinn nodded. "That shouldn't be too hard," she said. "What about this area here?"

"Yeah, that's the challenge," Remington said. "They haven't done a lot of upgrades on security."

Again, Quinn nodded. "The stage setup's gonna be different too, because it's a flat venue, not as deep," she explained.

"Yeah, we're gonna have to talk to the guys when we get there. I'm not sure how they're going to build around that."

"My bet is they'll go up," Quinn said. "That's what they did for a few of Xandy's shows, and that's usually the way BJ plans it."

Remington nodded. "Good to know."

As the bodyguards continued to talk, Xandy scrolled through Facebook and then got a message about a breaking story. She tapped the message, which took her to a newsfeed. She read it and grimaced, glancing over at Wynter who was sipping her coffee and looking out the window at the scenery flying by outside. She looked pointedly over at Quinn then. Quinn glanced up, seeing Xandy's look and raised her chin, asking a question without a word. Xandy tilted her head toward her iPad, and then tapped out a message, sending it to Quinn's phone.

"Story about Lauren on MSN, saying she's been seen making out with various women in West Hollywood!" was the message she sent Quinn.

"Bloody hell! Doesn't look like she knows," was Quinn's response.

"Should we tell her?" Xandy sent back.

"Wouldn't you want to know?" Quinn replied.

Xandy raised her head looking at Quinn, her look pained, as she nodded.

"Um, Wynter..." Xandy began hesitantly.

"Hmm?" Wynter murmured, looking over at Xandy and seeing her hesitant look. "What?" she asked worriedly.

Remington looked over at Xandy and Wynter to see what was going on having seen Quinn's tense look as well as hearing Xandy's tone.

Xandy turned her iPad around and pointed to the story in her news feed. Wynter leaned forward, setting her coffee down as she read the story. Remington could see Wynter's hand shaking as she lifted it to scroll further down on the story. She looked over at Quinn who grimaced shaking her head.

"What is it?" Remington asked Wynter, her tone purposefully gentle.

Wynter shook her head as she continued to read. After another minute, she pushed Xandy's iPad back to her and stood up, walking back to the bunks. Remington, who had stood when Wynter had, leaned forward slightly, watching her go and saw her crawl into the lower bunk.

"What was that about?" she asked quietly, looking between Quinn and Xandy.

"Lauren has been seen screwing around on Wynter," Quinn said.

Remington blew her breath out, nodding. "Who reported it?" she asked.

"TMZ," Xandy said.

"Okay."

Remington walked back toward the bunks. She squatted down next to the bunk Wynter was in, putting herself at her eye level.

Wynter was lying on her side, her arm up under her head, staring off into space.

"You okay?" Remington asked softly.

Wynter blinked slowly, then rubbed her face on her arm and shrugged.

"Xandy said it was on TMZ," Remington said, "and you know it could be complete fiction. Kind of like that story about you and me."

Wynter blinked again, then focused her look on Remington's face.

"Do you think that's what it is?" she asked, her voice toneless.

"I think you shouldn't believe it until you talk to Lauren," Remington said.

Wynter looked pensive but finally she nodded, and sat up to reach for her phone. Remington stood up and walked away, giving Wynter privacy to make her phone call.

Twenty minutes later Wynter walked back up to the table.

"She says it's all bullshit, that they saw her talking to one of her friends who was having a rough time with her girlfriend," Wynter said, sitting down.

Quinn and Xandy exchanged a quick look. Quinn's eyebrow went up slightly, she didn't believe it for a second, but didn't say anything.

Remington nodded, catching the look between Quinn and Xandy.

"Good," Xandy said, smiling.

An hour later, they pulled into Columbia, South Carolina. Xandy and Wynter looked out the windows. It looked like a small town.

"Why'd BJ book this?" Wynter wondered out loud.

"I don't know," Xandy said, "but it's sold out completely."

The buses pulled up to the venue. It was a historical-looking building, made up of red brick and white plaster. It didn't look impressive at all.

"Maybe there's been a mistake…" Wynter wondered.

"Let's go see," Quinn said, standing as the bus stopped.

When they got off the bus, they could hear Billy bitching immediately.

"What the fuck is this!" Billy yelled, standing with her hands on her hips.

Jerith moved past his lead singer and walked up the steps to the venue. Jordan and Dylan followed him, as did Wynter and Xandy. As they walked into the venue, past the front doors and into the main hall, they suddenly understood why BJ had booked it. It was an awesome venue!

"Oh my God, this is so cool…" Wynter breathed, glancing over at Xandy who was nodding.

"And they went up…" Quinn said, watching the work being carried out on the stage.

"You called it," Remington said, grinning.

The stage usually had a graduated platform for the various artists to move around during their performance. Since the stage in this particular venue wasn't as deep, the platform had been built using levels that went up, rather than out. It was something the artists were going to need to adjust for in preparation for the show and was why BJ had made sure they arrived early.

They spent the day doing the usual sound checks and working around the new stage setup. Remington and Quinn went through security, briefing the temporary help as well as the few guards with the tour.

By three that afternoon, everyone was tired and wanted to rest. The talent had rooms at a local inn and the rest of the group had rooms at a nearby hotel. The inn was an old Victorian-style home, with wood floors and individual rooms and, thankfully, private bathrooms for each room. The room Remington and Wynter walked into was simple, with absolutely no technology, no TV, no radio. The owner had proudly declared however, that they did have Wi-Fi. Once again, there was a single queen bed in the room. Remington made a short sucking sound between her teeth, but said nothing. Wynter did her best not to grin.

"Okay, I need noise," Wynter said, digging through the suitcase Remington had just set on the bed.

She pulled out a small speaker and used the Wi-Fi to connect it to her phone. Music soon filled the room, and Wynter danced around to the music as she pulled items out of her suitcase. Remington checked out the bathroom, noting there was a clawfoot tub with no shower.

"Espektakilè…" she muttered.

"What?" Wynter asked from behind her.

Remington stood back, nodding toward the tub.

"Oh, cute," Wynter said, then saw Remington's look. "Oh, I guess not cute for you huh?"

Remington gave a long sigh, shaking her head as she walked out of the bathroom. Wynter pressed her lips together grinning. She felt bad for Remington, but she also found her facial expressions endlessly amusing.

"What was that you said anyway?" Wynter asked, as she set some of her toiletries on the vanity in the bathroom.

"When?" Remington queried.

"Uh, when you walked into the bathroom…" Wynter said, walking back out into the room, seeing Remington's perplexed look. "You do realize you were speaking Creole, right?"

Remington quirked a grin. "Actually, no, I didn't," she said. "I said 'spectacular.'"

"Say it again," Wynter said, her look captivated, "in Creole."

Remington looked back at her quizzically for a moment, but then said, "Espektakilè."

Wynter smiled broadly, her eyes sparkling. "I just love your language," she said, "especially the accent."

Remington smiled bemusedly, inclining her head. "Well, thank you."

"And you really don't realize when you speak it instead of English sometimes?" Wynter asked.

Remington shook her head. "No, it's what we spoke primarily in our household growing up, so some things just come to me in Creole instead of English and it comes out."

"Interesting…" Wynter said, smiling and shaking her head. "I'd love to learn it if you're willing to teach me."

Remington's look flickered with surprise, but she nodded. "Sure."

"Cool!" Wynter said, smiling brightly. "I'm gonna go take a bath," she said nodding toward the bathroom. "Did you need it first?"

"I'm good, thank you," Remington said, shaking her head.

"I'm gonna leave the door open a little so I can hear my music, okay?" Wynter said then.

"Ah, you can take your music in there," Remington told her, her tone ever so slightly alarmed.

Wynter heard the tone and had to force herself not to giggle. "It's okay, I don't want to leave you stuck in all this silence," she said gesturing around the room with dismay.

Remington tilted her head, stretching her neck, trying to think of something, anything to say that would keep Wynter from leaving the bathroom door open. Unfortunately, her temporary silence was taken as acquiescence, so Wynter walked into the bathroom closing the door only part way. Naturally, the opening in the door faced directly at the bathtub.

"Li ap eseye touye m'mwen konnen li," she muttered under her breath. *She's trying to kill me I know it.*

"I'm gonna go talk to Quinn for a minute," Remington announced, pleased with herself for thinking of that. "Don't leave the room, okay?"

"Gonna be naked, Remi," Wynter said amused. "I doubt I'll leave the room!"

Remington looked heavenward, "Bondye ede m '," she said louder than she'd meant to.

"What?" Wynter queried from the bathroom.

"Nothing, I'll be back," Remington called and left the room as quickly as she could, picking up her cigarettes and lighter on the way out.

Remington made her way down to the front porch of the house, still mentally patting herself on the back for her quick escape. Quinn was down on the porch smoking as well.

"Hey," Quinn said, looking surprised to see her.

"Hey," Remington said, lighting a cigarette and taking a long drag, feeling the smoke fill her lungs.

Quinn noted the deep draw and raised an eyebrow.

"Problems?" she queried.

Remington shook her head. "Unless you count the fact that Wynter's trying to fuckin' kill me, no," she said wryly.

Quinn threw her head back and laughed. "Well, yeah that might count as a problem," she said, her Irish accent clear in the quiet of the porch.

"She's up there right now taking a bath, and she told me she was going to leave the door open…" Remington said, her voice trailing off a she took another drag.

"Why?" Quinn asked. "I mean, why did she say it?" she clarified at the deadpan look she got from Remington.

"She said it was because she didn't want to leave me in the silence, she's got her music going."

Quinn nodded, running her tongue over her teeth, grinning. "Do you prefer silence?"

"To taking the chance of catching sight of her naked, hell yes!" Remington exclaimed.

"What the hell is wrong with you?" Quinn asked seriously. "Do you know how many women would kill to see Wynter Kincade naked?"

"You included?" Remington asked, raising an eyebrow.

"Ah, no," Quinn said, holding up her hands in surrender. "I got my own star, thanks. Seriously though, Rem, why wouldn't you just go for that?"

Remington blew her breath out, shaking her head as she started to pace.

"I have a girlfriend, she has a girlfriend," Remington said.

"Yeah, she has a girlfriend that's fuckin' around on her," Quinn said derisively.

Remington looked back at Quinn sharply. "So you and Xandy don't believe that story Lauren told her?"

Quinn made a dismissive sound. "That little bouzzie is so full of shite her eyes should be brown," she said.

Remington chuckled at Quinn's statement.

"Yeah, it sounded like bullshit to me too," she said, "but if Wynter wants to buy it, who am I to argue?"

"You're right, it's not your place," Quinn said, nodding. "Regardless, if she wants to nail you…" she said then, her voice trailing off as she lifted her hands to indicate helplessness.

"I have a girlfriend," Remington said simply.

Quinn gave her a pointed look. "Have you and Katrina agreed to be exclusive already?"

Remington looked back at Quinn, putting her tongue against her teeth, finally shaking her head. "We didn't really discuss it, no, but that doesn't mean it's not expected."

"And you're just graspin' now," Quinn said with a knowing look.

Remington blew her breath out again, leaning her head back against the wall, looking up at the porch ceiling.

"I'm not looking to become some notch on Wynter's bedpost," she said. "That's not me."

Quinn frowned, but nodded. "So maybe she'd be a notch on yours."

Remington glanced sharply over at Quinn. "Definitely not my style."

Quinn narrowed her eyes at Remington. "I've seen the women 'round you, Rem, you leave 'em creamin' every time, don't pull that innocent shit with me."

Remington laughed at that. "I haven't done that intentionally," she said, qualifying it with, "lately."

"But before, what?" Quinn asked.

"Back in New York, yeah, all the time," Remington said, shrugging and shaking her head, "but not since I hit LA."

"And why the hell not?" Quinn asked, her look unabashed.

Remington shook her head. "How do you think I ended up with shit like the Akasha situation?"

"Oh ho…" Quinn said, her eyes widening. "So was there some truth to Akasha's statements about Sage Baker?"

"No," Remington said immediately. "Well, I admit I flirted with Sage, just like I flirted with half of the women in New York, gay or straight. But she did come on to me, not the other way around."

"And what happened there?" Quinn asked.

"She showed up at my apartment, saying she wanted to talk about Akasha. Got inside and dropped her coat wearing nothing but a smile."

Quinn gave a slow blink as her face reflected shocked admiration. "Damn… and I imagine she has the body to go with that incredible face?"

"Oh, she has a body that would make angels weep," Remington confirmed.

"And you didn't hit that?" Quinn asked, once again looking at Remington like she was crazy.

"She was someone else's girl, Quinn. I don't do that, not ever," Remington said.

Quinn gave a low whistle, shaking her head. "You got more self-control than me."

Remington gave a low chuckle. "For all the fuckin' good it did me. She went back and told Akasha I called her over to my place and tried to jump her."

"Bitch…" Quinn said, looking disgusted.

"You're tellin' me," Remington said. She glanced at her watch then. "How long do women usually take in the tub? Think I'm safe yet?"

Quinn chuckled. "Couldn't tell ya."

"Xandy doesn't take baths?" Remington queried, grinning.

"If she does, I'm usually in there with her, so… I don't really pay attention to time."

"Aw," Remington said, shaking her head and clearing her throat pointedly. "Did Xandy do this kind of shit to you when you were guarding her?"

"No," Quinn said, shaking her head, "Xandy wouldn't even consider that kind of thing, 'specially as she was straight back then."

"Oh, yeah," Remington said, nodding. "So you're no help at all."

"Sorry," Quinn said.

Remington pulled out another cigarette. "One more, then I'll go back up."

"Uh-huh," Quinn said, grinning. "So what's happening with Billy? She's eased up lately, hasn't she?"

"Thankfully," Remington said, shaking her head. "She just does it to piss Wynter off."

"And why do you think it pisses Wynter off?" Quinn asked with a pointed look.

Remington caught the look, and narrowed her eyes slightly. "I'm not sure," she said. "You know she told me that she says some of the shit she does to me, just to get me to react."

Quinn didn't look surprised by that comment. "And how do you feel about that?"

"Scares the shit out of me," Remington said, chuckling.

"Why?" Quinn asked.

"She wants me to react," Remington said, "and she's doing shit like what she just did in the room…" She shook her head. "She may get more of a reaction than she means to at some point."

"I doubt that," Quinn said skeptically.

Remington narrowed. "Are you trying to tell me something?"

"I'm not sayin' nothin'," Quinn said, holding her hands up in surrender.

Remington didn't reply, simply looking back at the Irishwoman with a searching look.

"So you gonna go home when we get that break for Thanksgiving?" Quinn asked to fill the silence that stretched uncomfortably.

"Home to Kentucky, yeah," Remington said. "We'll only be three hours from there when we break."

"How long's it been since you were home? It's your parents there, right?" Quinn asked.

"Yeah." Remington nodded. "And my little sisters too. It's been about six months," she said.

Quinn nodded.

"Your family's in Northern Ireland, right?" Remington asked.

"Yeah," Quinn nodded.

"Makes it a helluva lot harder to get home, huh?" Remington said, looking sorry for Quinn.

"Oh yeah," Quinn said, nodding, "but we'll probably try to head there after this tour."

Remington nodded. "Your family like Xandy?"

"They love Xandy," Quinn said, grinning.

"'Cause she settled you down?" Remington asked, knowing that's what her parents wanted for her constantly.

"That's part of it for sure," Quinn said, nodding, "but they really adore her too."

"That's good," Remington said, nodding.

"Yeah, it is," Quinn agreed.

Quinn and Remington had the same opinion about family; it was the most important thing in the world, no matter what.

"Well, I'm headed back up," Remington said, stubbing out her cigarette and picking up the other butts to deposit them in the trash. "See you two at six," she said.

"Later!" Quinn called, watching Remington walk away, shaking her head ruefully.

Remington opened the door to the room carefully, looking around and not seeing Wynter and thinking she couldn't possibly still be in the tub.

"Wynter?" she queried as she shut the door.

"Yeah?" came the immediate reply from the bathroom.

Remington rolled her eyes, shaking her head. "I'm back," she said simply.

"Okay," Wynter answered.

Remington busied herself with taking things out of her suitcase, dreading the idea of trying to get clean in a bathtub. Finally, she gave up and sat on the floor with her back against the bed, reading a book.

She heard water splash like Wynter was getting out of the tub. She kept her head pointedly turned away from the bathroom door.

Wynter walked out of the bathroom wearing a tank top and bikini underwear. She immediately saw Remington sitting on the floor, and laughed to herself at her bodyguard's sly tactics. She'd known that she wasn't likely to get Remington to stay in the room, let alone actually see anything she'd wanted her to see. She had to hand it to Remington, though, the woman remained impossibly obstinate.

Remington got to her feet as she noticed Wynter walk back into the room, and she sighed at her skimpy outfit. She didn't bother to say anything though because she knew the answer she was going to get. She caught Wynter's quick grin at her sigh. Wynter climbed onto the bed, lying down across it as Remington sat back down on the floor.

"Why are you sitting down there?" Wynter asked, propped up on her elbows, her head above Remington's.

"It's comfortable," Remington said.

"Uh-huh, sure," Wynter said, her tone disbelieving. "Well, it's your turn to choose music," Wynter said, holding her phone out to Remington, her arm right next to Remington's face.

All Remington could think was how goddamned good Wynter's skin smelled. It was a combination of jasmine and gardenias and it was heady. The woman had to be doing it on purpose, didn't she?

"I'm fine," Remington finally managed to say.

"Oh, come on!" Wynter said. "I know you hate my stuff."

"I don't hate all of it," Remington said, grinning.

"Just most of it, right?" Wynter asked, laughing softly.

"I wouldn't say that," Remington said, glancing up at Wynter.

Wynter was leaning down to hand Remington to her phone, just far enough that when Remington looked up, she could see down her shirt. She immediately averted her eyes, but not before she caught an extremely enticing glimpse of cleavage and the curve of what were likely to be perfect breasts.

"Bondye…" she muttered before she could stop herself.

"What does that mean?" Wynter asked. "I've heard you say that before, a lot in fact… so what does it mean?"

Remington looked back at her, pointedly keeping her eyes high so as not to see more than she could handle, literally. She contemplated lying and just not answering at all.

Wynter narrowed her eyes at Remington. "You don't want to tell me," she said, "which means it's something you don't want me to know…"

She brought her phone back up, starting to tap away on it. Remington knew she was screwed even before Wynter's eyes widened.

"It means 'God'?" Wynter asked sharply.

"Yes, it means God," Remington said, moving to stand.

"And why did you say that just now?" Wynter asked, sitting up as Remington stood up, keeping her eyes on her.

Remington didn't answer for a long moment, making a sucking sound through her teeth as she tried to decide exactly what to say.

"It's an expression of frustration," Remington said finally as she moved to lean against the dresser, her arms crossed over her chest, her legs crossed at the ankles.

"And you're frustrated why?" Wynter asked, her look expectant.

A wry grin curled Remington's lips and her hazel eyes narrowed slightly. Wynter could see a number of thoughts play across Remington's face, none of which she understood. Remington's eyes went from the floor to Wynter, then back to the floor, and back up again.

"Remi?" Wynter queried pointedly.

"I'm going to go check if Quinn and Xandy have a shower in their room," Remington said, moving off the dresser and turning around to pick up the things she'd set aside earlier. "Don't leave the room," she said over her shoulder as she walked out.

Wynter stared at the closed door, her mouth open in shock. She closed her mouth after a full minute and shook her head. Remington LaRoché could confound the most patient of saints and smartest of women, that was for sure.

Chapter 5

In the end, Remington came back just in time to take her to the venue. She had Xandy and Quinn with her. Wynter had a feeling that it had been on purpose. Remington had showered and changed; now she wore all black, a black oxford-style shirt, black slacks, and black leather dress boots. And sitting in the Escalade with her, Wynter found out how damned good she smelled too. With Xandy and Quinn in the back it was a bit crowded, so she had to sit close to Remington. Though it wasn't too much of a hardship.

Remington escorted Wynter to her dressing room and told her to text her when she was ready to head to the stage. With that, Quinn and she started to work ensuring everything was secure for the show. Twenty minutes before show time, Remington got a text from Wynter. She arrived at the dressing room expecting Wynter to be ready. Instead, Wynter answered the door wearing a very short silk robe.

"Uh," Remington stammered. "I think you've forgotten something." She averted her eyes from the low neckline of the robe.

"Funny," Wynter said, rolling her eyes, "I need your help. I can't get the zipper up on this dress… hold on…" she said as went to untie the robe.

Remington had a flashback of Sage that night in her apartment in New York.

"Kenbe!" Remington said, fortunately holding her hand up at the same time, which told Wynter what she was saying. "Shit, I mean hold up," Remington said, grimacing at the cuss word she'd just used. "I'm sorry," she said, squeezing her eyes shut for a moment. "Go over there"—she pointed to the screens set to the side of the room— "and put the dress on, then come out here, *fully covered*, and I'll help you zip it," she said, making sure Wynter understood what she meant.

Wynter looked back at her for a long moment, pursing her lips and looking like she wanted to rebel against Remington's instructions.

"Either that or I'll go get a prop guy…" Remington added with a chilly smile.

"Not funny, Remi…" Wynter said, narrowing her eyes.

"Then go over there… and do what I said," Remington said, her tone matching her narrowed eyes.

Wynter blew her breath out and did as she was told. She walked out wearing a black dress that hugged every curve of her body. It was short in the front and long in the back. The neckline was low, but not extremely so. Though it did reveal the scalloped lace of a very sexy-looking lace bra. The front of the skirt was cut at an angle, the highest point, being about seven inches above her knees the lowest being six inches above her knees. It revealed a nice expanse of perfectly tanned, toned and smooth leg, and was paired with high-heeled ankle boots.

Remington's mouth went dry when Wynter walked over to her and stood just inches from her, her ice blue eyes staring up at her from behind long thick black lashes. Her makeup was dark, but done in such a way that Remington couldn't even fathom what she wore. Her blue eyes appeared to glow and sparkled with glitter, and her lips, parted at the moment, were a rich tawny color. Her cheekbones were accented giving her already incredible face an unreal quality.

Wynter's black hair fell in long curly waves almost to her waist and shined with health. It was a dangerous combination and it was only made worse when Wynter turned around. The first thing to hit Remington was the scent she wore; it was much sexier and rich than she normally did. Added to that was the fact that Remington was now staring at her back, bare except for the slim strap of her bra, all the way down to just above her butt.

She glanced over her shoulder at Remington. "Can you get it?" Wynter asked softly.

It took every ounce of self-control Remington possessed to reach out and rather than slide her hand up that incredible expanse of skin, to take the zipper and slowly pull it upward. She was certain Wynter had to be able to hear her heart pounding in her chest.

Wynter turned around, smiling up at Remington, and was almost sure she saw the fleeting look of desire in those gold-green eyes of hers, but it was gone a moment later.

"All set?" Remington asked. She kept her voice completely normal, even as she clenched her fist behind her back to keep control of herself.

"Yes," Wynter said, nodding.

Remington stepped over to the door, opened it, and gestured for Wynter to precede her. Wynter did and Remington followed moments later. They stood on the side of the stage, watching Jordan do her set. Remington had on a wireless headset and would occasionally say something to one of the security team. At one point, Wynter moved to lean against the wall, thinking she should have waited longer before she came out. In truth, part of her had hoped to manage to seduce

Remington before the show, but as usual, Remington was a solid wall of rock.

When Jordan finally finished her set, Wynter went on. Remington watched Wynter as she moved and sang. It was obvious that Wynter was in her element when she was on stage. She moved so smoothly and with so much sex appeal that it was no wonder men and women alike wanted her. Remington did her best to concentrate on more than just Wynter, but she reminded herself that in truth, Wynter was the one she was supposed to be protecting, so she had every right to watch every tiny little thing the woman did.

Finally, Remington gave up trying to pay attention to anything else. She stood just off stage with her arms in front of her, her hands clasped in one another. Standing 'at ease' was the term Wynter thought of when she glanced over to where Remington stood. She couldn't help but wink at her bodyguard. Naturally that was caught on camera, as was the picture of Remington standing off stage watching Wynter perform. The entire show was being recorded.

Wynter was near the end of her set and the crowd was screaming. The stage in its altered state seemed to be working out quite well for the artists; it gave them more space to move around. Wynter had just gotten to the highest point of the stage when Remington noticed something sticking up from the stage floor to Wynter's far left. It was an odd angle, so she wasn't sure if it was just a trick of light or not. Nothing had been noticed earlier so it was probably nothing. She moved to get to a better angle as the section was near the back part of the stage. She'd just reached the very edge of the off stage area when she saw Wynter headed for that same part of the stage.

Suddenly, Wynter stumbled and started to fall. There was a screech of feedback from her microphone as she dropped it. Remington lunged, quickly covering the thankfully short distance between them to catch Wynter, banging her wrist on the scaffolding that supported the stage as she did. The crowd suddenly realized what had happened, and there were screams and people moving toward Remington as she quickly turned and strode off stage with Wynter in her arms.

Off stage, she took a knee holding Wynter and trying to look her over at the same time. She sat on the floor bracing Wynter against her left knee and her chest. She saw blood streaming from a cut on Wynter's forehead near the hairline. She yanked off her shirt, balled it up, and pressed it to Wynter's forehead.

"Remi?" Wynter said, sounding dazed and terrified at the same time.

"It's okay, babe, I got you, it's okay… you're okay," Remington said soothingly, even though her insides were shaking violently.

Quinn came on the run, having been on the other side of the stage. She slid to a stop, dropping to her knees as she looked both Wynter and Remington over quickly.

"Get an ambulance," Remington snapped.

"Already on their way in," Quinn told her. "Did she hit the floor?"

"No," Remington said, shaking her head, "but I'm thinking she hit her head on the edge of the stage."

"You caught her?" Quinn asked, looking stunned.

Remington nodded, not paying any attention to Quinn's look; her eyes were focused on Wynter.

"Remi?" Wynter queried again, hearing them talking and realizing what had happened. "I fell, Remi… What…" Her voice trailed off as she looked panicked.

"Wynter, it's okay, you're okay," Remington told her. "Just relax babe… Stay with me though, okay? Just keep talking to me."

Wynter's eyes grew wide as she heard people yelling and the ambulance backing into the dock not too far backstage.

"Remi!" Wynter exclaimed, terrified suddenly.

"Hey!" Remington said, putting her forehead against Wynter's. "Look at me, babe, okay? Just look at me… don't worry about all that… look at me, Wyn… it's okay…"

Remington felt Wynter grasping at her shoulder, her nails digging into her skin.

Quinn turned to yell to the paramedics. As they ran up, Wynter grew frantic. Remington's strength came in handy at that moment because she was easily able to control Wynter's movements with little effort. Her voice did more.

"Wynter, babe, it's okay… Look at me… right here, babe… it's okay…" she said, staring into Wynter's eyes and keeping her looking back at her.

Whenever Wynter's eyes strayed toward the paramedics who were pulling out their gear, Remington touched her chin, getting her attention back easily, especially when she unconsciously slipped into Creole. "Rete avek mwen bebe… rete dwa isit la siwo myèl … dwa isit la avè m '…" Remington said, continuing to talk to her.

Wynter didn't look away from her once while she spoke, mesmerized by her accent and the look in her eyes as she spoke the words that sounded so poetic.

The paramedics tried to take Wynter out of Remington's arms. Remington shook her head, her eyes still on Wynter's, still talking to her. She gestured with her hand to Quinn to have them check the cut on her head.

The cameras were still rolling during everything. The press fell in love with Remington LaRoché in the moment she started speaking Haitian Creole to Wynter Kincade. No one could deny that Remington held Wynter entranced with her words. They'd only fall deeper in love with Remington, as would every one of Wynter's fans, when they played back the tape of Wynter's fall and realized the fact that Remington had indeed caught her, keeping her from hitting the ground. The pictures of Remington sitting with Wynter braced against her bent knee and chest would hit every paper by the morning.

The video of Wynter's fall, and later of Remington ripping off her shirt to press it to Wynter's head, and then closer video of Remington's head bent to Wynter's, the Creole words rolling off her tongue like a song, were played on every station around the country. The videos were quickly picked up around the world, with helpful translation provided in subtitles. The world heard that Remington was entreating Wynter to stay with her, to stay right 'here' with her calling her baby and honey.

Wynter was pronounced extremely lucky by the paramedics. The cut on her head, although it had bled profusely at first, was not serious. Remington thought she'd pass out with relief. Quinn stood up, bending to take Wynter out of Remington's arms so she could stand up. Remington stunned her by shaking her head. Remington tightened her left arm around Wynter's shoulders and slid her right arm under Wynter's knees. She then used her enviable core strength to stand. It was yet another thing the press would later comment on; how Remington LaRoché wouldn't relinquish her charge for a moment.

"I'm going to get her back to the hotel," Remington told Quinn.

Quinn nodded, taking the jacket that Xandy handed her to put it around Remington's shoulders, since it was currently near freezing outside. She and Xandy walked with her as she strode toward the dock area where an Escalade had been brought around. Remington got into the Escalade, once again without putting Wynter down. Wynter was in and out of awareness. The paramedics and given her a painkiller, saying she was likely to have a nasty headache later.

A few minutes later, Remington carried Wynter into the inn and up the stairs. Quinn unlocked the room door and pulled the bed covers back so Remington could lay Wynter down carefully. Only then did she feel the deep ache in her wrist. She clenched and unclenched her hand feeling sharp pains as she did.

"You okay?" Quinn asked, seeing Remington's movements.

"Yeah," Remington said, nodding, "thanks."

"Good work tonight," Quinn said, grinning wryly.

"Just another day at the office," Remington said, curling her lips sarcastically.

Quinn laughed at that. "I'm gonna get you some ice for that wrist," she told Remington.

"Thanks," Remington said, sitting on the bed and leaning down to unzip her boots.

Quinn left and came back with not only ice in a bag for Remington's wrist, but a bucket of ice, a glass, and bottle of Knob Creek bourbon.

"I know it's not your favorite… but it should do the trick," Quinn began as she put ice in the glass, and poured the bourbon.

"I'll take it," Remington said, grinning as she put out her hand.

Quinn handed her the glass with a grin. Remington drained the glass immediately and held it out for more. Quinn poured obligingly. After two glasses, Remington set the third glass of the amber liquid down on the nightstand.

"Wrist is hurting less already," Remington said, grinning.

"Amazing," Quinn said, chuckling. "Alright, I'm gonna get out of here and go do some damage control. You need anything?"

"No, I'm good, thanks," Remington said, leaning her head against the wall behind the bed.

Quinn left and Remington settled herself against the pillows, sitting up with her left leg lying flat on the bed and her right knee bent with her foot on the bed. She looked down at Wynter and unzipped her boots, doing her best to take them off one-handed, since her wrist had begun hurting again. She pulled the covers up over Wynter and settled back against the pillows again, her arm up over where Wynter's head lay on the pillow. She fell asleep that way, unaware her name was becoming a household name overnight.

Wynter woke slowly the next morning, feeling groggy. It took her a few moments to remember what had happened. She remembered being onstage, and seeing Remington moving toward the back part of the stage, looking up toward her, but not at her. Then she remembered her boot catching on something and suddenly she was falling. She couldn't remember if she'd screamed or not. Then somehow Remington was holding her. She remembered feeling Remington's arms under her, and being jostled as Remington carried her somewhere. She then remembered looking up at Remington and hearing people screaming and the sound of a siren.

The next thing she could remember was Remington's voice talking to her, the soothing tone of Remington's accent, her gold-green eyes looking very worried as they stared down at her. She'd been so close to her, her face right next to hers and her voice had been so soft, so soothing. Wynter remembered wanting to ask Remington what she was saying in Creole, and did she realize she was speaking Creole, but the words wouldn't come out. She remembered feeling completely mesmerized by Remington's voice, by her eyes, by her words, even if she couldn't understand most of them.

It suddenly occurred to her that she'd fallen from the highest part of the stage, and that had to have been twenty feet. Remington had caught her… She had saved her life… That thought was still bouncing around in her head as she opened her eyes and looked up to see Remington looking down at her.

"You saved my life…" Wynter breathed her blue eyes wide.

A grin tugged at Remington's lips. "Bonjou," she said softly.

Wynter blinked a couple of times. "Bonjou," she repeated, her accent surprisingly perfect. "Now tell me how to say thank you."

"Mèsi," Remington supplied.

"Mèsi," Wynter repeated seriously. "Now tell me how to say I owe you my life."

Remington narrowed her eyes slightly. "Mwen dwe ou lavi m'," she said slowly. "But you don't," she added.

"Mwen dwe ou lavi m '," Wynter repeated perfectly. "And yes I do," she added sitting up, looking into Remington's eyes. "That part of the stage has to be twenty feet off the ground. I would have died," she said, "but you caught me… How did you catch me?" she asked then, shaking her head in wonder.

Remington looked back at her, her eyes searching Wynter's. "I saw something on the stage but I wasn't sure if I was seeing it or if it was a trick of light… I started to walk back toward that spot. I was in the right place at the right time."

"Remington, you caught me," Wynter said in awe. "You saved me."

Remington's look flickered and her lips twitched. Then she chuckled. "Well, that is what you're paying me to do, you know."

"Right, catch me when I fall twenty feet," Wynter said in a deadpan voice. "I'm sure I saw that in the contract somewhere," she said, narrowing her eyes at Remington.

"It was in the fine print," Remington said, grinning. "Under that five percent other duties as required."

"Catching random falling objects?" Wynter asked.

"Yeah, somethin' like that," Remington said, her eyes sparkling.

Wynter surprised her by reaching up to touch her cheek, laying her palm flat against it, her eyes staring into Remington's.

"Thank you," she said, her tone very serious.

She then leaned forward and kissed Remington's lips softly, then put her forehead against Remington's chin and her other hand on Remington's chest, right above her heart. Remington's hand covered

Wynter's hand on her heart, and then touched Wynter's back, moving back and forth soothingly.

They sat that way for a long while. Wynter feeling a sense of unreality, but at the same time a sense of completeness, like she was exactly where she was meant to be at that moment. Remington felt a sense of calm that she hadn't felt for a long while, the stillness of the moment, and the sincere gratitude she'd seen in Wynter's eyes served to cement her commitment to Wynter Kincade in whatever form that took.

The silence was broken by Remington's phone ringing.

"It's Lauren," Remington told Wynter, reaching over carefully to pick it up, wincing as her wrist screamed at her.

"What's wrong with your hand?" Wynter asked, immediately concerned.

"It's fine," Remington told her, handing her the phone.

Wynter set the phone aside and reached for Remington's hand.

"Remi, it's swollen..." she said, carefully lifting it. "Oh Jesus, that bruise is black!" she exclaimed.

"It's okay," Remington said gently. "I smacked it on the scaffolding, its fine."

"Remi, you might have broken it," Wynter said, refusing to let her hand go. "Did the paramedics look at it?"

"They were kind of focused on the girl that fell," Remington said, smiling.

"And of course you didn't bother to mention getting hurt yourself..." Wynter said.

"I didn't even remember it until we got you back here, to be honest," Remington said.

"Well, it needs to be looked at," Wynter said, as she looked around her.

"What are you looking for?" Remington asked, grinning.

"My phone," Wynter said.

"It's probably still at the auditorium," Remington said. "Things were just a tad hectic last night."

"You don't say?" Wynter said narrowing her eyes.

"Quinn might have picked it up when she went back, but that's also probably why Lauren is calling my phone. BJ might have called her."

"I'm not worried about that," Wynter said, shaking her head, as she picked up Remington's phone.

"What are you doing?" Remington asked.

"Calling Quinn," Wynter said putting the phone up to her ear.

Remington watched her with a look of mild amusement on her face.

"Hey Rem, how's Wynter?" Quinn answered.

"It's me, Quinn," Wynter said. "Remi needs a doctor, her wrist looks bad."

"I, uh," Quinn stammered, "okay, I'll get someone out here right away."

"Thanks," Wynter said, smiling.

Five minutes later, Quinn and Xandy were at the door and Wynter let them in. Xandy hugged Wynter.

"You scared a lot of people to death," Xandy told Wynter.

"And you're bloody famous," Quinn told Remington gleefully.

"Excuse me?" Remington said, looking surprised.

"Oh yeah," Quinn said, "you are all over the news, all over the papers, all over the Internet… You may have actually broken the Internet."

"You're enjoying that way too much, babe," Xandy told Quinn.

Quinn smiled with her tongue between her teeth.

"Don't mind her," Xandy said, smiling at Remington as she walked over to where she sat on the bed. "She's just happy she's not the only white knight around now. Now let me see that…" she said, her tone softening.

Remington smiled softly, as Xandy took her hand ever so gently. Wynter watched, seeing how easily Xandy handled the steely retired MMA fighter.

"Oh, Remi, this looks really painful… the doctor is coming to take a look soon, but I wouldn't really be surprised if you broke it."

Remington's lips twitched, then she looked over at Quinn.

"Have you talked to BJ?" she asked.

"About ten times now," Quinn said, grinning. "He thanks you for saving his star," she said, winking over at Wynter, "and warns you to get ready for fame once more."

"I purposely got out of that business," Remington said.

"Yeah, well, save a rock star, get famous," Quinn said, smiling benevolently. "That's apparently the way to fame these days."

"And you'd know," Remington said.

"Indeed," Quinn said, glancing over at Xandy. "Is it too early for a drink?"

"Yes," Xandy said. "Quinn, it's only ten."

"It's five o'clock somewhere…" Quinn said, grinning mischievously, holding the bottle of Knob Hill up to Remington, who nodded.

"Don't you even think about it!" Wynter warned the Irishwoman. "If she needs painkillers she can't be drinking."

"Sorry Rem," Quinn said, shaking her head as she opened the bottle.

Xandy reached over taking the bottle out of Quinn's hands. "You need a clear head for today, babe."

"Damn…" Quinn said, grinning unrepentantly. "Oh, and BJ said he's cancelling the next two shows, so Wynter can recover."

Wynter shook her head. "I'm fine, if he starts cancelling shows that affects everyone…"

"I think they'll understand," Xandy assured her.

Wynter looked at Remington, who nodded. "Well, let's see how Remi is, but if she's okay, I don't want two shows canceled on my account."

In the end, Remington's hand was surprisingly not broken, but badly bruised. The doctor recommended a brace for her wrist until the bruising subsided and prescribed painkillers, which Remington refused to even have filled.

"Remi…" Wynter had begun, her tone worried.

"Wynter, I've dealt with a lot more painful injuries and still fought," Remington assured her. "I'm okay."

"Fine," Wynter said, "then I want to head back up to New York today to make tomorrow night's show."

"No," Remington said seriously, "you do need to rest."

"I'm fine," Wynter said.

"Really?" Remington said, narrowing her eyes slightly. "Your head hurts, doesn't it?"

"Why do you say that?" Wynter asked.

Remington looked back at her, her look saying *really?* "You mean besides the fact that you answered a question with a question?" she said wryly. "Your eyes are darker than they usually are and that usually indicates pain."

Wynter pressed her lips together, looking away.

Xandy grinned, glancing at Quinn who nodded.

"Alright, let's say one show," Remington said then. "You guys can make that up easy once we're done in Pittsburgh."

Wynter looked pensive, looking at Quinn, then Xandy, and lastly Remington. She sighed, nodding.

"Okay, you win, one show," she said.

Remington looked over at Quinn. "Call BJ."

"You got it," Quinn said.

"I'm going to go get you some ice for your wrist," Xandy said.

"And some for the Knob Hill?" Remington queried hopefully.

Xandy looked back at Remington, seeing the wistful look on her face.

"Fine!" she said, shaking her head.

Wynter finally called Lauren back to tell her that she was fine and that all the news reports were accurate. Before long, however, Lauren couldn't seem to keep from making a nasty comment about Remington's face being everywhere all of a sudden, like she was "some kind of star."

"She saved my life, Lauren," Wynter said, sounding appalled at Lauren's attitude.

"Oh don't be all dramatic," Lauren said, her tone placating.

"I gotta go," Wynter said her tone turning cold suddenly.

"What? Wait…" Lauren started to say.

"Bye," Wynter said, hanging up the phone before she had to hear one more word.

Wynter and Remington spent the day in the room for the most part. They received visits from the other performers and band members. Remington received a great deal of accolades from everyone for her 'great save.' Wynter received a lot of comments about being the luckiest woman on the planet, and she agreed one hundred percent every time, looking over at Remington each time. By mid-afternoon a flat screen TV was brought up and connected through Wi-Fi, so they were able to watch some TV.

Wynter started seeing all the news stories on the incident the night before. She saw the video of Remington lunging forward to catch her. It made her wince every time she saw it, because she saw Remington's hand hit the scaffolding. It was indeed a miracle it wasn't broken.

"Strong Creole bones," Remington said, winking at her.

Wynter also saw the video where Remington pulled off her shirt to press it to her head. She glanced over at Remington at that point, and saw that Remington was pointedly looking down. Wynter reached out to touch Remington's hand, her look searching.

"There was a lot of blood. It scared the hell out of me," she said simply.

Wynter swallowed convulsively at the look in Remington's eyes.

Then Wynter saw the video of Remington talking to her, her head bent, her lips so close to her face. The audio was haunting because Wynter could remember hearing Remington saying those things; she could remember Remington's voice so close to her and so soothing. Hearing it again and combined with everything else she'd already seen, it simply overwhelmed her.

She moved to lie next to where Remington sat on the bed, putting her head on Remington's knee.

Remington glanced down at Wynter, seeing tears in her eyes. Without a word, Remington put her hand on Wynter's head, stroking her hair, careful to stay away from the cut. Wynter put her hand on Remington's leg, her hand alternately rubbing then grasping at the material of the yoga pants Remington wore.

Remington's phone rang and she glanced down at it, seeing that it was her father. She picked up the phone, smiling as she answered it. Wynter glanced up, seeing Remington's smile, watching as she talked, only hearing Remington's side of the conversation.

"Alo?" she said. "Wi papa… pa gen okenn li se amann, she's fine," she said then, winking at Wynter, which told her that she was translating what she was saying to her father. "Mwen menm amann twò, I'm fine too," she said then, chuckling warmly, "chans trape, lucky catch…

pa gen li se amann, it is fine," she said, holding up her wrist. "Mwen pwomèt, I promise… di manman mwen byen, tell Mom I'm fine… Wi mwen se tradui, yes I'm translating for Wynter," she said then, winking at Wynter. "Wi, li se isit la, yes she's here." She laughed out loud then, nodding her head. "Wi, li te rete apre tout, yes she stayed after all… Ah, wi," she said, looking down at Wynter. "My father says he's glad you are okay."

"Tell him 'mèsi'," Wynter said, shocking Remington momentarily.

"Li te di, 'mèsi'." She grinned then. "Wi, aksan li se yon bon bagay, her accent is good," she said, "very good." She smiled fondly then, "Mwen renmen w tou. Orevwa."

"Okay, I recognize that last word from one too many movies set in Paris… but what was that before?" Wynter asked.

"Mwen renmen w tou," Remington said, her hazel eyes looking down into Wynter's eyes. "It means I love you too."

"Mwen renmen w tou," Wynter repeated, once again her accent near perfect.

"Are you sure you weren't French in a previous life?' Remington asked, grinning.

"Why?" Wynter asked, smiling.

"Because your accent is almost dead on," Remington said, looking pleasantly surprised.

Wynter shrugged. "I've always felt that if I was going to speak someone else's language, I should give it the respect of doing it right, or not at all."

"Trè byen," Remington said, inclining her head, surprised and extremely impressed by Wynter's comment.

"Mèsi," Wynter said, smiling.

"And a damned quick study," Remington added with a smile, her eyes shining happily.

The bus ride back to New York was uneventful, except for a conversation Remington and Wynter had about the accommodation arrangements in New York. They were sitting in the small media area next to the bunks. Remington was icing her wrist and the TV was on.

"So," Remington began glancing over at Wynter, "we're not gonna stay in the hotel with everyone else in New York…"

Wynter looked over at her, surprised.

"We're not?" she asked. "Why?"

Remington grinned. "Well, my apartment in New York is right around the corner from the first venue, so…"

"You have an apartment in New York?" Wynter asked, not sure why she was surprised.

"Yeah," Remington nodded.

"Okay," Wynter said nodding.

"It's a two bedroom," Remington said, "and I figure we can stay there for the next five or six show dates. It'll be more comfortable than a hotel."

Wynter nodded, surprised by this turn of events, but also really curious to see what Remington's apartment would look like.

"You're kidding me, right?" Wynter asked Remington as the bus drove away and a doorman busily loaded their bags onto a trolley.

Remington looked back at her perplexed. "Uh, no," she said, her tone reflecting her confusion at Wynter's question.

"Your apartment has a doorman?" Wynter asked.

"It's New York," Remington said, grinning, "lots of them do."

"Okay…" Wynter said, following Remington into the building.

Inside, Wynter looked around. It looked very nice and far from what she'd expected.

"Ms. LaRoché, excellent to see you again, ma'am," the slim gray-haired uniformed man at the front desk said, bowing slightly to her.

"Thanks, James," Remington said smiling. "How's it been going?"

"Well, ma'am, it's definitely getting colder out there by the minute, early winter this year I think. How is California fairing for you?"

"It's had its trials," Remington said, grinning at Wynter. "Oh, and there was an earthquake not more than a week after I got out there."

"California, where natural disasters abound…" James said, his eyes twinkling with mirth.

"We like it," Wynter put in, grinning. "It keeps things interesting!"

James inclined his head politely to Wynter. "If you say so, miss." He looked over at Remington then. "Will you be needing your car later, Ms. LaRoché?"

Remington looked at her watch, and nodded. "Yeah, can you have them give it a quick clean, I'm sure it's got a huge layer of dust."

"Of course, ma'am," James said, nodding.

Remington led her to the elevator and the doorman followed at a polite distance. Wynter leaned against the wall of the elevator, her eyes searching Remington's. She sensed that she was about to be completely shocked by Remington LaRoché. Remington simply looked back at her, a slightly amused grin on her lips.

They walked off the elevator directly into a foyer, with marble floors and elegant wainscoted walls in earth tones. Remington walked through an open doorway and Wynter followed, suddenly finding herself in a room with the most incredible view of Central Park and the buildings on the other side of the park. They were seventeen floors up and Wynter could not believe what she was seeing.

The room was a long loft-style room with windows along its entire length. Looking from left to right, she saw a dining room, a living room area, and what looked like another sitting room to the far right. The furniture was all wood and earth tones, it definitely wasn't fussy or overly decorated, which was very much Remington.

"Fuckin' A, Remi…" Wynter breathed, unable to come up with any other suitable adjectives.

Remington chuckled, shaking her head at Wynter's comment, and turning to the doorman.

"Put those," she said, pointing to Wynter's bags, "into the second bedroom, please. My stuff can go in the master. Thanks," she said, smiling.

The doorman nodded, and headed off to the right.

Wynter turned to look at Remington. "This is a rental right?"

"No," Remington said, "why?"

"You own this?" Wynter asked, unable to keep the shock off her face or out of her voice.

Remington curled her lips, grinning as she nodded. Wynter reached out and swatted Remington on the arm. Remington laughed, putting her arm up defensively to fend off any other attacks.

"What?" she asked, laughing as she did.

"What?" Wynter repeated sarcastically. "You knew this was going to shock the shit out of me, didn't you?"

Remington was still smiling as she shrugged. "How was I supposed to know what you expected."

"Well, there was no way I was expecting this!" Wynter said, gesturing to the view of New York.

"Well, let me show you the rest then," Remington said, smiling warmly.

The kitchen off to the left of the dining room had butcher-block counters and stainless steel appliances. Behind the kitchen Remington had an enviable home gym, complete with treadmill, free weights, weight bench, stair climber, and a seventy-five-inch flat panel TV mounted to the wall.

Wynter shook her head, thinking that Remington was going to always be one surprise after another to her. Remington then led her to the other side of the apartment where the bedrooms were located. To the left was the 'guest bedroom' which featured three walls of windows, with low light colored wooden built in dressers under the windows on all three sides as well as built in bookcases filled with books. There were also comfortable chairs at the end of the bed that faced out toward Central Park. All of the rooms were decorated in earth tones: light beiges, some greens, and darker browns. There was nothing flashy or ostentatious about the apartment. The view itself was the key feature.

"Okay, now let's see your room," Wynter said, smiling.

Remington grinned, and gestured across the hall. Wynter walked into Remington's room, and once again thought that it was totally her. There was nothing too flashy, nothing too over-the-top, just sturdy wood furniture, and lots of built-ins. One of which was a full wall of drawers, shelves and doors with a large screen TV in the center. Even the comforter on the bed was white.

Wynter looked around, continuing to shake her head in complete awe.

"This place is absolutely incredible, Remi," she said, looking over at her bodyguard. "You never cease to amaze me."

Remington smiled softly, her expression pleased. "Thanks," she said simply.

"Never one to gush, are you?" Wynter said, shaking her head.

"Why don't you go get settled, and we'll go get some dinner," Remington said.

Going to 'get some dinner' turned out to be yet another shock for Wynter. As they walked out of the lobby, a bright orange Porsche drove up in front of them. To Wynter's utter shock, the young man got out of the car and walked around to hand the keys to Remington.

"Thanks," Remington said, smiling and handing the young man a folded bill.

"Anytime, Ms. LaRoché," the young man said, smiling widely as he moved to open the passenger's door for Wynter.

"Thank you," Wynter said, looking over at Remington completely floored.

Inside the car, Wynter turned to look at Remington as she got in on the driver's side.

"This is yours too, I take it?" she asked.

Remington chuckled at her tone. "Yes," she said, nodding.

Wynter shook her head once again. "So this is like your New York car?" she asked, grinning.

"I guess you could call it that," Remington said, as she pulled away from the curb and smoothly into traffic. "So, does seafood sound good?"

"I," Wynter stammered, "sure."

Remington nodded, changing lanes. Wynter watched as Remington drove; she looked very much at home behind the wheel of the sports car.

"What is this?" Wynter asked, gesturing to the car.

"It's a Porsche 911 GT3 RS," Remington answered.

Wynter blinked a couple of times. "So like… fast, fast car…" she said, her voice trailing off as she grinned.

"Or that," Remington said, smiling.

It took a half an hour to get to the restaurant, and Wynter was surprised to find that it was down on the water, and in Brooklyn. The restaurant had a valet. Remington got out, handing the guy the keys, and opening Wynter's door for her, looking around as she did.

The restaurant they walked up to was very unassuming looking, with a large number of potted plants on either side of black and glass paneled door. It was called "River Café." Inside, however, Wynter was wowed by the beautiful view of the New York skyline across the river.

"Remi, this is amazing…" Wynter said, feeling like she was saying that a lot on that particular day.

"Yeah, I love the view here," Remington said. "The food is excellent too."

"Handy," Wynter said, grinning.

They ordered their meals, and had an incredible dinner. Wynter enjoyed Remington's company. She felt like they were getting closer as friends, since the fall. Remington seemed a lot less formal, laughing and smiling more, and opening up by taking her to her home and what was obviously a favorite restaurant, since most of the staff seemed to know her.

Wynter Kincade, of course, didn't go unnoticed either. She received a lot of requests for autographs, and much to Remington's dismay, so did the retired MMA fighter. One woman was completely unabashed when speaking to Remington.

"I just think you are so amazing!" she said, smiling with bright white teeth and darkly painted lips. "The way you saved Miss Kincade here, it was just so fantastic!"

Remington inclined her head, blinking a couple of times. She never had any idea how to respond to compliments like that, and couldn't begin to extricate herself from the woman who was holding her arm tightly as she gushed.

"Yes, she's pretty incredible, that's why I love her…" Wynter said taking Remington's hand to make it look as though they were there on a date, so the woman would take the hint.

"Oh my goodness," the woman said, looking embarrassed suddenly. "I'm so sorry I'm interrupting your date…"

She hurried away shortly thereafter. Remington grinned at Wynter. "Our date?" she asked.

"Well, she wasn't going away any time soon and I figured you probably wanted her to, so…" Wynter said, shrugging.

"I've never known what to say to people like that," Remington admitted.

"That's because you're not a gloater," Wynter said. "You'd make a terrible rock star," she said, grinning.

"That and the fact that I can't sing or play an instrument," Remington said, grinning.

"Eh, there's lots of those out there," Wynter said, waving her hand to the 'outside.'

"You're not one of those, though," Remington said with a serious look.

"What? A talentless hack?" Wynter asked, grinning. "I'd like to think I'm not."

"You're not," Remington said, her tone sure. "The other night I was watching you perform…" She shook her head as her voice trailed off. "You were born to do this. You had those people in the palm of your hand, it was absolutely amazing."

"And then I fell," Wynter said, grinning.

Remington laughed, nodding. "There is that part too, yeah."

"Uh-huh…" Wynter murmured, her look chagrinned.

"That experience should show you just how many people care about you," Remington said, her tone earnest. "You've had so many of those 'hits' things on Facebook and all that… People don't do that for talentless hacks, they do that for people they adore."

Wynter looked back at Remington for a long moment, debating whether or not to say what came to mind. She wasn't sure if it was the candlelight, the wine, or the amazing view of the New York city lights, but she felt all soft and warm inside in that moment.

"What that experience showed me was one thing that was important to me, Remi…" Wynter said, her look searching.

"What's that?" Remington asked, picking up her wine and taking a drink.

"That you care about me," Wynter said softly. Though she wondered if she was crazy to tell Remington.

Remington tilted her head looking somewhat pained. "You didn't know that before?" she asked, her voice reflecting the look on her face.

Wynter looked back at the woman who was her bodyguard, this incredibly strong, beautiful and gentle woman, and shook her head.

Remington blew her breath out, grimacing slightly. "Well, then I wasn't doing a very good job of expressing myself," she said, her tone matter of fact. "I do care about you, Wyn," she said. "I know that things have been difficult sometimes, because you and I are extremely different, but I do care. You should know that."

Wynter smiled softly, nodding her head.

"I care about you too, Remi," Wynter said, "and I'm really glad that you're becoming more open with me. I feel like we're finally becoming friends."

Remington smiled. "Yes, I think it's safe to say we are."

"Good," Wynter said, nodding. "Now… what kind of nightlife do you New Yorkers have?"

"Well, there are a few bars," Remington said. "One I usually go to in the West Village… Did you want to dance, drink or what?"

"Tonight?" Wynter said, thinking about it. "Tonight I think just drinking would work."

"Then I know where to take you," Remington said, smiling.

They ended up at a bar called The Cubbyhole in the West Village. Wynter wasn't too shocked to hear people hail Remington with hellos. A number of women came up to her shaking her hand, or pounding her on the back. They all were happy to be introduced to Wynter Kincade. They ended up staying out until two in the morning.

The next morning, Remington was awake long before Wynter stirred. Wynter finally walked out of the guest bedroom, finding Remington sitting with her feet up on the windowsill in the dining room, drinking coffee and reading the paper.

As soon as she saw Wynter entering the room, Remington dropped her feet to the ground and stood, looking over at her charge.

"You look like you need coffee," Remington said, smiling.

"Oh yes, please…" Wynter said, smiling as she sat down at the dining room table, looking out over the park. "This is such a beautiful view…" she said wistfully.

Remington handed her coffee a couple of minutes later. Wynter sipped it and smiled blissfully.

"So good…" she said, sighing, then she looked over at Remington. "We still have most of a day to ourselves," she said, smiling. "What's on the agenda?"

Remington looked over at her. "Well, I need to get a workout in or the next time you decide to fall, I might be too weak to catch you."

"Yeah, like that's ever going to happen," Wynter said, shaking her head. "You ever weak… ha!"

Remington chuckled at her tone. "I can work out here, or I can show you where it all started…"

"Oh, definitely option B, please," Wynter said, smiling. "I want to see all your old haunts…"

"I don't think we'll go that far…" Remington said, rolling her eyes.

"Chicken," Wynter said, grinning.

"You got it," Remington said simply.

An hour later, Remington was driving up to an old brick building. She pulled around to the alley and parked in the dock area. Getting out of the car, she walked around to open Wynter's door, and then went to take her gear bag from the trunk.

"You aren't going to get in trouble parking back here?" Wynter asked, pointing to the huge 'no parking' signs.

Remington grinned as she looked at the signs and popped the gum she was chewing.

"It'll be fine," she said, nodding toward the opening of the alley and getting Wynter to precede her.

As they walked up the alley, a man wearing a T-shirt that said "Billy's Bar" and jeans was walking toward them.

"The prodigal daughter returns," the man said slyly.

"Shut up, Billy," Remington said, grinning as they passed him.

"You know him, I take it?" Wynter asked.

"Oh yeah," Remington said, nodding.

She knew a lot people as it turned out, including the owner of the gym, Jack Sands.

"And there's my long-lost partner!" a sandy-haired man called, walking up to Remington on the street and hugging her.

"Hey Jack, it's good to see you," Remington said. "Jack, this is Wynter Kincade, Wynter this is Jack, he owns the place."

Jack extended his hand to Wynter, smiling widely. "Remi's half-owner, she just won't tell anyone."

"No point in it," Remington said simply.

"Hell, if you'd let me put 'Remi LaRoché used to live here' on the sign, I'd triple my business!" Jack said, guffawing at his own joke. "Come on inside, you training this morning?"

"That was my plan," Remington said, nodding. "Got anyone good I can spar with?" she asked as they walked up the stairs.

"I got a few youngsters that could use the workout, and the ass kicking," he said, with a wink. "Speaking of ass kicking..." Jack began.

"No, no, don't start that shit," Remington said, grimacing and glancing down at Wynter. "Sorry," she said softly.

Wynter shook her head smiling.

"You can't let that little bitch talk trash about you like that!" Jack exclaimed. "You need to shut her up."

"She'll shut up eventually," Remington said, looking unconcerned.

"Not soon enough for my tastes…" Jack muttered.

The word was already running through the gym that Remington LaRoché was there, and slowly but surely people started to make their way over to talk to her and joke with her. Wynter looked on, seeing the way that Remington took in what people said, but never got cocky. Even when others were talking about how amazing she was, how awesome, how cool… Remington never agreed with them, or seemed to preen in the slightest. In fact, while people talked around her, Remington stood talking and nodding, but also taping her hands, flexing her muscles, and stretching.

"Okay, I need to work out guys," she finally said, grinning.

People stepped back then, and Remington began her workout. Wynter found a chair, and started looking at her phone. She could hear people talking about Remington the entire time. She never heard one single negative thing said about the woman. Everyone talked about her talent, her speed, her strength, her stamina. It was astounding to Wynter, but then again, she realized she shouldn't be surprised; Remington wasn't the type of person that spawned negativity. Wynter was sure that was why her friends were so determined that Remington needed to shut Akasha Salt up.

The last thing Remington did was climb into the ring, pulling on her gloves. One of the men Jack had tapped to spar with Remington was a good half a foot taller than her, and looked like he outweighed her by about fifty pounds. Wynter moved to the side of the ring, like many others and watched, feeling nervous. No agreements had been made not to hit or make major contact, which had her feeling even more nervous.

Remington bounced on the balls of her feet, and then dropped a foot back in a fighter's stance. Bringing her hands up, she motioned to the man with her fingertips, her eyes watching him closely. The man rushed in, and Remington immediately threw a punch, catching him on the jaw, but she pulled it at the last second, so it didn't impact as hard.

"Shit!" the man exclaimed, stepping back.

"It's okay," Remington said, "don't ever come in that hard, it's a fast way to lose."

The man nodded, rolling his neck to get himself back in focus.

Remington waited. He brought his hands up, moving to Remington's left, and she tracked him with her eyes, her body at the ready. He attempted a right hook, which Remington dodged easily, shifting back and to the right. He followed quickly with a jab with his left, but once again, Remington avoided it, and was able to get in a quick leg kick in, making him stumble slightly.

"Don't leave your left open that far," Remington instructed

The man nodded, taking in what she was saying. Then he did a quick fake to the left, coming at Remington from the right, his fist flying. It glanced off Remington's shoulder, but she avoided a full face hit with fast footwork.

"That was good," Remington said, nodding.

Wynter noticed that Remington's voice never became condescending, it was always even, or positive. She really liked that about her. Remington was still herself, even in the ring.

After about a twenty-minute session, the man held up his hand, breathing heavily. Remington immediately relaxed her position and walked over to shake his hand. Remington took a break then, grabbing her water and a towel to dry off with.

Wynter walked over to her. "That was pretty impressive."

Remington grinned. "You liked that?" she asked, sounding surprised.

"Yeah," Wynter said, smiling. "I like seeing my bodyguard in action," she said, winking at Remington.

Remington chewed at the gum in her mouth looking amused.

"What?" Wynter asked.

"Nothing," Remington said, shaking her head.

She'd been thinking that Wynter didn't strike her as the type to like things like fighting, so she wasn't sure if Wynter was simply humoring her or if she was just wrong about what Wynter liked. It never occurred to her that Wynter only liked the fighting because it was Remington doing it.

When Remington climbed back into the ring, music was playing in the background. Remington recognized the song that started and circled her finger in the air to get Jack to turn it up. He did as she wanted. The young guy that climbed into the ring was all muscle and bulk. He had a look about him that told Remington that he was going to be more of a challenge than the first guy. She pursed her lips, listening to the song playing; it was Limp Bizkit, "My Way."

The first lines seemed to be quite apropos in this case. "You think you're special, you do, I can see it in your eyes…" It's exactly what Remington was thinking this kid thought about himself. He was all tatted up, and already doing the puffing up and making grunting noises. She glanced over at Jack, giving him a wry look and raising her eyebrow, as if to say *really?* Jack grinned and mouthed the words, "Put him down hard." Remington nodded, getting the message.

Remington took a deep breath, blowing it out slowly, focusing herself. Once again, she brought her hands up and motioned with her fingertips for her opponent to begin. The kid did a lot of bouncing around, a lot of fake outs. Remington shifted, keeping her eyes on him at all times. She knew this kid wasn't going to pull any punches, so she resolved that she wouldn't either. It was obvious by the look in his eyes that he wanted to score a victory on Remington LaRoché; it wasn't the first time she'd faced someone that was determined to change her undefeated record even if it wasn't an official fight. It would be bragging rights, and a guy like the kid she was currently facing would always be looking for those.

His friends were yelling encouragement, and it was pumping up his ego.

"Get her, Charlie! Take her!" one of his friends yelled.

"Tap that ass!" another yelled.

Wynter's head snapped around to identify that particular big mouth.

Giving a yell, the kid charged at Remington, putting his head down expecting to catch her in the ribs, Remington danced aside, easily avoiding his first pass, but not clearing his longer reach. His arm whipped out grabbing her throat, Remington brought her fist up from under his chin in a sharp upper cut, and he gave a yelp and let her go. Remington jumped back, crouching as he started cussing and swinging. She avoided every punch, stepping in as the last swing passed her, jabbing him in the kidneys and giving a sharp side kick a quick second later.

He surprised her by spinning and sweeping her legs out from under her, a completely dirty move. She hit the mat hard, but rolled to the side to keep him from dropping on her. He outweighed her by a good hundred pounds, so if he was able to pin her, she was done and she knew it. He stunned her by soccer kicking her in the side, not once but twice. She heard Wynter scream her name, but shook her head. He drew his foot back a third time this time aiming at her head. She waited, giving him the confidence to try it. When his leg lashed out, she grabbed it, and, using the strength she was known for, she twisted his foot, hearing his knee pop out of place. She took him down to the mat, and brought her elbow down on his midsection brutally, moving over him and punching him in the face. She dropped low, putting her forearm against his throat, her eyes blazing as she looked down at him.

Wynter could feel Remington's fury from where she stood on the side of the ring.

"You fucking think you're gonna take me down?" Remington growled at the younger man. "You think you got what it takes? You've got shit," she snapped, and began increasing the pressure on his throat until he finally threw his hand out, smacking the mat with his hand, tapping out. Remington kept her arm over his throat, her jaw twitching as she clenched her teeth, staring him down. Finally, she moved to stand, throwing his friends a sneering look, then turning and walking to the other side of the ring where Wynter stood.

"Are you okay?" Wynter asked her immediately.

"Yeah, I'm okay," Remington said, nodding.

She glanced up as she saw Jack climb into the ring.

"Get the fuck outa my gym!" Jack was yelling at the kid as he climbed slowly to his feet. "I don't go in for that dirty fighting here, you get the hell out and take your friends with you!" He strode over to the where Remington stood. "You okay, Rem?"

"I'm fine," Remington said, nodding.

"I'm sorry, Rem," Jack said, shaking his head ruefully.

"It's cool, Jack, don't worry about it," Remington said.

Remington walked over to pick up her bag, looking down at Wynter who had followed her and was looking up at her worriedly.

"Wyn, I'm okay, really," she said. "I'm going to go take a shower." She glanced around. "You'll be safe out here."

"You're sure?" Wynter asked.

Remington quirked a grin. "You think anyone here will mess with you after that?"

Wynter's eyes widened, she'd just heard the slightest hint of an ego from Remington. She shook her head. "Probably not."

"Probably not," Remington repeated, grinning and winking at her. "I'll be out in a few, okay?"

"Okay," Wynter said.

In the end, Wynter decided she didn't like the looks the men in the gym were giving her, so she made her way to the women's locker room. She walked around the corner, and saw Remington standing in jeans, black leather boots, and a black exercise bra, her back was to

Wynter. It was an enticing sight, but then Remington turned around and Wynter saw the dark bruises on Remington's torso.

"Oh my God!" Wynter said, striding over and reaching out to touch the bruises gently. "Remi…" she breathed, her eyes showing concern.

Remington smiled down at her. "It's just a bruise, Wynter, I've had much worse."

"Well, I haven't seen much worse on your body before, okay?" Wynter said, her tone strident.

Remington smiled tenderly. "Okay, I'm sorry, "but it's really okay."

Wynter smoothed her hand extremely gently over the bruise, feeling Remington shudder and thinking that it was in pain. She glanced up, as Remington reached over to pick up her shirt, and pulled it on.

"Let's get out of here," she said, nodding towards the door as she tucked her shirt in and then picked up her jacket and her bag.

Wynter preceded Remington out of the locker room. Back in the car, she looked over at Remington, noting that she was moving gingerly. "Maybe we should just go relax today, so you can be up for tonight," she said.

Remington's lips twitched, but she nodded, agreeing that it was probably for the best.

That night the show, at Radio City Music Hall, went off without a hitch, except that the fans demanded Remington's presence on stage. Quinn laughed, knowing exactly how that felt; she'd had the exact same problem after she and Xandy had gotten together. She more or less pushed Remington out onto the stage. The audience screamed and stomped their feet. Wynter walked over to Remington, looking up at her, her eyes searching Remington's. She reached up, putting her hand to Remington's cheek, as she had in the room the morning after her fall, and put her other hand to Remington's heart just as she had. Remington smiled down at her, and put her hand over Wynter's hand on her heart. Wynter kept her eyes on Remington as she spoke into the microphone.

"Okay so many of you know that Remi saved my life a few nights ago…" she said, smiling as the crowd cheered, and Remington shook her head, rolling her eyes. "What most of you probably don't know is that Remi is a Queensrÿche fan. So…" she said, smiling. "Hopefully I can do Geoff Tate's incredible voice some justice… but this is for my bodyguard and my friend."

Jerith Michaels walked out on stage and started playing his guitar. Dylan Silver joined in on the base guitar. Wynter stayed where she was, her hand staying on Remington's chest as she began to sing. The words talked about being there for Remington through thick and thin and that she promised to do so with her hand on her heart.

As the song ended, Wynter took a step in closer to Remington and kissed her lips softly, then pulled back to look up at her.

"Mèsi," Wynter said softly to Remington.

"Toujou pou ou," Remington replied, her voice equally soft, but the microphone Wynter held picked it up anyway.

Wynter gave her a perplexed look. "What does that mean?" she asked, not caring that people were watching.

Remington leaned down, whispering in her ear, "Always for you." She kissed Wynter's ear, then stepped back, smiling down at her.

The crowd cheered, and Remington turned to them, putting her hands up in front of her chest in prayer form, inclining her head to the crowd, as she had done when she was still fighting. Many people in the crowd recognized it and yelled even louder. With that, Remington pivoted on her heel and walked off stage, leaving Wynter staring after her shaking her head slowly.

Chapter 6

In Los Angeles, Jet and Skyler were sitting out on the patio at The Club smoking.

"Uh," Skyler stammered as she looked across the patio. "Isn't that Wynter's girlfriend?" she asked, nodding her head toward the short-haired blond making out with another girl.

Jet followed Skyler's indication and looked shocked. "It's supposed to be, yeah."

"Isn't that Wynter's girlfriend?" Devin asked as she walked out onto the patio with a beer for Skyler.

Skyler chuckled, nodding. "We were just saying that."

Fadiyah walked out to the patio a moment later with drinks in hand as well. She looked over at the two girls making out and shot Jet a quizzical look.

"Yep," Jet said, nodding to her wife.

"That is not right," Fadiyah said shocked.

Jet and Skyler exchanged a grin.

"Woah," Dakota said as she and Jazmine walked out to the patio.

"Yeah, we know," Jet said, grinning.

Before long most of the group was outside, and more or less glowering at Lauren. When Lauren turned around, it was obvious that she'd known full well that they'd be there. Her look was rebellious, even as she put her arm around the girl she'd been making out with and walked by the group and back into the bar.

"Okay, who's texting Wynter?" Jet asked.

"I'll text Remi," Kashena said, pulling out her phone.

****

Remington and Wynter had just gotten back to Remington's apartment when Remington's phone chimed. She pulled out her phone and read the message from Kashena.

"Lauren at The Club, sucking face with some random chick and she knew we saw her."

Remington grimaced, glancing at Wynter, who had turned to look back at her.

"What?" Wynter asked, seeing Remington's grimace.

Remington handed her the phone and Wynter read Kashena's message. Wynter lips tightened, as she nodded, her eyes blazing. She looked up at Remington then.

"I want to go out," she said, "take me out."

Remington widened her eyes, but then nodded.

They ended up at a club called the Bum Bum Room, pronounced 'boom boom.' It was a salsa dance club. Remington kept a watchful eye on Wynter as she cut loose, drinking and dancing with whoever asked. Whenever one of the women at the club would get too insistent, Remington would step in to back the woman off. At one point, she'd done just that, as a slow song began and Wynter grabbed her hand.

"Dance with me," Wynter said, her eyes a bit glassy.

Remington knew she couldn't say no. Wynter was hurting and she needed to be there for her. Moving to take her charge in her arms, Remington put her lips against the top of Wynter's head, leaning down as they began to move.

"Are you okay?" she asked solicitously.

Wynter didn't answer, only nodding. Remington gave her a gentle squeeze and held her a little closer.

The song playing was Adele's "Love in the Dark." Wynter sang the words, her head resting against Remington's shoulder. One of the verses stuck in Wynter's head, making her throat clog with tears as she sang it. It talked about the one person that mattered the most being the person she would run to when she needed someone the most.

Remington felt Wynter trembling and knew she was crying. She reached up between them, putting her hand to Wynter's cheek. She had no way of knowing that Wynter wasn't crying about Lauren. She was crying because she was afraid she was never going to be in love.

They continued to dance, but it became obvious to Remington that Wynter needed to get out of there for a bit. Stepping back, she took Wynter's hand and led her off the dance floor and out to the club's balcony. She started talking to the bouncer out there. The bouncer had already told Remington earlier that he thought she was a "helluva fighter." Remington traded on that fame for once, getting him to clear the balcony temporarily.

Remington moved to sit against the railing, putting Wynter in front of her.

"Talk to me, Wyn…" she said, her eyes searching Wynter's.

Wynter shook her head looking sad. "You know, in seven years, I never cheated on her… never…" she said, her tone haunted. "I mean, I know the stupid tabloids always claimed I was screwing this girl or that girl… but I never did… never."

Remington nodded, grimacing, hearing the pain in Wynter's voice.

"And she went to The Club… where she knows my friends are going to be… Why? Is she just trying to hurt me? She can't hit me from this far away, so she's going to hurt me some other way?"

Remington shook her head. "I don't know, babe… li se yon timoun," she said, then rolled her eyes "She's a child," she translated.

Wynter smiled slightly at Remington's slip. "Do you do that when you're irritated?"

Remington grinned. "Yeah, sometimes," she said.

"Good to know," Wynter said, nodding.

"You should try to call her," Remington said.

"Why?" Wynter asked. "I mean, she denied it the first time, but I believe Kash."

"I know, and you should, but maybe she can explain it," Remington said.

"How?" Wynter asked, her tone sarcastic. "I slipped and stuck my tongue down someone else's throat?" she said, shaking her head. "No, I'm done."

Remington took a deep breath and blew it out slowly. "Okay."

"And now I'm going to go get drunk and stupid," Wynter said.

"Okay," Remington said again.

Wynter laughed as she grabbed Remington's hand and dragged her back inside. Wynter spent the next two hours getting really drunk. In the end, Remington had to carry her home and put her to bed.

The next four nights were spent the same way; after the concerts, Wynter would drag Remington out to whatever club was around. They both got very little sleep, and on the drive to the next show, it started to take its toll on Remington. She had been coughing for a couple of days, but had dismissed it as 'just one of those things.' She and Quinn were discussing the security for the next few dates and she'd gone to the back of the bus at one point to grab her laptop. She had a coughing fit that left her breathless, and then she felt dizzy and suddenly everything went black.

Wynter, who had just glanced toward the back of the bus to see where Remington went, saw her go down.

"Remi!" Wynter yelled, jumping up from where she sat and running back to where Remington lay on the floor kneeling on the floor. "Quinn!" she screamed, her voice sounding terrified.

Quinn came on the run.

"Let me get in there," Quinn told Wynter. Wynter stood to get out of Quinn's way. "Remi!" Quinn called, jostling Remington's shoulder.

Remington groaned slightly, moving her head.

"Come on," Quinn said, picking Remington up off the floor, and sitting her down on the closest bunk.

"I'm okay…" Remington said, not looking at all like that was true. She was pale and looking dazed.

"Yeah, right," Quinn said unconvinced.

Remington blinked slowly wavering a bit as she did.

"Okay, okay, lay back, Rem," Quinn said, pushing her friend back, glancing over at Xandy who was watching worriedly.

Remington complied, lying back on the bunk, her breathing slightly labored.

"Okay, you get some rest," Quinn told Remington. Then she looked at Wynter. "You," she said sternly, and then gestured with her head for Wynter to go up front.

Wynter saw anger in her green eyes and was surprised by it. She nodded, turning to walk toward the front of the bus. Quinn pulled off Remington's shoes and pulled the cover up over her. Straightening, she looked over at Xandy, shaking her head and blowing her breath out.

Xandy and Quinn had already discussed how much Remington was overdoing it with letting Wynter drag her out every night while they'd been in New York. Quinn had seen how exhausted Remington was getting and it had worried her, which had served to annoy her. Xandy knew Quinn was about to lay into Wynter, and she tended to think it was what Wynter needed at this point. She nodded supportively to Quinn.

Quinn turned to walk up to the front of the bus. Wynter was sitting at the table. Clamping down on her desire to yell, Quinn moved to sit across from Wynter and Xandy sat next to Quinn. Putting her hand on the table between them, Quinn looked at Wynter.

"You do get what just happened back there, right?" Quinn asked, her Irish accent thicker in her restrained anger.

Wynter looked back at Quinn, surprised by her tone and the anger she saw in Quinn's eyes. She shook her head slowly. Quinn gave a short laugh, shaking her head and looking at Xandy. She scornfully looked back over at Wynter.

"You've run her into the fucking ground with your bullshit," Quinn snapped, her eyes flashing in anger.

Wynter was shocked by not only by what Quinn had just said, but by the venom in her voice. She started to shake her head, thinking that Remington was just getting sick and that had been what had caused her to faint.

"We've stayed out late a few times, but—"

"What what?" Quinn asked, cutting her off. "You thought she went to sleep when you did? She couldn't, she was working, she's always working."

Surprise was evident on Wynter's face. Then she closed her eyes as she thought about what Quin was saying. Yes, she had assumed that Remington had gone to sleep when she did but they'd been in separate rooms, so she couldn't have known for sure. But Remington had always stayed up later than she had working on plans for the next tour date. There'd been shows every night when they were in New York, and Remington had had to plan the security for those.

"I..." Wynter stammered, shaking her head. "I'm sorry..." she said, feeling horrible suddenly. "I never even thought—"

"No, you didn't think," Quinn interrupted again, "you were busy licking your fucking wounds over that cunt Lauren."

Wynter winced at Quinn's sharp words, but she knew she was right.

"Quinn, you have to know that I never meant to hurt Remi," Wynter said, her look solemn.

"Okay, but you did," Quinn said, her words short, not looking placated.

Wynter nodded, accepting the blame. "What can I do to fix it?"

Quinn thought about it for a moment.

"You're gonna need to convince her to rest tonight instead of doing the show. She needs a break."

Wynter nodded. "I can do that."

"You think it's gonna be easy?" Quinn asked, raising an eyebrow. "Remi takes her protection of you very seriously. She's not just going to willingly sit this one out."

"I'll convince her," Wynter said, looking determined. "Even if I have to be a complete bitch to do it."

Remington slept on the bus for the next six hours. They arrived in Chicago at five in the evening and the show was at seven that night. The intent was to leave after the show and head to their next stop in Noblesville, Indiana. Another three-hour drive. When the bus pulled up to the venue, iWireless Center, Wynter was sitting on the bunk next to Remington.

Feeling the bus stop and the front door open, Remington stirred, moving to get up.

"Uh, no," Wynter said, putting her hand on Remington's shoulder to stop her from getting up.

"What?" Remington asked, looking perplexed.

"You're taking the night off," Wynter said simply.

"Like hell..." Remington said, giving her a shocked look and moving to sit up again, this time avoiding Wynter's hand.

Wynter stayed where she was, blocking Remington from being able to climb out of the bunk.

"Wynter," Remington said, gesturing for Wynter to move.

Wynter folded her arms in front of her chest, shaking her head.

Remington gave her a narrowed look, blowing her breath out when that didn't change Wynter's stance. "Wyn, I'm fine, okay? I just needed a little bit of sleep. I'm good now, and time's a wasting."

"You're taking the night off, Remi," Wynter told her, her tone brooking no argument.

"And I say I'm not," Remington replied her tone equally inflexible, moving again to get out of the bunk.

Wynter moved to block her from doing so.

Remington gave her a stern look. "Don't make me move you."

"Don't make me smack the shit out of you," Wynter replied seriously.

She saw a flicker of a challenge flare in Remington's eyes, and then she saw Remington clamp down on the thought, her eyes dropping below Wynter's as she fought to control her apparent annoyance.

When she raised her eyes to Wynter's again, she was calm.

"I'm fine, Wynter, I need to do my job," Remington reasoned

"And I'm saying you don't need to do your job tonight," Wynter said. "Quinn is going to walk me in and keep an eye on things here."

"It's not Quinn's job…" Remington said, her tone lowering in her ire.

"Well, she's just as good as you, so, I'm going. Stay here I won't need you tonight," Wynter said off-handedly, looking away as she stood up dismissively.

Remington was so stunned by her statement she didn't move. Wynter was gone a moment later.

As she walked off the bus Wynter had tears in her eyes. Quinn looked at her and glanced back to see if Remington was following but she wasn't. Quinn nodded, putting her arm around Wynter, guessing easily that Wynter had had to be nasty to get Remington to stay put.

"You okay?" Quinn asked, as she, Wynter and Xandy walked toward the doors arena's back door.

Wynter shook her head. "No, I feel like shit, and I was just so nasty to her that she's probably going to be mad at me for a while…" Her voice trailed off as a stricken feeling came over her.

She'd pointedly stood up and walked away so she couldn't see the look on Remington's face when she'd said what she had. She knew that she'd just minimized what Remington had done back in South Carolina, and she felt horrendous about it. It affected her performance that night, and when the audience chanted for Remington, Wynter left the stage in tears. Xandy, who was on after Wynter, had told the crowd that Remington wasn't feeling well that night and was therefore taking a well-deserved rest.

That night when Wynter climbed onto the bus, she noted that Remington was sleeping with her back to the opening of the bunk. After changing into her sleeping clothes, she climbed into the bunk above Remington, doing her best to keep her teeth from chattering; it was snowing. She bundled up as best she could, but found that she deeply missed Remington's arms around her. Not just because of her body heat, but because she missed the closeness she felt with Remington when they slept next to each other on the bus.

It was six o'clock in the morning when the bus pulled into Noblesville, Indiana. It had taken longer due to accidents on the roadway. The buses pulled into the parking lot of the hotel where they'd been booked for the day.

When Wynter crawled out of her bunk, feeling sore and unhappy, she noticed that Remington was no longer in the bunk. She wasn't even on the bus. Looking out the windows, Wynter finally located her talking to Quinn. She sat down at the table on the bus, not wanting to approach Remington at that point, dreading having to do so.

She wasn't surprised when Remington's manner was all business. Remington had walked past her on the bus, picking up both of their bags, and walking back down the aisle. She waited for Wynter outside the bus without a word.

Wynter walked off the bus, forcing herself to maintain her composure. They walked into the hotel together, and Remington led her up to the room. At the room door, Remington put the card key into the lock and then opened it, gesturing for Wynter to precede her. Wynter did, and noted right away that there were two queen beds in this particular room. She wondered if fate had done that to teach her a lesson. She hadn't made any arrangements for the rooms to have one bed, she'd figured that it had been fate all along.

In the room, Remington put Wynter's bags on the bed closest to the windows, and set her bags down, pulling out the few things she needed.

"I'm going to go over to the venue with Quinn," Remington said without preamble, "please don't leave the room." With that she turned and walked out, pocketing one of the card keys.

Wynter stood in the room, feeling terrible and wanting to cry. She pulled her overnight bag out, and took it into the bathroom with a change of clothes. She took a long hot shower and let herself cry. When she climbed out, she dried off, and blow-dried her hair and put on the clothes she'd taken into the bathroom. It was silent in the room when she walked out. She thought about turning on music, but she just didn't want to. She lay down on the bed, staring out the glass door onto the balcony, watching it snow.

She was asleep when she heard the door open. She didn't move, listening to Remington move around the room. She heard the bathroom door close and the shower start a few minutes later. Turning over onto her back, Wynter stared up at the ceiling. She had no idea how to bridge the sudden distance between her and Remington. Part of her wondered if she had the right to even try. It had been her desire to drink and party and forget about what was happening with Lauren that had caused Remington to get sick, so saying what she had for Remington's own good didn't excuse the reason for it in the first place.

Wynter got up, picking up her phone, headphones, and cigarettes. She then pulled on warmer clothes and Remington's leather Affliction jacket that she'd doggedly kept thus far on the tour. She walked out onto the balcony, fortunately blocked from snow actually landing on it. She put her headphones in her ears and sat in one of the chairs cranking her music and smoking.

Remington emerged from the bathroom, tensing when she realized Wynter wasn't in the room, but then saw her on the balcony. Remington watched Wynter smoking, her lips twitching in consternation. She knew that it was snowing outside and well below zero, and that Wynter shouldn't be out in the cold like that. Part of her wanted to do what she would normally have and tell Wynter to come back inside. The part that was still feeling stung by Wynter's comment the night before, however, reminded her that Wynter was an adult and could decide for herself if she should be outside.

It dragged at her that she was allowing her personal hurt feelings to interfere with what she saw as her job. Protecting Wynter Kincade sometimes meant protecting her from herself as well. Remington couldn't begin to think of a way to address the situation without sounding angry, because the fact was, she was angry. It bothered her no end that she'd allowed Wynter's comments to hurt her feelings, but they had hurt, and she couldn't seem to get past it at that moment. Blowing her breath out, Remington sat on the bed, and pulled out her laptop. She concentrated on starting to look at the next leg of the tour, after their break, to see where there might be issues or things to be addressed.

Part of her wondered if she'd even continue on the tour after the break. She wondered if it might be better if she asked John to replace her. It had been going around in her head since the night before that maybe she was just getting too close to Wynter, and that it was interfering with her objectivity. She thought that it might be better in the long run if Wynter was protected by someone that was better able to cope with her changeable moods. Bodyguard work had just been one of the ideas she'd had as a career choice and she was beginning to wonder if it had been a mistake. Her time back in New York had reminded her that she had other options. She'd never sold her apartment in New York because she hadn't been sure she'd stay in Los

Angeles. She was hoping her trip home in two days would help her make some decisions about where her life was going.

Before long, it was time to get ready to the show. Remington was dressed and waiting for Wynter when she came in from the balcony.

"I just need to change," Wynter said softly, keeping her eyes averted from Remington.

Remington nodded, sitting back down on the bed and opening her laptop again.

Wynter was ready twenty minutes later. Remington led her out of the hotel and onto the bus without comment. Ten minutes later, they arrived at the venue. Remington led her to her dressing room, telling her to text her when she was ready to go to the stage. Wynter nodded, closing the door to the dressing room softly.

Again, that night Wynter's performance was affected by her depressed mood. Once again, the audience cheered for Remington's presence. Remington stood offstage, standing in an 'at ease' position, when Wynter looked over at her to see if she was willing to come onstage. Remington simply shook her head stoically.

"Sorry, guys," Wynter said, sadly. "Remi's busy at the moment. But thank you for a great night," she said, but it was obvious her heart wasn't in it.

She walked off stage, the opposite side from where Remington stood. Xandy met her backstage and hugged her. Wynter cried in her arms for a few minutes.

"She hates me now…" Wynter said sounding lost.

"She doesn't hate you," Xandy said, "she's just mad. Give her time, she'll get over it. Do you want me to have Quinn talk to her?"

Wynter shook her head vehemently. "No, I made this mess, I'll deal with it."

Later that night they were back in the room. Wynter had taken a shower to clean up after the show. When she emerged, she saw that Remington was lying on the bed she'd chosen near the door, one arm over her eyes.

"Can we talk?" Wynter asked softly.

Remington dropped her arm, turning her head to look at Wynter, her look considering. Finally, she nodded, moving to sit up, putting her back against the headboard. Wynter moved to sit on the bed facing her.

"What I said the other night in Chicago," Wynter said, "I didn't mean it. I was worried about you because you had fainted, and I knew that you needed to rest…"

Remington looked back at her for a long moment. "I told you I was fine," she said evenly.

"I know," Wynter said, "but you weren't fine, Remi. I could see how tired you still were…" Her voice trailed off as she reached out to touch Remington's hand that rested on the bed between them. "Quinn pointed out that it was my fault that you were so tired, because I kept dragging you out in New York."

Remington gave a short, frustrated laugh. "Does it ever occur to you that Quinn doesn't know everything?" she asked, her tone slightly derisive.

Wynter narrowed her eyes. "Yes, it does, but the fact was I did drag you out every night and you weren't apparently sleeping much during the day while I was…"

Remington didn't answer that, simply looking back at Wynter. Finally, she shook her head unhappily.

"I just think things are getting skewed here…" Remington said then.

"Skewed how?" Wynter asked, surprised by the statement.

"I just…" Remington started to say, grimacing slightly as she felt emotions churn up in her again. "I think we need to think about whether or not this is really working."

"This?" Wynter asked, her eyes searching Remington's.

"This, me protecting you," Remington said.

"I—" Wynter began, her look suddenly panicked. A knock at the door interrupted whatever she was going to say.

Remington stood up and went to open the door. Wynter couldn't see who was at the door because Remington's body blocked the way.

"What are you doing here?" Remington said, her tone far from friendly.

"I came to see Wynter, just get her," Wynter heard Lauren say.

Remington dropped her arm from the door where she held it and moved to stand back, gesturing for Lauren to enter the room.

Lauren walked in, her eyes finding Wynter immediately.

"Lauren, what are you doing here?" Wynter asked, her eyes going from Lauren to Remington and then back to Lauren.

"I came to talk to you," Lauren said, her tone earnest, "to apologize, to make it up to you…"

Wynter looked warily at Lauren for a long moment.

"Don't look at me like that, babe. I'm sorry!" Lauren said, her tone beseeching. "I just lost my shit… I saw all that stuff about you and her," she said, gesturing angrily at Remington, "and I just lost it… I'm sorry… I love you…" Lauren said, stepping in to take Wynter in her arms.

Wynter's eyes went immediately to Remington. Their eyes connected for a second, then Remington broke the contact. She walked over to her nightstand, picking up her cigarettes, lighter, and phone.

"I'm gonna give you two some privacy," Remington said, not looking at Wynter.

"Where will you be?" Wynter asked worriedly, as she stepped back from Lauren.

"Not sure, I'll text you with my location," Remington said with her back to Wynter as she opened the door.

Remington walked out of the room a moment later, realizing belatedly that she hadn't grabbed a jacket.

"Modi li…" she muttered, saying 'damn it.' Sighing, she shook her head and walked away.

Twenty minutes later she climbed onto the tour bus and went to lay down on the bed Quinn and Xandy usually slept in. She laid back on it staring up at the ceiling of the bus. She texted Wynter that she was on the bus, then lay back again.

She was still lying there, half asleep when she heard a voice say, "What the hell!"

She levered herself up on her arms, looking over at Billy Montague who was standing with her hands on her hips looking at her.

"What are you doing here?" Billy asked disdainfully as she gestured to the bus.

Remington rolled her eyes, dropping back down on the bed and blowing her pent-up breath out.

"Lauren showed up, I gave them the room," she said simply. "What are you doing down here?" she asked.

"I was getting something out of my bus when I saw a light on over here," Billy said, then she gave Remington a derisive look. "Are you fucking crazy?"

Remington craned her neck to look over at Billy. "Not that I'm aware of," she answered mildly.

"Why the fuck would you let Lauren near Wynter again?" Billy asked.

"She's Wynter's girlfriend…" Remington said, feeling like she was stating the obvious.

"They broke up, remember?" Billy said.

"Not officially," Remington countered.

Billy stood staring at Remington and after a long minute she shook her head.

"You know, Remi, I pegged you for smarter than this," Billy said bluntly.

"I'm sorry?" Remington said, not following Billy's train of thought.

"You have the chance to fuck a rock star and you're stupid enough to throw it away?"

Remington blinked slowly, her face reflecting a stunned reaction to Billy's brash statement. She opened her mouth to respond, but realized she had no idea what to say to the outrageous singer.

"You don't get it, do you?" Billy asked, her tone haughty.

"Get what, Billy?" Remington sighed, as she turned her head back to face the ceiling, already tired of trying to keep up with Billy Montague.

Billy shocked Remington by crawling onto the bed on all fours, and positioning her body above Remington's seductively, her blue eyes staring down into Remington's hazel eyes.

"What are you doing?" Remington asked shocked.

"I'm showing you what you're missing," Billy said simply.

Without warning, Billy leaned down, her lips moving over Remington's in a sensuous kiss, pressing her body close to Remington's as she did. Remington's immediate reaction was to put her hands on Billy's waist, ostensibly to move her off of her, but that thought never completely made it to fruition. Billy kissed Remington's lips for what seemed like forever, and Remington allowed the kiss, but when their lips finally parted and Billy leaned up, Remington's look was sardonic.

"So," Remington said, her tone matter of fact, "that's what I'm missing?"

"That's right," Billy said confidently.

Remington nodded, her look inscrutable. Then Billy was shocked when Remington's hand came up, sliding through Billy's long hair, grasping a handful as her hazel eyes stared up into Billy's.

"This is what you're missing," Remington said, pulling Billy's head down to hers, and kissing Billy with the passion and strength she usually kept at bay.

Billy was stunned by the strength of Remington's kiss; the woman could really kiss! Her body lit up, every nerve coming alive and screaming all at once. She moaned against Remington's lips, her hands grasping at Remington's shirt, and her body pressing closer. Remington's lips continued to move over hers, sucking and parting and taking possession again and again. Billy was sure she was about to come when suddenly Remington stopped, pulling back, and looking up at Billy, their faces only an inch apart.

"Now," Remington said, her voice low and heated, "go back upstairs to your husband and let him finish the job."

Billy let out a gasp of pure frustration, her eyes staring into Remington's. "Or you could just finish the job yourself," she said breathlessly.

Remington shook her head slowly, a look of near malice entering her eyes.

"You're married, Billy, I don't mess with that," she said seriously.

Billy drew in a sharp breath, then nodded, knowing she'd just been bested at her own game, and feeling admiration for Remington LaRoché starting in her. Climbing off the bed, Billy looked down at Remington her look both admiring and still a bit seductive.

"You win that round, Remi," she said, grinning with her eyes sparkling. "But we'll see who wins the war," she said with a wink.

Remington rubbed her index finger over her lips thoughtfully, and simply smiled back at Billy.

"Good night, Billy," Remington said.

"Good night, Remi," Billy replied with a wide smile.

Wynter was stunned to see Billy walking out of the bus. As she walked toward the bus, Billy smiled at her, making a gesture of buffing her nails on her shirt with a confident smirk on her face. Wynter stood openmouthed staring after Billy, watching her disappear into the elevator. She climbed onto the bus and walked back to the sleeping area.

"What the fuck was Billy doing in here?" she snapped.

Remington's head snapped around to look at her.

"What the hell are you doing down here?" Remington asked.

"I asked you a question," Wynter said, putting her hands on her hips, her eyes blazing.

Remington looked back at her for a long moment, then she turned her head back towards the ceiling. "She was getting something from their bus when she saw the light on over here."

"Uh-huh…" Wynter said her tone disbelieving.

Remington propped herself up on her elbows, looking over at Wynter. "Again, what are you doing down here?"

Wynter looked back at Remington, just wanting everything to be back to right with them. Blowing out her breath, she threw caution to the wind and climbed onto the bed, lying down next to Remington like she would have before their fight.

"We had a fight, I left, I'm done with her," Wynter said simply, putting her face against Remington's shoulder.

Remington turned her head to look down at Wynter. "And you left the room…" she said.

"Yes, I left the room. I walked straight from the room to the elevator and from the elevator here, no one accosted me along the way, I promise," Wynter said, her tone glowering.

Remington looked back at her for a moment, then a slow grin spread across her lips.

"I meant," she said, her tone holding humor, "that you left a room that was heated, to come to a bus that we're likely to freeze to death in overnight… and you left your now ex-girlfriend in said heated room… Kalite fou."

"What does that mean?" Wynter asked, grinning.

"Kind of crazy," Remington said, smiling wryly.

"Wi," Wynter said simply.

They both were silent for a few minutes. Remington lay back on the bed, lifting her arm so Wynter could snuggle closer, and then pulling the covers up over both of them.

"What really happened with Billy?" Wynter asked after a few minutes.

"Let's just say I beat her at her own game," Remington said, smiling in the semi-darkness of the bus.

"How?" Wynter asked, leaning up on her elbow to look down at Remington.

"Not important," Remington said, smiling slightly.

Wynter knew she wasn't hearing the whole story, and the fact that she wasn't hearing it meant there was something about it that Remington felt she needed to be discreet about. There was a long moment during which Wynter debated arguing further, but she decided that it wasn't worth possibly destroying the fragile truce they seemed to have at that moment.

"Can I ask you a totally different question?" Wynter asked then.

"Sure," Remington said.

"Why have you kept your apartment in New York? I mean, that's a lot of money to spend on a place that you're not living in, right?"

Remington shrugged. "If I decide to stay in LA, I'll look into selling it, but not until then."

Wynter moved to sit up, looking down at Remington in alarm.

"What do you mean *if* you decide to stay in LA?" she asked.

Remington looked back at her for a long moment. "Wynter... I haven't decided where I'm going to live. LA was just my first stop."

"But..." Wynter began looking crestfallen.

"But what?" Remington asked gently.

"I just thought... I mean, I figured you were staying in LA..." Wynter said, her voice trailing off as she bit her lip.

Remington shrugged. "Like I said, I haven't decided yet."

Wynter took a deep breath, feeling a knot in her stomach as she nodded, and moved to lie back down next to Remington. Remington glanced down at her, surprised by Wynter's reaction.

They both lay lost in their own thoughts, finally falling asleep an hour later.

The question of what had happened with Billy was resolved the following evening just before the show. They were in Indianapolis,

Indiana. Wynter was in her dressing room when she heard a knock on her door. She opened it to find Billy standing there. After a brief moment where she considered shutting the door in Billy's face, Wynter finally sighed and stood back to allow Billy entry into the dressing room.

Billy walked in, looking around at Wynter's dressing room, then over at Wynter.

"So, what's up, Billy?" Wynter asked, already on her guard.

Billy looked at her for a long moment, then grinned, shaking her head. "So tense for someone so young…"

"What do you want?" Wynter asked impatiently.

"It isn't what I want," Billy said then, her look pointed. "It's what you want."

"What?" Wynter queried, scowling at the other woman.

"Remington," Billy said simply.

"What about her?" Wynter asked, her tone instantly sharp.

Billy started to smile. "She's pretty hot, huh?" she asked suggestively. "I mean, I know now, just how hot…" she said giving Wynter a pointed look, her grin leering.

Wynter stared openmouthed at Billy, knowing that this had everything to do with whatever had happened on the bus the night before.

"What the fuck did you do?" Wynter snapped.

Billy chuckled, her eyes sparkling mischievously. "Oh, it wasn't all me, honey…" she said. "Remi had everything to do with it, and she did it so damned good…"

Wynter's mouth opened in pure unadulterated fury, her hands clenched in fists and she was ready to pummel Billy Montague into the ground.

"Woah, woah, woah!" Billy said, holding up her hands, knowing she was about to be attacked by this girl. "Hold on…" she said, smiling. "I'm really seriously here to help you out."

"Get the fuck out of my dressing room, Billy," Wynter gritted out.

"Wynter," Billy said, her tone placating now, "what I'm telling you is this… If you want Remington LaRoché you're going to need to grab her with both hands and not let go, no matter what."

"And why would you tell me that?" Wynter asked.

"Because she laid a kiss on me last night that lit me up like the Fourth of July. I kept Sky up for three hours with the remnants of it… So if you're smart, and I think you are, you'll see that she's not going to take what's not offered, so you're just going to have to hand it to her."

Wynter stared back at Billy, warring with the desire to kill the other woman for getting that kind of kiss from Remington, and also the desire to hunt Remington down and kick her ass for giving in to Billy Montague's ways.

Billy could see the thoughts churning in Wynter, and took that opportunity to leave, figuring she'd done her good deed for the day, maybe even for the year.

Later that night after the show, Remington and Wynter were back in the room. Wynter had gone to take a shower as usual. Remington was sitting on the bed, working on her laptop. She heard the door to the bathroom open, but didn't see Wynter pass her. She glanced up and thought her heart would stop.

Wynter stood a foot from her on her right side wearing absolutely nothing.

"What are you doing?" Remington asked, her voice breaking slightly.

Wynter looked back at her, smiling softly. Without a word she walked over to take the laptop off Remington's lap, and set it aside. She moved to straddle Remington's waist, her eyes looking down into Remington's.

Remington's hands went out to the sides, as she glanced sharply up at Wynter.

"Wynter…" she began, her tone chiding. "Go put some clothes on."

"No," Wynter said simply, putting her hands on Remington's shirt, and starting to unbutton it.

Remington turned her head down and to the side, squeezing her eyes shut, her hands still up and out to the sides of Wynter.

"What are you doing?" Remington asked again, not looking at Wynter.

Wynter continued to unbutton Remington's shirt, until she was able to lay the sides open. She then slid her hands over Remington's skin, pressing closer to her.

"Bondye…" Remington breathed, her voice a husky whisper. Her body trembled under Wynter's hands.

Wynter moved her hands under Remington's shirt, to grasp her shoulders, as she looked down at Remington.

"Remi, look at me," Wynter commanded.

Remington's eyes were open, but averted from Wynter's body. She shook her head.

"Please look at me," Wynter asked then, her tone softening.

Remington grimaced, unable to deny Wynter's second request. She turned her eyes up to look directly into Wynter's. Her breathing was coming in short gasps as her body was reacting to Wynter's proximity.

Wynter looked down at Remington, her blue eyes searching. "Tell me you don't want me, Remi…" she said softly. "Tell me you don't want me and I'll leave you alone."

Remington drew in an unsteady breath, then shook her head ruefully. "I can't do that."

"Then kiss me like you did Billy last night," Wynter said, her voice soft but strong.

Remington slid her hands into Wynter's still damp hair and pulled her head down to take possession of her lips forcefully. She dumped all of her pent-up passion and need into the kiss, sliding her other hand up Wynter's bare back, and pulling her body closer. Within minutes, they were both crying out in their release but neither of them pulled away. Instead, Wynter removed Remington's shirt, sliding her hands over Remington's skin, their lips still meeting over and over again. Remington grasped at Wynter, her fingers biting into her skin, which only incited Wynter more.

Wynter reached between them to unbutton Remington's pants. Remington obliged her by taking them off, their lips never losing connection. As soon as Remington lay naked under her, Wynter pressed her body along the entire length of Remington's, reveling in the feel of her skin and the feel of her muscles shifting and flexing against her skin. She shifted her body against Remington, pressing harder against her in her need. Remington responded by groaning out loud and grasping at Wynter and dragging her closer, moving to Wynter's rhythm.

Wynter cried out as she came again, and Remington groaned loudly, pressing her mouth against Wynter's neck as she reached her release again. As she breathed heavily, she began kissing and softly biting Wynter's neck, as Wynter caressed her skin. Before long, they were both grasping at each other as they were overwhelmed again. They lay together for a few minutes, both trying to catch their breath, each of their hands caressing and moving over the other's skin.

"Mwen pa ka jwenn ase nan ou…" Remington breathed. "I can't get enough of you…"

Wynter smoothed her hand over Remington's skin, answering with her body that she was having the same problem. At one point, Wynter moved to Remington's side, wanting to pull Remington up over her. Remington obliged, shifting to put herself over Wynter, keeping most of her weight off her by bracing her arms to either side of Wynter's body. She pressed against Wynter, shifting her body against hers, sliding over her. Wynter's nails bit into Remington's shoulders as she grasped at her, pulling her down.

They spent the next four hours making love almost constantly, their hands and bodies intertwined, their lips meeting over and over. When they were finally sated, Wynter lay in Remington's arms. Remington lay on her side, her arms around Wynter, her right hand up at Wynter's face, her thumb stroking Wynter's cheek. Their eyes met and they both smiled, both of them still breathing somewhat heavily.

"When are you supposed to leave to head home?" Wynter asked.

Remington glanced at the clock. "In about an hour," she said, with a grin. Then her look grew serious. "I want you to come with me."

Wynter's eyes searched Remington. "You want me to come home with you?"

"Wi tanpri," Remington said, smiling. "Yes, please."

Wynter smiled. "How do you say, 'I'll go anywhere with you'?"

Remington chuckled softly. "Mwen pral ale nenpòt kote avèk ou," she said, her eyes sparkling.

"Yeah," Wynter said, grinning, "that."

"Oh, come on…" Remington said smiling, repeating the phrase for her bit by bit until she was able to say it. "Now, say it all," she said, her smile enchanted.

"Mwen pral ale nenpòt kote avèk ou," Wynter said in a perfect accent yet again.

Remington closed her eyes, listening to Wynter speak her language. This felt so good… so right. Opening her eyes, she saw that Wynter was looking at her.

"What were you just thinking?" Wynter asked softly, her eyes searching.

Remington hesitated, not sure what she wanted to say. "I was thinking that this feels good…"

Wynter looked back at Remington, her hand sliding up Remington's arm. "It does, doesn't it?" she asked. "It just feels… right."

Remington couldn't hide the surprise on her face, or the wonder that followed it. "You think it feels right too? I thought it was just me…"

"You didn't say it though," Wynter said.

"Because I chickened out," Remington said.

Wynter's eyes widened. "Did I just hear you right?"

Remington pursed her lips in humored mortification. "Yeah, you heard me right," she said.

Wynter licked her lips. "Would you have ever made a move?" she asked. "On me, I mean."

Remington thought about the question for a long moment. "I'm not sure," she said, shaking her head, "you intimidate the hell out of me."

"I intimidate you?" Wynter asked, stunned by that admission. "Why?"

"Because of how strongly I react to you," Remington said. "You make me feel so… crazy sometimes."

"Crazy?" Wynter asked, a slight grin on her lips. "Crazy how?"

Remington narrowed her eyes at Wynter. "You know damned good and well how," she said, her tone low with accusation.

Wynter laughed out loud. It was a bright, warm sound. Then she nodded. "I admit I was desperately trying to seduce you a few times."

Remington bit her lower lip and curled her nose up at Wynter in a kind of snarl. "You were modi sa ki mal," Remington told her, putting a finger to Wynter's lips. "Damned evil."

Wynter smiled with her tongue sticking out playfully.

Remington leaned in, kissing her, sucking on her tongue sensually. That got Wynter going all over again. It was another hour before they even managed to get out of bed. And still another before they were able to get ready to leave. Even then, they had a hard time taking a shower together. At one point, Remington walked into the bathroom to check on when Wynter would be ready. Wynter was applying eyeliner in the mirror. Remington stood staring at Wynter's reflection. Wynter was wearing boot cut jeans, high-heeled boots, and a bra, but no shirt at that point. The picture she presented was far too enticing.

Remington moved to stand behind her, watching Wynter in the mirror over her head, her hands sliding over Wynter's slim hips, bending her head to kiss Wynter's neck. She felt the vibration of Wynter's low moan under her lips and that only incited her more. A moment later Wynter was dropping the eyeliner pencil and turning in Remington's arms, pulling Remington's head down to hers to kiss her deeply. It was another half hour before Wynter was able to complete her makeup. Fortunately, they managed to get out of the hotel room before there were further incidents. But they were both grinning like teenagers as they walked out of the hotel lobby.

Remington had picked up an envelope at the front desk, as they walked out of the hotel. She opened the envelope, taking out paperwork and a set of keys. She shoved the paperwork in her laptop bag that was slung over her shoulder and glanced around the lot, then headed toward a black Mercedes. She opened the trunk, setting her laptop case inside, then walked over to the passenger door and opened it for Wynter. The bellboy brought out their other bags, and Remington handed him a folded bill, thanking him for his help.

Wynter looked over to Remington as she got in on the driver's side.

"Do you ever do anything halfway?" she asked.

Remington grinned. "I try not to," she answered.

Wynter looked around the car. The seats were leather and smelled very new.

"You didn't buy this did you?" Wynter asked.

Remington chuckled, shaking her head. "No, just a rental this time," she said, smiling.

Wynter nodded, grinning.

It was snowing as they pulled out of the parking lot. Fortunately, the car already had the cables installed on the tires.

"So how long is it to get home?" Wynter asked.

"About three hours, normally," Remington said. "Not sure with the snow though."

Wynter nodded, looking over at Remington. She looked extremely good that day as far as Wynter was concerned. She wore very faded jeans that fit her quite snugly, outlining her leanly muscled legs, leather boots with a slight heel, and a gray and black thermal Affliction shirt with a gothic cross on it. Over it she wore her recently reclaimed Affliction jacket. Wynter now wore her Marine's bomber jacket.

Wynter wearing her jacket hadn't gone unnoticed.

"Am I ever going to fully possess any of my jackets again?" she asked, not sounding too put out by the idea.

"Not as long as they smell like you, you won't." Wynter said.

Remington glanced over at her again, as she entered the freeway. "Is that why you've held on to my Affliction one all this time?"

"Yep," Wynter said unabashedly.

Remington smiled. "For some reason, I really like that…"

Wynter smiled too, enjoying this new closeness with Remington. It really did feel good.

As they drove they talked about whatever came to mind. At one point, the conversation turned to family.

"Okay, remind me again, it's your mom and dad… what are their names?"

"Delphine and Andre," Remington said.

"Okay, and your sisters? Two, right?"

"Right," Remington said, nodding. "Lisette and Justine. Lisette is the baby, she's only seventeen. Justine is thirty and married."

"Okay," Wynter said, nodding, feeling nervous. "And do they only speak Haitian Creole?"

"They primarily speak Creole," Remington said, "but they also speak English just fine and believe me, they won't insult you by speaking Creole in front of you unless they slip like I do all the time."

"Okay, but how do I say, 'it's nice to meet you' in Creole, or will that be insulting if I try to speak your language?"

Remington smiled warmly. "Not the way you speak it, it won't be," she said. "The easiest thing to say is 'anchante.' "

"Anchante," Wynter repeated.

Remington nodding, smiling. "I have to tell you that I love the way your voice sounds when you speak my language."

Wynter smiled brightly. "Then I should tell you I love the way your voice sounds when you speak your language."

"You do, huh?" Remington asked.

"Oh yes…" Wynter said, reaching over to touch Remington's arm, her look sincere. "The way you sound when you speak Creole…" she said, her voice trailing off as she shivered. "It goes right through me.

Remington moved her arm to take Wynter's hand in hers. She lifted Wynter's hand to her lips and kissed the back of Wynter's hand, interlacing her fingers with Wynter's.

"So, tell me about your family," Remington said then.

"Not much to tell, it's just my mom," she said shrugging.

"Do you see her?" Remington asked, looking over at her.

"Yeah," Wynter said. "I mean, I do, but not a lot."

"Where does she live?" Remington asked.

"In Westwood," Wynter said.

Remington looked over at her, her look perplexed. "Isn't that in LA?"

"Yeah," Wynter said, grinning.

"And pretty close to Brentwood where you live…" Remington said. "Do you not get along with her?"

"I do, yes," Wynter said.

Remington sensed the undercurrent to that answer. "Lauren didn't get along with her?"

"My mom has never liked Lauren. Not even when we were eighteen."

"Oh," Remington said, making a face.

Wynter caught the look and started laughing, shaking her head. "I saw that."

"I didn't hide it," Remington said mildly, her grin wry.

She looked over at Wynter a few moments later. "I'd like to meet her when we get back to California."

Wynter was surprised by her statement, but realized she shouldn't be. She'd already found that, to Remington, family was the most important thing.

"Okay," Wynter said, smiling. "I think my mom would love to meet you."

"It will be my pleasure," Remington said.

"I love how you say things like that," Wynter said.

Remington looked over at her, smiling. "You don't think it's too old-fashioned?" she asked, winking at Wynter.

Wynter laughed softly, shaking her head. "Speaking of which…" she said, looking tentative suddenly. "Your parents are old-fashioned, aren't they?"

Remington looked thoughtful for a moment. "My father is, for sure, my mother isn't as much."

"So I need to be careful with my language," Wynter said, looking worried.

Remington glanced over at her, seeing the nervousness Wynter was starting to feel.

"Siromyèl…" Remington said softly.

Wynter smiled and her eyes twinkled.

Remington canted her head, then closed her eyes momentarily. "Sorry, see? I do it all the time. I think it's proximity to home. It means 'honey,' " she said.

"So it's likely I'll understand you less and less over the next week?" Wynter asked, grinning.

Remington laughed. "Either that, or you'll learn a lot of Creole," she said winking. "Anyway, what I started to say is that you need to be yourself. That's who I'm with, okay?"

Wynter pressed her lips, reveling in the feel of having Remington referring to her that way.

"Thank you," Wynter said, smiling over at Remington. "How long has it been since you've been home?"

"About six months," Remington said. "It's been awhile."

"That's a while to you?" Wynter asked looking surprised.

"I usually come home every three months or so," Remington said. "The only other time I've been gone more time than that was when I was in Iraq."

"Were the four years all in a row?" Wynter asked.

"I had breaks in between tours, but they were about twelve to sixteen months each, depending on the assignment."

"And what did you do over there?"

"Infantry," Remington said.

"So, like…" Wynter said, her tone leading.

Remington chuckled. "I guess you don't know much about the military, huh?"

"Nope," Wynter said, shaking her head.

"Basically, I carried an M16 and shot where I was told to," Remington said, grinning.

"Oh," Wynter said, widening her eyes, "but I'd bet you were damned good at it."

Remington inclined her head. "I did pretty good."

"Uh-huh," Wynter said, not looking convinced by the underplay. "So how did you end up getting into MMA fighting?"

"I found out in the marines that I liked fighting," Remington said, grinning.

"How did you discover that?" Wynter asked.

"Well, marines are kind of a competitive bunch, and the men do not like us little girlies comin' in and showing them up… so they talk a lot of crap… I got tired of it and knocked a couple of them down, and figured out that I liked the way it felt."

Wynter's eyes widened. "Now that I would never have guessed," she said shaking her head. "In fact, when I've seen your fights, you always get worried when you actually knock girls out."

"'Cause that's girls," Remington said, her look amused.

"Okay, so knocking guys down or out is okay, but hitting another girl is not as fun?"

"Well, technically they sign up to be hit when they step in the ring, but…"

"But you don't like thinking you hurt someone," Wynter said.

"Well, permanent damage yeah," Remington said.

"I saw a fight where you kneeled at the edge of the ring and waited until they told you that the girl you'd just knocked out cold was okay. In fact, you reached over to shake her hand when she came to…" Wynter said, her look admiring.

Remington's lips twitched as she inclined her head.

Wynter smiled, shaking her head. "Remington LaRoché we have got to do something about your lack of ability to brag about yourself."

Remington shook her head. "I told you, I don't talk about stuff, I just do it."

"Like catching a singer before she hits the ground?" Wynter asked.

"Like that, yeah," Remington said, smiling.

They were both quiet for a while again. At one point, Remington looked over at Wynter and saw that she'd fallen asleep. She smiled fondly. She had no idea what was going to happen with this woman, but she knew that she wanted to find out.

Chapter 7

Wynter woke up, opening her eyes, and seeing Remington's profile as she drove. She looked her over, admiring the way she looked, her long legs outlined by the faded denim, her strong jawline, her long braids. She was sitting with her legs wide apart, her long and tapered fingers tapping the steering wheel as she drove. And then there were those lips… Wynter couldn't stop thinking about those lips and how they'd kissed her and made her breathless and so excited she could barely stand it. Looking at them now, she realized how sexy they were. They were smooth, but they had a strength to them and kind of sexy half pout to their shape.

As if she knew she was being watched, Remington glanced over at Wynter.

"I fell asleep," Wynter said, grimacing. "I'm a terrible traveling companion."

Remington quirked a grin. "Yes, you are."

"It's not my fault, you wore me out," Wynter said primly.

"I wore you out…" Remington said wryly.

"Uh-huh," Wynter said, grinning. Then she looked around and saw nothing but countryside. "Holy cow, where are we?"

"Near home," Remington said.

"How near?" Wynter asked her look worried.

"'Bout ten minutes."

Wynter immediately opened the visor using the lighted mirror to check her makeup, then she reached for her bag behind her.

Remington glanced over at her. "What are you doing?" she asked, grinning.

"Checking my makeup," Wynter said. "I don't want to meet your parents looking all frazzled."

"You look beautiful, babe, you don't need to worry."

"Uh-huh," Wynter said, sounding unconvinced. She started looking around again. "They really live out in the middle of nowhere," she commented.

"You usually don't raise horses in the city, Wyn," Remington commented.

"Oh, yeah, true," Wynter said, nodding.

They drove for a few more minutes.

"Look over there," Remington said, pointing to the right.

Wynter turned her head, seeing a huge beautiful white house with dark green shutters set back far from the road. The land it sat on was surrounded by a white rail fence. It was what Wynter thought of when she thought of the South.

"Wow, that's beautiful…" she said, shaking her head. "What is that?"

"Home," Remington said simply.

Wynter's head snapped around so fast it was a wonder it didn't come off.

"You just said what?" she asked stunned.

Remington pressed her lips together in amusement at Wynter's astonishment. "That's home."

"You need to stop this car right now…" Wynter said looking dead serious.

Remington obliged her by pulling over to the side of the road. Wynter climbed out of the car and started pacing on the side of the road, her boots crunching in the snow. Remington retrieved the bomber jacket and handed it to Wynter who took it with a narrowed look She put it on as she continued to pace. Remington leaned against the trunk of the car, her legs crossed at the ankles as she watched Wynter with an amused look on her face. Eventually she pulled out a cigarette and lit it, taking her time smoking as Wynter started muttering to herself. Remington imagined that if any of her parent's neighbors happened by, they'd wonder why Remington LaRoché was out with a crazy person.

Wynter stopped pacing and stood looking at Remington.

"Why didn't you tell me?" she asked.

"Tell you what?" Remington asked, her look mild.

"That you lived…" Wynter stammered, then gestured at the house. "There!"

"Would you have known where *there* was?" Remington asked, grinning wryly.

"Don't be a smart ass, Remington!" Wynter exclaimed. "You know that I had no idea…"

"Once again, I can't know what you assumed…" Remington said patiently.

"And god knows you don't brag…" Wynter said, rolling her eyes. "But a little, gee Wynter, I just so happened to grow up in a frigging mansion, would have been a handy little heads up!"

Remington put her hand up to her mouth, trying to hide the grin that started.

Wynter narrowed her eyes. "Don't you dare start grinning…" she said, her tone low and threatening. "Remington, I mean it…" she said, a grin starting on her lips too.

Remington reached out, sliding a hand around her waist, and dragged her over to her and up against her side. She leaned down to kiss her lips. Wynter immediately wrapped her arms around Remington's neck, kissing her back.

"Now, can we go, before we freeze to death?" Remington asked, grinning.

Wynter sighed, nodding her head.

The minute they were back in the car though, Wynter was nervous again.

"I can't do this, Remi…" she said. "I can't…"

"Yes, you can," Remington said.

"I'm just a kid from Reseda…"

"Honey, my parents have no idea where Reseda is or even what Reseda is."

"Okay, but," Wynter said then.

"Babe, stop…" Remington said. "You are beautiful, smart, and talented. You're a damned rock star… that's who you are."

Wynter bit her lip, smiling at Remington as they drove up the long drive to Remington's family home. A home that sat on an immense piece of land, and looked like something out of "Gone with the Wind."

"What kind of horses did you say your family raises?" Wynter asked absently as Remington stopped the car in front of the huge house.

"Thoroughbreds," Remington said, grinning as she got out.

"I'm gonna kill her…" Wynter muttered under her breath as she saw the front door open and people, who had to be Remington's parents, come running out.

Remington had just opened Wynter's door and had her hand out to help her out of the car when her mother threw herself into her other arm.

"Alo manman," Remington said while hugging her mom with one arm. "Mwen te rate ou. I have missed you."

Remington helped Wynter out of the car then, smiling at her.

A man, who Wynter guessed easily was Remington's father, stepped forward and extended his hand to Remington. She took it, inclining her head respectfully. "Papa…" she said, smiling.

Then she turned to Wynter. "Manman, Papa, this is Wynter Kincade. Wynter this is my mother Delphine LaRoché and my father Andre LaRoché."

"Enchante," Wynter said smiling, her accent absolute perfection.

Delphine and Andre both looked surprised, and glanced at their daughter who grinned proudly.

"Wynter's been learning a few things," Remington said, her eyes sparkling proudly.

"I told you her accent was good, Delphy," Andre said, smiling as he stepped over to Wynter, reaching for her hand.

Wynter gave him her hand, and he surprised her by bowing his head and kissing the top of her hand. It was a very old-world gesture and Wynter could immediately see Remington in him. She smiled brightly, glancing at Remington and seeing her grinning.

There was a loud exclamation from the front door, and suddenly a young woman came running right at Remington. Remington had the good sense to brace herself, right as the girl jumped on her, both arms and legs wrapped around her. Remington smiled broadly, hugging the girl tightly. It was obvious to Wynter that this was Lissette, her little sister. Lissette clearly adored her big sister, she was so excited to see her.

"Whoa!" Remington said as Lissette barreled into her, smiling all the while, and hugging her baby sister close. "How are you baby girl?"

"So happy you're home!" Lissette said, her petite frame still wrapped around Remington's. It was obvious she did this frequently, there didn't seem to be a concern whether or not Remington could hold her.

"Why has it been so long since you've been home?" Lissette asked then, leaning back to look up at her sister pouting.

"I've been busy, Lis," Remington said, nodding toward Wynter.

Lissette's head snapped around, ready to be angry with the person who had kept her sister from coming home, and then she saw who it was. Her eyes practically bugged out of her head as she stared at Wynter.

"You're Wynter Kincade…" Lissette said, dropping to her feet, her eyes still on Wynter.

Wynter nodded, smiling at the younger girl.

"O Bondye…" Lissette breathed.

"Steady now…" Remington said from behind her sister, feeling her sister waiver slightly. She reached out putting her arm around her sister's waist. "So, Wynter, this is obviously my baby sister, Lissette."

Wynter stepped toward Lissette and extended her hand to the girl. "It's nice to meet you," she said, smiling again.

Lissette put her small hand in Wynter's, staring at Wynter with wide eyes that were very much like Remington's.

"I…" Lissette stammered. "I'm a huge fan," she said in awe. "Your music is so great… and you are just so… you are even prettier in person than you are on TV…"

"Mèsi," Wynter said, inclining her head, like she'd seen Remington do so many times. "You have yourself a fairly incredible sister."

Lissette smiled broadly, glancing back at Remington with pride. "Mem's awesome."

"Mem?" Wynter queried, glancing at Remington.

"Lis could never say my name when she was little, she always called me 'Memi,' " Remington explained, shrugging. "It just kind of stuck."

Wynter nodded, smiling. "I like it."

"Well, come inside!" Delphine said, gesturing to the house. "Remington and Andre will get the bags."

Lissette moved to walk next to Wynter, and Delphine led the way into the house. The entry to the home was through double mahogany doors with etched glass semi-circular panels. Inside, Wynter was completely awed by the marble floors and sweeping split mahogany staircase with intricately carved spindles, rail, and posts. The entry was two stories and a huge crystal chandelier hung over their heads.

"This is so beautiful…" Wynter breathed, looking around with wide eyes.

"Mèsi," Delphine said, smiling, "we are very happy here. Come into the sitting room, it is much warmer there."

The sitting room was another incredible room with a huge marble and mahogany fireplace that dominated one wall. There was antique mahogany furniture that looked very sturdy, but still beautiful with warm brown upholstery that wasn't overly fussy. It was apparent that Remington had gotten her taste from her family home.

Wynter shrugged out of Remington's jacket, folding it over her arm.

"This is Remi's, isn't it?" Lissette asked.

"Yes," Wynter said, smiling. "I've been stealing her jackets on the tour. She just got her Affliction jacket back today," she said, winking at Remington as she walked into the room.

"I'm just gonna buy you your own," Remington said, grinning.

"Uh-uh," Wynter said, shaking her head, smiling, "'cause then it won't smell like you."

Lissette glanced sharply at Wynter and then at Remington.

"Are you two…" Lissette began looking shocked.

"Lissette Marie LaRoché!" Delphine exclaimed. "That is your sister's business and not your place to ask," she said, her tone chastising.

Lissette looked immediately contrite, lowering her eyes and folding her hands in front of her. "I'm sorry, Remi," she said quietly. "I apologize Ms. Kincade."

Wynter looked over at Remington, surprised by the formality. She noted that Remington also looked displeased with Lissette's presumption to ask what she had. It was obvious that the LaRochés took propriety seriously. She asked Remington about it later as they walked up a second flight of stairs to Remington's old bedroom located at the top of the house. The room itself was huge and because it was at the top of the house, it had slanted ceilings and a huge window set into the ceiling just above the bed, as well as windows that looked out over the vast property. It was painted a warm beige, with accents of navy blue and darker brown. The room also had its own master-sized bathroom complete with a steam shower and soaking tub.

"Wow…" Wynter said, looking around the room. "This is bigger than the apartment I grew up in."

Remington grinned, setting the bags down. "I was the oldest, so I got to pick out my own room. I liked being up here."

"I can see why," Wynter said, smiling as she moved to look at the windows. "Is that the barn over there?" she asked pointing to the large building set farther down the property.

"Those are the stables, yes," Remington said, leaning her arm above Wynter's head looking out the window as well. "We'll go see them later if you'd like but I personally need to lay down for a bit."

Wynter turned to look up at her, her eyes searching Remington's. "Why was Lissette asking about us improper?"

"Because it was a very personal question asked in front of a visitor," Remington said.

"But she was asking about you…" Wynter asked.

"And you," Remington said.

"And that was what was wrong?" Wynter asked, trying to understand.

"Yes," Remington said, nodding, "if it had just been a question about me, it would have been alright, but since the question related to you as well, it was too personal a question to ask."

Wynter nodded. "Okay, I understand now. I guess I have a lot to learn about how your family is…"

Remington looked at her for a long moment. "I know it's strange to you."

Wynter reached up, touching Remington's cheek. "It's not strange, Remi, it's just different. I just don't want to embarrass you."

"How could I ever be embarrassed by you?" Remington asked, her look searching Wynter's face.

"Oh, I'm talented, I can figure out a way," Wynter said, grinning.

Remington shook her head, grinning. She leaned down and kissed Wynter's lips. Wynter slid her hands up Remington's chest and pressed closer. The fire between them caught immediately and before long, Remington picked Wynter up and carried her to the bed, their lips never parting.

Laying Wynter down, she reached up and shrugged off her jacket and kicked off her boots, then moved to lie next to Wynter on the bed. Wynter pulled at her as they began to kiss again.

"I want you over me," she told Remington huskily.

Remington obliged and began kissing then moved lower as she unbuttoned Wynter's shirt. Wynter's hands grasped at Remington's head, and she moaned as Remington's lips moved over her skin and found an already hard nipple.

"God... god..." Wynter muttered as her body trembled under Remington's hands and lips.

Remington unbuttoned Wynter's jeans, slid them down, and tossed them aside. Wynter grasped at Remington's shoulders, trying to pull her up over her. Remington resisted, kissing up Wynter's legs, eventually reaching the spot where Wynter lost all control. She grabbed a pillow to press over her face as she screamed over and over again in ecstasy. Then Remington was removing her own clothes and moving to lay over her, moving against her, making her come again quickly.

Wynter pressed Remington back, looking down at her, her blue eyes heated as she leaned down to kiss Remington again and again, pressing her body to Remington's. Remington's hands slid over Wynter's skin, pulling, grasping, and caressing roughly, which only excited Wynter more. Wynter slid her hand between them, touching Remington and groaning at the heat and wetness she found there. Remington groaned loudly, her mouth capturing Wynter's as she pressed her body harder against Wynter's hand.

They came together, kissing all the while, which fortunately muted their loud moans and groans. Afterward, Wynter lay over Remington, both of them breathing heavily. Remington closed her eyes, shaking her head.

"Bondye, sa w ap fè m '..." she breathed.

"God, what?" Wynter asked, only recognizing the one word.

"What you do to me..." Remington told her huskily.

Wynter leaned up, looking down at Remington. "What do I do to you?" she asked in a sultry voice.

"You drive me absolutely crazy," Remington said, though not looking displeased about it.

Wynter bit her lip sexily. "That's because you make me so damned hot."

"I do?" Remington asked, her look wondrous.

"Oh my god, you don't know that?" Wynter said, sounding shocked. "Yes, Remi, you excite the hell out of me. If I'd have known how much sexual chemistry we'd have, I would have jumped you a lot sooner than I did."

"But you were tempting me long before that," Remington said, her look pointed.

Wynter grinned unrepentantly. "Yes, yes I was, but you just wouldn't take the bait. I couldn't get you to react."

"I reacted, believe me," Remington said. "I just didn't let you see it."

Wynter narrowed her eyes. "Pretty good at that... too good."

Remington shook her head. "I react far too strongly to you."

"Why do you say that?"

"Because I don't want to hurt you," Remington said looking worried.

"You mean emotionally?" Wynter asked, looking surprised by that possibility.

"No," Remington said, shaking her head, "physically. I'm sure I've already bruised your skin a few times…" she said, grimacing.

"But I love that you react to me that way," Wynter said.

Remington shook her head. "It's dangerous, and it scares me."

Wynter blinked a couple of times. "Remi, you won't ever hurt me that badly, I know you won't."

"How do you know?" Remington asked.

"Because you're the most controlled person I've ever met," Wynter said.

"Not when it comes to you," Remington said, shaking her head.

Wynter bit her lip, her eyes glowing happily. "I know it's wrong of me to say it, but I absolutely love that."

"And you're going to continue to use that, aren't you?" Remington asked though she already knew the answer.

"Yup," Wynter said, nodding. "Just like I did last night."

"And exactly what prompted you to do that in the first place?" Remington asked.

"Billy," Wynter said simply.

Remington looked shocked. "Billy?"

Wynter nodded, then pinned Remington with a look. "What really happened on the bus the other night?" she asked, her eyes reflecting worry. "Did you sleep with Billy?"

"No," Remington said immediately, looking directly into Wynter's eyes. "I would never do that. She's married."

"She never seemed to care about that when she flirted with you," Wynter pointed out.

"I cannot control what others do, only what I do," Remington said. "And I would not do that."

Wynter nodded, loving that Remington was so ethical even when it came to sex.

"So what happened?" Wynter said. "Billy said you kissed her."

Remington looked mildly surprised. "Did she say she kissed me first?"

"Of course not," Wynter said rolling her eyes.

"She was telling me how stupid I was for not 'going for it' with you," Remington said wryly.

"And to prove her point she kissed you?" Wynter asked, glowering at the idea. "The woman is unreal!"

"Well, she said she was going to show me what I was missing by not sleeping with a rock star."

"Uh-huh…" Wynter said, still not looking pleased. "So how did that go?"

Remington pressed her lips together, widening her eyes and waggling her eyebrows. "It was definitely enticing, I won't say that it wasn't."

"'Cause you've had fantasies about her for years…" Wynter supplied, her tone still sounding displeased by the very idea.

"Yes," Remington said, her tone placating. "I can't help that now, can I?"

"No," Wynter said, sighing. "So why did you kiss her?"

"To prove a point," Remington said, her hazel eyes sparkling.

"What point?" Wynter asked.

"That she should be careful who she messes with, because sometimes messing with the wrong person can buy you more trouble than you can handle."

"So you kissed her," Wynter said, "like you did me last night?"

Remington inclined her head, her eyes widening slightly.

"She said you lit her up like the Fourth of July."

"And then I told her to go back upstairs to her husband so he could finish the job," Remington said mildly.

Wynter laughed, nodding her head. "She said she kept Sky up for three hours because of that kiss."

Wynter looked her look astounded. She started to smile.

"You are the hottest thing on the planet, Remington LaRoché, and I absolutely love that."

Remington looked back at Wynter, her lips curled in a cynical smile, her eyes reflecting doubt about her 'hot' status. Instead of responding, however, she pulled Wynter down to kiss her lips, just as she had kissed Billy that night on the bus. Her lips moved expertly over Wynter's lips, sucking at them. Her thumb moved to Wynter's mouth parting her lips, her tongue sliding between them making Wynter groan with the sheer sensuality of it. Within minutes, Wynter was coming and grasping at Remington, her body shuddering uncontrollably.

"Jesus!" Wynter exclaimed, leaning down to kiss Remington's neck. "No one has ever excited me like you do, Remi, no one."

"Good," Remington said, her tone low.

Wynter moved to look down at her, looking shocked. "What was that?" she asked, her smile reflecting her surprise.

Remington merely smiled back at her.

"'Cause that sounded just a little bit possessive Remington LaRoché," Wynter said.

Remington nodded. "That's because it was."

Wynter took a deep breath, reveling in the excited feeling that ran through her. "Do you want to possess me, Remington?" she asked, her eyes sparkling.

"Yes, I do," Remington said with a direct look.

"Good," Wynter said, smiling.

Dinner that evening was interesting to Wynter because Delphine and Andre regaled her with tales from Remington's childhood, much to Remington's chagrin.

"Was she strong as a child?" Wynter asked at one point.

"Oh yes," Delphine said, nodding, "she always lifted things that even some of the boys could not. She was always challenging them to races and contests of strength."

Wynter looked over at Remington, who was leaning back in her chair drinking coffee and doing her best to keep out of the conversation.

"Kind of like the guys in the marines, huh Remi?" Wynter asked.

Remington nodded, smiling. "Practice," she said.

"I always hoped that Remington would take over the farm someday…" Andre said wistfully.

Remington lips twitched, knowing that it was her father's greatest disappointment, and that always bothered her. Wynter caught the movement and guessed that was the problem.

"Li se pa m ', Papa, Mwen swete li te," Remington said, her tone sad.

"Ah wi mwen konnen," Andre said, waving his hand dismissively as he shrugged. "Goumen se ou," he added, making Remington grimace and look away.

Lissette, who'd chosen to sit next to Wynter, leaned over, turning her head to talk in Wynter's ear without being seen.

"This is an argument they have all the time. Our father doesn't understand why she won't take over the farm when he retires, and Mem doesn't understand why he doesn't get that she's not a breeder."

"It hurts her that he's disappointed," Wynter whispered to Lissette.

"I know," Lissette said. "I don't know why Papa refuses to see that too."

Lissette turned back to the table and saw that Remington was watching her with slightly narrowed eyes. She looked back at her big sister and shrugged.

After dinner Remington walked over to where Lissette and Wynter sat talking. She leaned down, her elbows on the back of Wynter's chair, her look narrowed once again.

"What was that about?" Remington asked Lissette.

Lissette looked back at Remington. "You and papa were being rude speaking Creole in front of Wynter."

Remington tilted her head, her eyes narrowing more. "Because it's family business."

"It is rude to speak Creole in front of people who do not understand," Lissette insisted.

Remington lips tightened, but then she blew her breath out, shaking her head.

"I apologize," she said to Wynter, "it's just a sore spot with my father and me."

Wynter nodded. "I understand," she said, reaching up to put her hand over Remington's.

Later, they were back in bed after having made love again. Wynter was laying on her back, with Remington on her side next to her, her head above hers on the pillow.

"So, what do you want to do while we're here?" Remington asked Wynter.

Wynter's fingers were intertwined in Remington's, and she was examining how incredibly sexy her fingers were. She glanced up, surprised by the question.

"I'm here with you," she said. "I'll do whatever you want."

Remington grinned. "Okay, do you ride?"

Wynter looked mystified for a moment, then said, "You mean horses?"

Remington pressed her lips together, Wynter assumed in an effort not to reply with something smart assed. "Yes, I mean horses. You are on a horse farm, babe."

Wynter made a face at her. "I know that, thank you," she said, "and no, I've never ridden a horse in my life. They don't have horses in Reseda."

"I see," Remington said, "have you ever been around horses?"

"Does being in a parade where there were horses present count?" Wynter asked.

Remington shook her head, grinning. "No, that does not count," she said. "Are you afraid of horses?"

"I don't think so," Wynter said.

"Well, we'll just take it slow till we know for sure," Remington said.

"So I guess you ride, huh?" Wynter said.

"Since I was three," Remington said, grinning.

"Three?" Wynter asked, looking stunned.

Remington nodded.

"Wow," Wynter said, shaking her head. "Do you have your own horse?"

"Yes, I do," Remington said.

"Is it a thoroughbred?" Wynter asked.

"No, he's a Friesian," Remington said. Then she chuckled seeing Wynter's perplexed look. "It's another breed of horse. They come from the Netherlands originally. I like them because they're spectacular-looking creatures."

"Okay," Wynter said, nodding.

Remington pointed to picture of a black horse on the wall opposite the bed. In the picture the horse was rearing on its hindquarters with a dark forbidding looking storm cloud behind it. The horse's black coat was incredibly shiny, and its mane and tail looked extremely long. It also had long hair at its feet.

"That's a Friesian?" Wynter asked.

"That's my Friesian," Remington said proudly.

"That's a seriously beautiful horse," Wynter said, nodding.

"Mèsi," Remington said, smiling.

"What's his name?" Wynter asked.

"Satan," Remington said.

"Seriously?" Wynter asked.

Remington chuckled, nodding. "He threw me a few times; it's what I started calling him after about the third time when I broke my arm."

"He threw you?" Wynter asked, her look shocked.

"That's just part of horses, babe, you learn to get back up pretty quick."

"I guess… but you broke your arm?" she asked.

"In two places," Remington said, not seeming bothered by it.

"Ouch," Wynter said, grimacing. "And you want me to ride a horse?"

Remington laughed. "I would never put you on a horse that would throw you," Remington said, "but if you are too nervous about it, you can just ride with me."

"Hmmm…" Wynter murmured grinning.

"What?" Remington asked, seeing the look Wynter was giving her.

"I'm thinking you on a horse… and me in front of you…" Her voice trailed off suggestively.

Remington looked immediately affected by the mental picture Wynter had just painted.

"You're trying to kill me, right?" Remington said, her tone husky.

"No ma'am…" Wynter said, shaking her head. "Just answering your question."

"Ou se sa ki mal," Remington said, narrowing her eyes.

"I understood that," Wynter said, batting her eyes up at Remington.

"Bon," Remington said.

"Which is…" Wynter said.

"It means good." Remington told her.

"Bon," Wynter said.

"Trey bien," Remington said, smiling.

"Mèsi," Wynter countered.

Remington just shook her head, smiling.

"Oh, there is one thing I want to do while we're here," Wynter said.

"What's that?" Remington asked.

"I want to see you get your braids redone," Wynter said.

"Why?" Remington said.

"You said that the lady that does it here is the one you prefer," Wynter said.

"She is," Remington said, nodding. "But why do you want to see it?"

"Because I want to see you with your hair out of the braids," Wynter said.

Remington looked back at her for a long moment. "And what will that accomplish?"

"Probably give me all new fantasies for months," Wynter said, winking at her.

Remington rolled her eyes, shaking her head. "If you say so."

"I do," Wynter said.

The next morning, Remington woke before Wynter. She climbed out of bed, pulling on her jeans and taking a black cable knit sweater out of a drawer. She laced up her books and grabbed her Affliction jacket, checking to ensure her cigarettes and lighter were in the pocket. She walked over to kiss Wynter on the cheek then left the room quietly.

Lissette found her out on the back porch smoking and drinking coffee.

"Bonjou," Lissette said, putting her arms around Remington's shoulders and leaning down to kiss her sister's cheek, hugging her from behind.

"Bonjou," Remington responded, smiling up at Lissette.

"Where's Wynter?" Lissette asked, perching in the chair next to where Remington sat.

"Still asleep," Remington said, glancing over at her sister. "Why?"

Lissette shrugged. "You two are a couple, aren't you?"

Remington thought for a moment before answering. "Yes, but just recently, like two days ago."

"But you liked her long before that," Lissette said.

"Why do you say that?" Remington asked.

"Come on, Mem. I saw those videos like the rest of the world did, but I know you," Lissette said smiling warmly. "When you were talking to her in Creole I could hear it in your voice. Mom and Dad heard it too."

Remington licked her lips, her look contemplative. Finally, she sighed, nodding. "Yeah, I've liked her for a while."

"I knew it!" Lissette said, smiling. "She's really beautiful, and so talented!"

"Oke fasil kounye a," Remington said, her eyes widening at her little sister, telling her 'easy now.'

"Mom and Dad like her," Lissette said then. "I heard them talking."

"Eavesdropping?" Remington said, her tone chiding, even as her eyes narrowed.

"Oh, come on, like you never did!" Lissette said, shaking her head. "That time you were caught with Genevieve and you were trying to figure out how mad they were?"

"You aren't supposed to remember that," Remington said, grinning.

"Well, I do, so…" Lissette said, sticking her tongue out at her sister. "Anyway, they think it's a good match, you and Wynter."

"Well, let's hope they're not planning a wedding or anything," Remington said, rolling her eyes.

"Why?" Lissette asked, looking crestfallen. "You wouldn't marry her?"

Remington looked at her sister. "You just want to be able to say that Wynter Kincade is your sister," she said wryly.

"Well, yeah!" Lissette said, laughing. "But I want to see you happy too and she seems to make you happy…" she said, her voice trailing off as she rolled her eyes heavenward, her look telling Remington that she knew something.

"What is that look about?" Remington asked.

"Let's just say that the air vent in your room feeds directly into mine, and… well you two are not exactly quiet," Lissette said, looking far too gleeful for Remington's comfort.

"O Bondye… tiye Mwen," Remington said, squeezing her eyes shut and shaking her head ruefully.

"What does that mean?" Wynter asked from the door to the patio.

Remington got to her feet immediately, extending her hand to Wynter. Wynter stepped down onto the patio taking Remington's hand, smiling. Remington pulled her close and kissed her softly, then pulled back to look down at her.

"Good morning," Remington said softly.

"Bonjou," Wynter said, her voice equally soft. "Now, what did you just say?"

"I said 'kill me,' " Remington told her, pulling a chair over to where she was sitting.

Wynter sat down, giving Remington a shocked look. "And why did you say that?"

Remington sat in her chair again, glancing at Lissette who was doing her best to suppress her laughter. Remington narrowed her eyes at her sister.

"Because Lissette just informed me that she's got far too good hearing and that I need to have our parents change her room," Remington said, smiling tightly at her sister.

"Not fair!" Lissette said laughing. "I told her that I can hear you two, um… you know," she told Wynter, once again rolling her eyes heavenward.

Wynter looked at Remington with her mouth open slightly. "How did you say that?"

Remington chuckled. "Tiye Mwen," she said.

"Oh yes, please…" Wynter said, shaking her head.

"O wi tanpri," Lissette supplied in Creole.

Wynter exchanged a look with Remington, both of them shaking their heads in embarrassment.

"So, you know the family is coming to Thanksgiving…" Lissette said, stepping into the silence that ensued, unaware of how mortified Wynter and Remington were that she'd heard them having sex.

"So your sister and her husband?" Wynter asked Remington, who was looking at Lissette with a look that Wynter didn't understand.

"They are?" Remington asked Lissette.

Lissette smiled broadly, nodding her head.

"Oh mèt…" Remington breathed.

"Ou ta dwe konnen," Lissette said her tone chiding. "Pote lakay li nan jou fèt la."

"Ou gen rezon," Remington said, shaking her head and grinning at the same time.

Wynter looked back and forth between them, not understanding a word they were saying.

"Uh, excuse me," Wynter said, holding up her hand. "Didn't you say it was rude to speak Creole around someone who didn't speak it?" she asked, looking pointedly at Remington.

Remington folded her upper lip under her teeth, closing her eyes, knowing she had been caught by her own words.

"Yes," she said, "I apologize, but Lissette just kind of shocked me."

"Okay," Wynter said, "I'll forgive you this time if you tell me what you two were saying."

Remington blew her breath out, looking like she really didn't want to do that.

"She's somehow surprised that the whole family is coming for Thanksgiving this year," Lissette said. "I told her that she should have known that it was going to happen that way since she brought you home."

Wynter looked at Remington who'd just lit another cigarette and took a deep drag, blowing the smoke out a full minute later.

"Why is that a big deal?" Wynter asked.

"Our family is rather large," Lissette said, grinning.

"How large?" Wynter asked, look cautious.

Remington smiled weakly. "The house will be full."

"O bondye…" Wynter said with such shock and in such perfect intonation it made Remington burst into laughter.

"Well said," Remington said, when she was able to talk again, nodding with a huge smile on her face.

"Okay," Wynter said trying to cope with this information, "but they've met other women you've dated, right?"

Wynter and Lissette exchanged a look then they both looked at Wynter and shook their heads.

"Mem's never brought a girl home before," Lissette said, grinning broadly.

"So your family's never met anyone you've dated?" Wynter asked.

"Well, they've met the ones that live around here," Remington said, "but not the others."

"Wait, wait, wait…" Wynter said, holding up her hand. "The ones around here?" she queried pointedly.

"I've lived here my whole life, Wyn," Remington said, a wry grin on her lips.

"Are they still here too?" Wynter asked, her look more pointed.

Remington looked at Lissette, who widened her eyes slightly, and then looked back at Wynter.

"I don't really know for sure…" she said hesitantly.

Wynter looked at Lissette. "How many of them still live here?"

"Well, there's Genevieve and Britt, oh and Alisana and Bettina of course, she lives down the road," Lissette said, glancing at Remington's glowering face.

Wynter looked at Remington, her look contemplative. "That many? Just here?"

"Well… I mean…" Remington stammered. "Gena and Britt were high school."

"Uh-huh," Wynter said, "you had two girlfriends in high school? When did you come out?"

"When I was about fifteen," Remington said.

"So two girlfriends in three years…" Wynter said.

"Two years," Lissette corrected. "Mem graduated a year early."

"Ou pa yo ap ede," Remington muttered to Lissette.

Lissette grimaced. "Sorry," she said.

At Wynter's pointed glare, Remington looked contrite. "I just told her that she's not helping," Remington said.

"Oh, but she is," Wynter said, smiling evilly.

"Wyn…" Remington said, her tone reasoning, "these girls were a long time ago."

"And apparently rather abundant," Wynter said. "No wonder you're so…" she started to say, but stopped herself.

Remington gave her a questioning look.

"Bon," Wynter said, her look pointed.

Remington laughed, dropping her head and shaking it, even as Lissette looked at them perplexed.

"Okay, so now I need to go shopping too," Wynter said.

"Why?" Remington asked.

"If you're whole family is coming, I need to look good," Wynter said.

"Babe, you look good in jeans and a T-shirt," Remington said.

"Yeah… and I'm betting this isn't a jeans and T-shirt kind of holiday here, is it?" Wynter asked, narrowing her eyes at Remington.

"Well, no," Remington said.

"You're on my list right now, so you need to just smile and agree to whatever I ask for at this point, okay?" she said, smiling sweetly, her eyes sparkling with malice.

"I think you better take her shopping," Lissette said to Remington.

"I think you're probably right," Remington said, nodding.

"Can I come?" Lissette asked brightly.

Two hours later after breakfast, the three climbed into the Mercedes and headed out.

"Where did you say we were going?" Wynter asked as she looked around.

"Louisville," Remington answered. "That's apparently where they keep the girly stuff," she said, winking at Wynter.

"Not in Lexington?" Wynter asked.

"According to my mother, Louisville is better," Remington said.

"Well, she has great style. I can already see that, so I'll take her word for it," Wynter said smiling.

"Wow…" Lissette said from the back seat a little while later.

"What?" Remington asked, glancing in the rearview mirror at her sister.

"You and Wynter are blowing up the internet right now," Lissette said, grinning.

"Already?" Remington said, glancing over at Wynter who was already looking it up on her phone.

"Oh yeah..." Wynter said, nodding and chuckling.

"What are they saying?" Remington asked.

"Basically, what I've said," Wynter said, grinning. "That it's about damned time!"

Remington rolled her eyes, shaking her head.

Wynter glanced down at Remington's phone that was sitting in one of the cup holders plugged in to the car's stereo.

"Remi, have you checked your messages this morning?" she asked, grinning.

"No, why?" Remington asked, already looking over at Wynter with trepidation.

"May I?" Wynter asked, gesturing to Remington's phone.

"Of course," Remington said, nodding.

Wynter picked up Remington's phone and started to scroll through the messages.

"Okay, let's see..." she said, grinning as she saw who all had texted Remington. "We've got Quinn, of course, saying that you finally got it right... I do love her... and Xandy who of course is thrilled and says congratulations... Um, oh... Mackie said, and I quote 'Seriously? You're killin' me, Remi!' but then he has a wink at the end of it... So, I think you're safe there… Jericho and Zoey send congrats. Jet says good job… I'm a job now? Wow… yeah pretty much everyone else happy for us, congrats, and all…"

"Gotta love the internet," Remington said, shaking her head.

"You really didn't think this was going to stay a secret, did you?" Wynter asked.

"It would have been nice to have some privacy," Remington said wryly.

"Welcome to my world," Wynter said, winking at Remington, "nothing I do is secret… Oh lovely…" she said then, her tone changing significantly.

"What?" Remington asked, glancing over at her.

"Lauren is talking shit already…" Wynter said.

"What's she saying?" Remington asked her tone low.

Wynter glanced over at Remington and could see that her eyes were narrowed.

"She's just complaining about how she knew I was having an affair, blah, blah, blah… She's playing up the 'poor me' angle. Sadly, I'm not surprised at all."

Remington made a sucking sound through her teeth. "She's talking about you having an affair? With me? She's really pushing her luck at this point."

"She's not the only one talking sh—I mean stuff," Lissette said, correcting herself before she got into trouble with Remington.

"What do you mean?" Remington asked.

"Akasha's talking about you again," Lissette said, her tone disgusted.

Remington sighed, shaking her head. "That's nothing new."

Wynter was looking on her phone and Lissette handed over her own phone. Wynter took it, smiling back at the girl. Then she read the article.

"Well, this time I'm included in her tirade," Wynter said, rolling her eyes.

"What?" Remington asked sharply. "What is she saying about you?"

"Oh, let's see," Wynter said, scrolling back up on the story. "She's quoted as saying that 'Remington LaRoché just seems to keep getting lucky with women… too bad she won't hold onto this one either…' Oh lovely, she says that maybe she needs to come take care of me for you…" Wynter's voice trailed off as she saw Remington's face change, going from being slightly amused to being downright furious.

She hit the hands-free button on the car's Bluetooth. "Call Salio," she practically growled.

Wynter glanced back as Lissette who was now smiling broadly.

"Her manager," Lissette mouthed to Wynter, even as the line started to connect.

"Well, it's about fucking time!" exclaimed a man's voice when he answered the phone.

Remington gave the dashboard a glowering look, waving her hand dismissively. "Yeah, yeah, don't start all the shit, Salio… I've been hearing it for over a month now… But now she's pissed me off, so get me the fight."

"You got it," he said, sounding extremely happy, "when?"

"Get me some dates from her people. I'm still on this tour after this break, so I need to stay with it."

"Okay, how much do you want for the fight?" he asked then.

"This ain't about money, Salio. It's about shutting that bitch up for good," Remington said sharply.

"She talked shit about your new girl, I saw that…" Salio said, looking at his computer with the picture of Akasha Salt talking to the press.

"And she went too far," Remington said. "So now I'm going to jam that shit right back down her throat."

Salio laughed, sounding very pleased to hear it. "Good to have you back."

"I'm not back, this isn't about my title, this about honor," Remington said, glancing over at Wynter who was watching her with wide eyes. She'd never seen this side of Remington, and she really liked it. "Oh, and Salio, get me a trainer, I need someone who can travel with the tour."

"Who're you thinking?" Salio asked.

"If you can get Kai, do it, she's good with fast results," Remington said.

Salio gave a low whistle. "If I can even get her, she'll cost you a fortune."

"Don't care, I need the best right now," Remington said.

"Okay, sis, you got it, I'm on it. I'll call you back with details."

"Thanks Salio," Remington said, nodding.

"I've missed ya, kid," Salio said.

Remington chuckled, nodding. "Missed you too, Salio."

They hung up a couple of minutes later.

"So, let me get this straight…" Wynter said in the ensuing silence after the phone call. "She talks all kinds of shit about you," she said, circling her finger to encompass all the things Akasha had been saying for months. "But that's not a matter of honor?"

Remington curled her lips in grin as she shook her head.

"But she talks shit about me one time, and now you're going to kick her ass?"

"Yes, ma'am," Remington said. At Wynter's perplexed look, she explained, "When I got into MMA I knew that other fighters would talk garbage, that's what a lot of them do, especially Akasha. And I accepted that as being part of the sport. When I retired, I knew I'd still hear some crap, and that's okay with me too. But someone starts talking about you… That's not okay with me. You didn't sign up for that like I did."

"Actually, becoming a rock star means you sign up for whatever people want to say about you, babe," Wynter said, winking at Remington. "I'm used to it too."

"Yes, well, I can't do anything about what others say or have said, but I can do something about Akasha's mouth, and I'm going to," Remington said.

Wynter looked back at Remington and smiled fondly. It was definitely a different feeling having someone stand up for her. Lauren had never stood up for her; she'd just told her to get thicker skin. Remington made her feel protected and appreciated. It was a great feeling.

The shopping trip ended up taking longer than expected because Wynter couldn't find anything she liked. At one store, while Wynter was in the dressing room making noises about nothing looking right, Remington called her mother. When Wynter emerged from the dressing room, still having found nothing she liked, Remington stood up.

"Come on," she said, nodding toward the front of the store.

"Where are we going?" Wynter asked, glancing over at Lissette as she followed Remington.

"My mother had a suggestion, I want to check it out," Remington said, offering Wynter her arm.

"Okay," Wynter said, smiling as she took Remington's arm with both of her hands.

Ten minutes later, they were standing in front of a vintage clothing store.

"I think I love your mother…" Wynter said as she looked at the clothes in the window.

A half an hour later, Wynter had bought a dress and shoes that she wouldn't let Remington see.

"I want to surprise you," Wynter told Remington.

"Alright," Remington said, grinning.

They had an early dinner at a local Italian restaurant where many of the people seemed to know Remington. Apparently, she'd come to Louisville a lot over the years. Wynter found it refreshing to be the 'girlfriend' of a star, instead of the star. She sat back and watched

Remington smile and talk to people. She seemed much more comfortable here than she had in New York. It was a really nice day.

The following day was much more surprising. Wynter got the opportunity to see how good of a horsewoman Remington really was. Apparently, riding since she was three years old had given her an extremely good command of the art. The first thing that surprised her was the attire Remington wore: knee-high leather boots and leather gloves, a collared button up shirt, jeans, and her leather Affliction jacket. Wynter found it very attractive, and so very different from what she'd seen Remington in previously.

As they walked to the stables, Remington told her things about the farm, what they did, how they operated. Wynter found it all extremely interesting.

"We've had four Kentucky Derby Winners come out of LaRoché farms," Remington proclaimed proudly.

Wynter nodded, smiling. She wasn't sure she understood how big of a deal it was but from the look on Remington's face, it must have been a big deal. Inside the stables, Remington walked over to one of the stalls on the end, giving a low whistle as she approached it. A huge black head immediately stuck out over the stall door.

"Gen ti gason m', there's my boy…" Remington said, smiling as she stepped up next to the large horse's head, reaching up to stroke his neck and patting him.

The horse tossed his head, turning it to Remington and nuzzling her shirt.

"I know what you're looking for," Remington said, grinning.

She put her hand in her pocket and pulling out sugar cubes, holding one up in the palm of her hand. The horse immediately took the cube, snorting happily. Remington looked over at Wynter.

"You want to come over here and pet him?" she asked solicitously.

Wynter nodded, biting her lip nervously.

"It's okay," Remington said softly, putting her hand out to Wynter.

Wynter took her hand, allowing herself to be drawn closer to the big animal, her eyes widening. She reached up tentatively, stroking the side of the horse's neck.

"He's so soft," Wynter said, smiling.

"That's because he's spoiled and gets bathed and brushed all the time," Remington said, grinning.

Satan responded to Wynter's presence, as if he sensed she was new at this. He turned his head slightly, regarding her with dark eyes. He put his muzzle under her hand, and Wynter looked at Remington.

"He wants you to stroke his muzzle," Remington said, reaching over to show Wynter how to do just that.

Wynter smiled as Remington showed her.

"You can go all the way up to his forehead there," Remington said, showing Wynter, "and he'll probably love you forever if you use those nails of yours."

Wynter did what Remington suggested, and Satan immediately pressed his head closer to her.

"Oh boy…" Remington said. "I think I've just lost my mount," she said, grinning.

"What?" Wynter asked, looking over at Remington.

"I think he's in love," Remington said, smiling, her hazel eyes sparkling.

"He likes me?" Wynter asked, smiling happily.

"He does," Remington said, nodding.

"Is it okay to stand in front of him?" Wynter asked.

"Yes, just don't get too close to the stall door, if he moves his head too fast he'll knock you down."

Wynter nodded, stepping over to stand in front of Satan's head. The horse immediately lowered his head to her. Wynter reached up, using both hands and started scratching his face, from his muzzle up to his forehead. Remington watched, feeling her heart tug at the picture of Wynter standing with her horse.

"You're putting him to sleep…" Remington told Wynter softly.

Wynter glanced around to see that Satan's eyes were indeed closing. She also saw his lips flutter.

"What does that mean?" she asked, nodding toward his lips.

"It means he's in heaven," Remington said, smiling. "You have the touch."

"The touch?" Wynter asked softly.

"With the horses… just like other animals, they can sense a person's intent and their soul…" Remington said softly, staring into Wynter's eyes. "And he recognizes yours as kind and gentle."

Wynter felt tears sting the backs of her eyes; no one had ever spoken to her in the way Remington just had. She nodded, unable to think of an appropriate response. She looked back over at Satan, putting her face against the warm muzzle.

Remington saw Wynter's reaction to what she'd said, and it drew her another step down the path to loving this woman deeply.

A little while later, Remington went to saddle Satan, joking that if she continued to scratch his head, she'd put him into a coma. Wynter watched Remington in fascination as she hefted the saddle over Satan's large back.

"Is he really big for a horse?" Wynter asked. "I mean he seems huge to me, but I don't have a basis for comparison, so…"

Remington grinned, nodding. "Yeah, he's eighteen hands high," she said and saw Wynter's blank look immediately. "You measure from the withers, which are here," she said, putting her hand at the top of Satan's back where his neck met the back. "Then it's four inches per hand. So basically he's six feet from here to the ground."

"Wow," Wynter said, smiling.

When Remington had saddled Satan and put on the halter, she opened the stall door and led him out of the stall. Wynter stood back, staring up at the large horse astounded. Remington continued to lead Satan out to the yard. Wynter watched as Remington stuck her feet in the stirrup and, holding onto the pommel on the saddle, pulled herself up onto Satan's back.

"Come here," Remington told Wynter.

Wynter walked over to stand next to Remington. As she did, Remington leaned down, extending her hand and arm to Wynter.

"Put your hand up to my forearm and hold on," Remington said.

Wynter did what Remington told her and was shocked at how easily Remington lifted her off her feet and swung her up behind her on the saddle.

"Wow," Wynter said, wrapping her arms around Remington from behind. "I don't know how I ever managed to forget how strong you are…"

"Comes in handy," Remington said, turning her head to smile back at Wynter. "So just keep ahold of me, okay?"

"That won't be a problem," Wynter said, putting her head against Remington's back happily.

Remington took things slow at first, instructing Wynter on what each type of step was. They did walking, trotting, and cantering.

"Now, are you ready for a run? Or do you want to go back?" Remington asked Wynter.

Wynter squeezed Remington's waist excitedly. "Let's run," she said, her eyes glowing in her excitement.

"Okay, hold on tight," Remington told her, "don't loosen your grip on my jacket no matter what, okay?"

"Okay," Wynter said, grasping two handfuls of Remington's leather jacket.

"Now, lean forward with me," Remington said, as she raised up in the stirrups.

She clicked her tongue and Satan began walking then changed into a canter.

"Hold on," Remington told Wynter again. Then she gave Satan a gentle kick to his sides and said, "Ha!" and Wynter felt the shift of Satan's muscles under her.

Suddenly it was like they were flying, and Wynter could not believe the amazing feeling of it. She held on tight to Remington's waist and jacket, and felt exhilaration sweep through her. When the finally slowed to a canter and then a walk again, Wynter found she was breathing heavily.

"How you doing back there?" Remington asked, turning her head.

"That was the most incredible feeling I've ever had!" Wynter said smiling widely.

Remington smiled, inclining her head. "Yeah, there's not a lot that beats that," she said.

Remington walked Satan over to an area lined with trees, where the snow didn't completely cover the ground. She dismounted, and then held her arms up to help Wynter off Satan's back. Remington tied the reins to a tree and gave Satan a quick rub. She pulled the rolled blanked off the saddle that she'd placed there earlier, and then spread it on the ground for them to sit down.

Wynter sat down, moving to snuggle into Remington's arms immediately.

"Are you cold?" Remington asked.

"A little," Wynter said.

Remington immediately shrugged out of her jacket putting it around Wynter's shoulders.

"Remi, you'll freeze," Wynter said worriedly.

"No, I won't, I'm used to this kind of weather," Remington said, grinning.

Remington sat with her knees up, and pulled Wynter back into her arms and between her legs so Wynter could rest against her chest. Lying against Remington's chest was fast becoming one of her very favorite things. She listened to Remington's heartbeat, sliding her hand around Remington's waist and inhaling her scent.

Remington bent her head to rest against the top of Wynter's head, closing her eyes at the feeling of Wynter's hand around her waist. She marveled at how incredibly good she felt at that moment. It was far from what she would have expected with Wynter in the beginning. Now she couldn't imagine anything else. She just hoped it would stay this way for a while.

At one point, Wynter shifted so she could look up at Remington. Remington leaned down to kiss Wynter's lips softly at first, and then with more heat. Wynter wound her arms up around Remington's neck, pressing closer as they kissed. They were out in the middle of nowhere; there were no people on the grounds because the next day was Thanksgiving. It was just them.

Remington's hands slid up under the sweater Wynter wore, caressing her back, and pulling her closer to her. Their lips met over and over again, with increasing passion each time. Remington gathered her ever closer, her hands grasping at Wynter's skin, breathing heavily. Wynter moaned against Remington's lips, wanting her more than anything in the world at that moment.

"Remi... please..." Wynter pleaded softly, her voice full of so much longing it caused Remington to groan.

Then Remington was laying her back on the blanket and making love to her, and Wynter couldn't feel anything but Remington's hands on her and the incredible sensations running through her body. When they both came, shouting and crying out, their hands and their bodies were intertwined, even almost fully clothed.

Remington rolled to her back, pulling Wynter over her as she gasped for breath. Wynter lay against Remington's chest, her head against the hollow of Remington's shoulder.

"Well, that's a first," Remington said, grinning.

"What is?" Wynter asked, glancing over at Remington.

"Doing that out here," Remington said.

"Really?" Wynter asked, looking surprised. "I'd have thought it would have been one of your signature moves," she said, winking at Remington.

Remington glanced over at her. "Out in the open, on my parent's farm?" she asked, raising an eyebrow at Wynter.

"I guess not," Wynter said, looking contrite, but her eyes sparkled mischievously.

"And you like that you got me to do it, don't you?" Remington said, her eyes narrowed slightly, even as a grin played at her lips.

"Oh hell yes!" Wynter exclaimed, grinning.

Remington shook her head slowly. "You're going to be trouble for me, I just know it…"

"Aren't I already?" Wynter asked.

Remington nodded. "Yes, you have been," she said, smiling, "but it's worth it."

"Bon," Wynter said, widening her eyes.

"Trey byen," Remington said.

After a while, they decided to start back because it looked like it was getting ready to snow, according to Remington. Remington helped Wynter up onto Satan first, then pulled herself up behind Wynter, putting her arms around her to hold the reins. Wynter laid her head on Remington's shoulder, thoroughly enjoying the feel of Remington's body surrounding hers, and rested her hands on either of Remington's thighs. It was a very sensual feeling. Wynter unconsciously rubbed her hands up and down on Remington's thighs, her eyes closed as she remembered what they'd done earlier. She felt Remington's hand brush against her breast and breathed heavier at the excitement that stirred in her. She pressed back against Remington, her hands grasping at Remington's thighs.

Remington felt Wynter's hands on her thighs, and felt her press back against her, and suddenly she couldn't think, her body was alive with sensations. This woman was going to drive her insane, she knew it! She turned Satan away from the direction of home, knowing that there was no way she was getting close to home in this state. Tying the reins off on the pommel and giving Satan his head, she slid her arms around Wynter's body, her head bent to kiss her neck. Wynter's hands slid higher on her thighs, coming together to touch Remington as Remington's thumbs brushed up over hard nipples. Minutes later another first occurred, for each of them. For Wynter it was being made love to on a horse, and for Remington it was making love to a woman on a horse.

The snow was just starting to fall as they both reached their release.

"Great, we're going to die out here in the snow," Remington muttered, as she nuzzled Wynter's neck.

"If I gotta die, I'll go this way, happily," Wynter said, grinning, her hands sliding over Remington's hands that were around her waist.

"Let's actually get back now, though," Remington said, grinning. "I really don't want to have to explain to my father why he had to send out a search party on his own land…"

Wynter laughed at that comment.

Chapter 8

Thanksgiving dawned at the LaRoché house. Wynter woke in Remington's arms and snuggled closer to her. Remington stirred and opened her eyes, looking at Wynter.

"Bonjou," Remington said, as Wynter found she did whenever they woke together.

"Bonjou," Wynter replied.

"Are you ready for today?" Wynter asked then.

Remington smiled. "Why wouldn't I be?" she asked.

"I'm just thinking you're going to have to spend the day explaining to your family why you're dating me," Wynter said, her voice belying the concern she really had.

"Well, that'll be easy," Remington said.

"Really?" Wynter asked, her blue eyes sparkling in the morning sunlight.

"Yes," Remington said, nodding, "I'll just tell them to take one look at you."

Wynter narrowed her eyes at Remington, but then smiled. "Smart answer there, Remi."

"And the truth," Remington said, her look soft. "So when do I get to see this dress?"

"When I put it on later," Wynter replied primly.

"Okay," Remington said, shaking her head. "Let's go grab some breakfast and find out when everyone is supposed to get here."

They got up, pulling on clothes, managing to avoid kissing too much in the process. They'd discovered that when they started kissing, it was when they got themselves in most of the trouble. It wasn't always the case, but it tended to be the fastest way to cause the fire to start between them. They grinned like kids at each other as they walked down the stairs together.

In the kitchen, Delphine was already working on the turkey.

Remington walked over to her mother, hugging her and kissing her on the cheek. "Pase yon bon jou Aksyondegras," she said.

"Pase yon bon jou Aksyondegras, ou two," Delphine replied. "Happy Thanksgiving, Wynter," she said smiling over at Wynter.

Wynter looked at Remington. "How do I say that again?" she asked.

"Pase yon bon," Remington said.

"Pase yon bon," Wynter repeated, nodding.

"Jou Aksyondegras," Remington said then.

"Jou Aksyondegras," Wynter repeated.

"Let's hear it," Remington said.

"Pase yon bon jou Aksyondegras," Wynter said, grimacing hoping she was getting it right.

Delphine clapped, nodding her head. "Trey byen!" she exclaimed. "You are a natural!"

Wynter smiled, innately pleased by Remington's mother's praise. "Mèsi," she said.

"There is coffee, and there are sweet rolls in the oven, Remington," Delphine told her daughter.

Wynter leaned on the counter, looking over at what Delphine was doing, not seeing what she was used to seeing with the preparation of a turkey.

"Is this a Haitian way of doing the turkey?" Wynter asked.

"Wi, we use bell peppers, garlic, lime juice, coconut milk," she said, holding different things up.

"Ohhh… that sounds so good," Wynter said, smiling.

Remington glanced at her mother and saw the approving nod she gave. Lissette had been right, her parents did like Wynter. She poured coffee for Wynter, handing it to her with the cream and sugar that she knew she liked in her coffee.

"Do you want a roll?" Remington asked, knowing that Wynter didn't always eat much for breakfast.

"Sure," Wynter said, nodding.

In the end, Wynter sat at the breakfast bar watching Delphine prepare the turkey the entire time, asking questions and tasting things that Delphine handed her to try. Remington wandered out onto the patio, sitting down to smoke. Wynter noticed Remington had left the room, and she looked around until she located her. Seeing her sitting on the back patio, she smiled fondly.

"I see that smile…" Delphine said slyly.

Wynter looked back at Delphine, her blue eyes shining as she did.

"She's so much more relaxed here," Wynter told Delphine. "I like seeing her this way."

"She is happy with you," Delphine said. "It blesses my soul to see it."

Wynter smiled softly. "And I am so happy with her," she said. "She is so… different from what I am used to."

"Different how?" Delphine asked. Then she grimaced slightly. "I'm sorry, if it is okay for me to ask."

"It's totally okay," Wynter said, her eyes trailing back over to Remington. "She's so calm, so smart, so patient, and so gallant." She shook her head, her look wondrous. "She treats me with so much care and tenderness, I didn't think that was ever possible with someone."

"Remington was raised to respect women, when we realized that she wasn't like other girls, Andre knew he needed to instill in her the teachings traditionally reserved for our young men… I believe it has served her well."

"You are very right about that," Wynter said. "She is the most gentlemanly person I've ever met, and it's so ingrained in her, she's amazing."

Delphine smiled, looking very pleased by what she was hearing. She reached over the counter, taking Wynter's hand in hers.

"I hope that you and Remington have a long relationship. I believe that you are very good for my daughter, as it sounds like she is good for you. Andre and I very much approve of your relationship," she said, then rolled her eyes. "I know that is a very old-fashioned thing to say in this day and age, but it is true."

Wynter looked pensive for a moment. "Can I ask you a question?"

"Of course," Delphine said.

"It's about Remi, and if it's not something that I should ask, please tell me."

"Go on," Delphine encouraged.

"Did you approve of other girls she's dated? I mean the ones that you know?" Wynter asked, thinking she was probably about to be told to mind her own business.

Delphine looked thoughtful for a moment, then she shook her head. "It is not that we didn't approve of them, it was that they did not make her happy, as you do. She was more restless and tense when she was with others."

Wynter bit her lip, nodding. She looked over at Remington again, thinking that nothing was dissuading her from falling head over heels for this woman. She sighed softly. Delphine heard it and felt her heart swell.

Later that day as guests started to arrive, Remington stood at the windows of her room looking out as people arrived. She wore dove-gray slacks that fit perfectly, outlining her legs and butt nicely, and a bright white button up shirt, with a tailored gray sports jacket that nipped in at the waist. At her throat, she wore a black leather cord with a silver and black dog tag style pendant with a fleur-de-lis on it, and her black leather Phillippe Patek watch. She also wore black leather dress boots with a two-inch heel on them. She heard heels on the floor behind her and grinned.

"Am I allowed to look now?" she asked.

"Yes," Wynter said.

Remington turned around and was sure that her heart skipped a beat. Wynter stood wearing a cream-colored vintage 1920s dress with an Art Deco pattern done in gold sequins and pearl beads. The dress stopped just above her knees and her tanned skin glowing against the material. Her hair was pulled back in a clip that closely matched the colors and style of the dress, and she wore strappy heels the same color as the dress. Her makeup was light, but done in a way that made her blue eyes stand out, and her cheeks and lips glow.

"Oh my God you are so beautiful…" Remington breathed, her eyes reflecting her awe.

Wynter smiled, walking over to Remington, sliding her hand up the lapel of her jacket.

"And you look so handsome, it's unreal… You just get sexier and sexier…" she said, her eyes shining.

Remington reached out, touching Wynter on the chin, and taking a step closer, she leaned down kissing her softly on the lips.

"I will be so proud to call you mine today," Remington said reverently.

Wynter couldn't believe how good it felt to hear that from Remington.

"And I am yours, Remi," Wynter said. "So completely yours."

Remington's eyes stared down into hers as her thumb brushed back and forth on her cheek. Moving forward, she took Wynter into her arms, hugging her close and feeling so good at that moment, she had no words to describe it. Instead, she simply held Wynter against her caressing Wynter's back.

Wynter stood in Remington's arms, and pressed her face against her jacket, thoroughly enjoying the embrace. She closed her eyes and breathed in Remington's scent, and felt the strength of her arms around her. At that moment, Wynter felt like the luckiest woman alive.

When they finally parted, Remington reached down, taking Wynter's hand to lead her out of the room. At the top of the split stairs, Remington paused looking around at the family members milling about. She glanced at Wynter, who looked terrified suddenly. Remington pulled Wynter back to her chest, and holding her from behind. She lowered her head, putting her head down by Wynter's ear.

"They will all love you because you are the most incredible woman I've ever met…" she told Wynter, her voice a soft whisper against her ear.

Some members of Remington's family spotted them and started nudging each other. Many of them watched as Wynter turned in Remington's arms to look up at her, putting her hand to Remington's heart as she had at the concert the night she'd thanked her. Everyone recognized the gesture and fell in love with Wynter Kincade in that moment.

"Uh…" Remington murmured, as she noticed the hushed silence and glanced behind Wynter.

Once again, Wynter turned in Remington's arms and looked down at the group gathered below. The picture that they made in that moment, with Wynter's cream dress, long flowing dark hair, and bright blue eyes standing in front of Remington's taller broader frame, in her dove-gray suit, crisp white shirt and her hands on Wynter's waist, was something no one would ever forget. Someone in the group had the good sense to take a picture.

"Get down here girl!" called one of Remington's uncles, making everyone laugh, including Remington and Wynter.

Remington took Wynter's hand and led her the rest of the way down the stairs and began introducing her to family members. Each and every family member was so kind to Wynter that she felt like she'd been worried for no reason at all. Remington never left her side, keeping her hand at Wynter's back, or her arm around her shoulders, or her hand in hers. Remington also frequently leaned over to kiss her lips softly, or kiss her cheek, or temple, or to whisper something in her ear. Wynter felt completely special the entire day, she'd never felt so loved and accepted.

At one point, Remington took her over to meet Justine, her other sister.

"Wynter, this is Justine, Jus this is Wynter," Remington said, smiling.

Justine had green eyes and brown hair. She was small like Lissette; it seemed that Remington had inherited their father's height, since Andre was almost six feet.

"It's really lovely to meet you," Justine said. "Lissette's been talking non-stop about you since you got here," she said smiling. "She's right, you really are much prettier in person."

Wynter smiled. "Thank you. You and Lissette are just as beautiful, like your mother."

"Mèsi," Justine said.

Wynter looked to Remington, who seemed to read her mind. "Byenvini," she supplied for 'you're welcome.'

"Byenvini," Wynter said. "I'm practicing my Creole."

Justine smiled warmly. "And doing well," she said.

Later they were sitting talking to one of Remington's oldest aunts, Wilamena.

"You have such a beautiful voice, dear," she said holding Wynter's hand in both of hers.

"Mèsi," Wynter said, smiling.

The older woman's eyes widened, looking up at Remington.

"Li se trè bon, wi? She is very good, yes?" Remington said, translating for Wynter.

"Wi, trey byen," the older woman said, nodding at Wynter.

"I'm trying to learn," Wynter said. "Remi is a very good teacher."

"She learns by me forgetting myself and speaking Creole all the time," Remington said, smiling.

"Like that night you spoke to her when she fell," Remington's aunt said, grasping Remington's hand. "You were so gallant, Remington, so very gallant. We were very proud of you that night for sure," she said, her dark eyes sparkling proudly.

"Mèsi, matant," Remington said, smiling fondly.

"Matant?" Wynter asked.

"It means aunt," Remington told her.

"Matant," Wynter repeated, testing out the word.

"So smart!" Remington's aunt said. "You should marry this one, Remington!" she proclaimed. "When else are you going to find a woman who is not only beautiful, smart, and talented, but also with a love of your culture?"

Remington looked back at her aunt, surprised by what she'd said. She looked at Wynter and saw that Wynter was simply smiling softly at her aunt. It was something Remington thought about the rest of the day.

Later that evening, after dinner, Remington and Wynter sat by the fireplace with many of the family members still chatting and drinking wine. Remington had removed her jacket and laid it on the back of the couch, rolling up the sleeves of her white shirt. They sat on the wood floor. Wynter had taken off her shoes and they sat next to the couch. Remington had her knees up and Wynter was sitting between them, her legs curled under her demurely. Remington had her arms around her as she leaned against Remington's chest her head on Remington's shoulder.

Justine was sitting with their parents and looked over at them. She nudged her mother, who nudged, Andre. The three watched Remington and Wynter avidly. They made such a handsome couple, it was almost impossible not to watch them. They were talking about something, Remington's head was bent saying something and Wynter smiled, shaking her head then said something in return. As they talked their fingers intertwined, and Wynter put her other hand to their joined hands, touching Remington's fingers affectionately, even as they continued to talk. At one point, Remington threw her head back, laughing. It was a warm, rich sound and it made Delphine, Andre, and Justine smile. The family definitely approved of Wynter Kincade.

Later, Remington and Wynter lay in bed, each on their side facing each other. Remington's arm was under Wynter's neck, her hand coming around to stroke back and forth on Wynter's forehead as they talked.

"My family absolutely adores you," Remington said smiling.

"Your family is awesome, Remi," Wynter said, her eyes glowing with happiness. "I've never been around so many nice people before in my life."

"That's 'cause you've lived in Los Angeles your whole life," Remington said, winking at her.

Wynter chuckled. "Yeah, that's true," she said, rolling her eyes.

"Did you get along with Lauren's family?" Remington asked curiously.

"Oh…" Wynter said, shaking her head, "her family was a nightmare, she avoided them if she could."

"That bad?" Remington asked, not sure why she was surprised.

"They were… well… they were really white trash," Wynter said. "I know that sounds unkind, but they were just bloodsucking leeches, always looking for a handout."

Remington looked disappointed at that. "So it's really just been you and your mother for a long time?"

"Yeah," Wynter said, "we haven't seen my dad since I was like two, and even then, I guess he was never really part of our lives."

Remington shook her head. "I can't even imagine that," she said. "I've always had so much family underfoot. I wouldn't know that to do without them."

"Fortunately, you don't have to worry about that," Wynter said, smiling, "and I have to say, that I felt very privileged being a part of your Thanksgiving." She laid her hand on Remington's cheek then. "Thank you so much for bringing me here with you, it really means a lot to me."

Remington searched Wynter's eyes looking pensive.

"What is it?" Wynter asked.

"Something my aunt said earlier today," Remington said.

"That doesn't really narrow it down, Remi," Wynter said, grinning. "You have like eight or so…"

Remington laughed softly. "True, but this was about you loving my culture," she said.

"Oh, that was your aunt Wilamena," Wynter said. "I really liked her, she was so sweet."

Remington shook her head, her look wondrous.

"What now?" Wynter asked, smiling.

"The fact that you remember names, that you remember the Creole I've taught you… it's just… amazing." Remington said.

"Of course I remember, Remi, it's important," Wynter said softly. "And Wilamena was right, I do love your culture, because it's who you are," she said, her eyes gleaming with emotion. "It's how you talk, it's how you think and how you act, it's you."

Remington looked back at her for a long moment. "No one's ever said that before," she told Wynter.

"That doesn't mean they didn't think it, Remi," Wynter said. "Expression isn't something everyone is good at."

"Or maybe they didn't think the way you do," Remington said. "Maybe they didn't see me the way you do."

"Maybe you didn't save their life a couple weeks ago," Wynter said, smiling softly, "and maybe they didn't get to see everything you've shown me. I mean, there seems to have been a million of them, but…" she said, grinning as her voice trailed off.

Remington narrowed her eyes in mock anger. "There weren't millions," she said pointedly. Then her look softened, as she pulled Wynter into her arms, sighing deeply. "And no one has ever felt this good in my arms."

Wynter pressed her face against Remington's neck, enjoying the thrill that went through her at hearing that.

"No one has ever felt so right," Remington said, leaning down to kiss Wynter's temple. She kept her lips near Wynter's ear as she whispered, "I love you. I know it may seem too soon to say, but—"

Her words were stilled when Wynter raised her head and kissed her lips deeply.

"If you just want me to shut up…" Remington murmured against her lips.

"Shut up," Wynter said, pressing closer to Remington and deepening the kiss.

They were making love moments later, doing their best to be quiet this time, even though they'd stacked pillows and a suitcase on the air vent.

Afterwards, as they lay trying to catch their breath, Wynter levered herself up on one elbow, looking down at Remington.

"I love you too," she said softly.

Remington reached out her hand, smoothing it over Wynter's cheek, her eyes staring up into hers. "You do?"

"How could I not?" Wynter asked. "You are the most amazing person I've ever met."

Remington pulled her close then, kissing her lips once more. Her phone pinged at that moment. She reached over to pick it up and looked at the message.

"What is it?" Wynter asked.

"Salio's got the fight set… for Christmas Eve," she said, shaking her head ruefully.

"Seriously?" Wynter asked.

Remington chuckled. "Yeah, I think he's seen Rocky IV too many times," she said, shaking her head. "And it looks like the trainer will be here tomorrow at ten."

"Did you get the one you wanted?" Wynter asked.

"Yeah, he managed to get Kai. She's probably the toughest trainer out there. She will literally kick my ass, but if I'm going to be ready in a month, I need it."

"I can't believe you think you're out of shape, Remi," Wynter said, sliding her hand over Remington's leanly muscled abs, abs many women would kill for. "There isn't an ounce of fat on you."

Remington grinned. "It isn't about fat, babe," she said. "It's about muscle memory and reaction time. Not reacting fast enough in the ring is what gets people knocked out."

Wynter nodded, alarmed by what Remington had just said. "She's going to travel with the tour too?"

"Yep," Remington said, nodding. "So I'm likely to have no free time for the next month."

Wynter nodded, looking unhappy at that thought, but knowing that it was what Remington needed to do.

They fell asleep a little while later.

The night of the fight in Madison Square Garden arrived. Wynter accompanied Remington into the arena, to the screaming of thousands of fans. Akasha Salt entered from another side of the arena with a woman on either arm. Wynter thought that Akasha looked like she'd been taking steroids, she seemed almost twice the size she had been before.

"Is that for real?" Wynter asked Remington. "She's huge all of a sudden!"

Remington moved her neck around, looking over at Akasha with barely veiled contempt.

"She's probably been doping," Quinn said from Remington's side.

"Well that's illegal isn't it?" Wynter asked.

"Yeah, but you gotta prove it," Remington said, her lips curled in displeasure.

They went to the center of the ring. Akasha stood a foot taller than Remington and seemed to dwarf her. Wynter watched from the sidelines, having a really bad feeling in the pit of her stomach.

"Are you guys sure she's ready?" Wynter asked Quinn.

Quinn nodded. "Yeah, she's ready," she said, looking at Wynter like she'd lost her mind. "Don't be negative, she don't need that shit right now."

Wynter was shocked by Quinn's sharp words and shook her head as she looked back to the ring. The referee was giving instructions, and then had Akasha and Remington touch gloves, which they did. They then backed up as the referee made the gesture to start. Akasha charged Remington, punching her in the face twice. Remington fell back and Akasha advanced and hit her again. Remington stumbled. Akasha continued to advance, punching her again and again.

Wynter screamed, looking over at Quinn. "Do something!" she told Quinn.

Quinn shook her head, shrugging. "Nothing we can do."

"What the hell do you mean! Stop this!" Wynter screamed as she saw Remington go down.

Akasha jumped on her, punching her over and over again. There was so much blood!

Wynter screamed as she saw Akasha's fist come up again. Remington wasn't moving.

"No!" Wynter screamed as Akasha's fist drove home.

Akasha was quickly pronounced the winner by Total Knock Out. Wynter scrambled through the ropes to get to Remington but Quinn got there first. Quinn was on her knees next to Remington's head. She looked up at Wynter ran up.

"She's gone," Quinn told her.

"What!" Wynter screeched.

"She's dead," Quinn said.

"Too bad," Akasha said with a sneer on her face, "guess she wasn't as good as she thought."

"No!" Wynter screamed.

"Whoa! Wynter!" Remington yelled, as Wynter started awake screaming.

Wynter was breathing heavily, shaking her head, tears streaming down her face.

"Wynter, what is it?" Remington asked, touching her face looking worried.

"Oh my God, oh my God…" Wynter said over and over again, as she started realizing that she'd been dreaming.

"Babe, what is it?" Remington asked, her eyes searching Wynter's.

Wynter dropped back against the pillows as she tried to calm her pounding heart. There was a knock on the bedroom door then.

"Is everything okay?" called Andre.

"Yeah, Dad, we're okay, I think she just had a nightmare," Remington said, looking down at Wynter. "Babe, are you okay?"

Wynter nodded, still breathing heavily, closing her eyes slowly and then opening them again when the image of a bloody, broken Remington flashed in her head again.

"Do you want to talk about it?" Remington asked solicitously.

Wynter's lips trembled as tears appeared in her eyes again.

"Oh honey…" Remington murmured as she took Wynter in her arms again, holding her and stroking her back soothingly.

It took a full ten minutes for Wynter to calm down long enough to tell Remington about the dream.

"It felt so real," Wynter said, looking pained.

"It wasn't real, babe. I'm right here," Remington said softly.

Wynter shook her head, still looking very haunted. "I can't lose you Remi…"

"You aren't going to lose me, Wynter." Remington said.

"I love you…" Wynter said, reaching for Remington's face. "Nothing is worth losing you for."

"Babe, there's been four whole deaths in the history of MMA and it's been around for more than two decades. Nothing is going to happen to me, okay?" Remington said, her tone sure.

Wynter put her head to Remington's shoulder, trying to push the vision of Remington from her dream out of her head. She shook her head. "I'm never going to forget that picture of you…" she said tearfully.

"I'm sorry, honey…" Remington said. "It was probably the reference to Rocky IV that did it."

Wynter nodded. "Probably, that part where Apollo Creed gets killed… It did have the kind of feel to it."

Remington kissed her forehead, closing her eyes slowly. "I'm sorry, honey."

They lay together for the next hour until Wynter could finally go back to sleep. Fortunately, she didn't dream again.

The first thing they heard about the next morning was that the picture of them on the stairs at the Thanksgiving celebration the night before had managed to go viral.

"Apparently someone in the family sent it to someone else in the family and they posted it on Facebook…" Wynter said, grinning as she looked at her phone. "You're famous again, babe," she said, winking at Remington.

"Great…" Remington said, not sounding thrilled in the slightest.

Later that morning, Kai Temple stood keenly watching Remington do sprints, her muscled arms folded over her chest.

"Knees up!" she yelled and saw Remington respond instantly. "Okay, bring it in," Kai called.

Remington moved back to stand in front of the trainer, breathing heavily.

"Let's do some body work," Kai said.

Wynter walked out to where Remington and the trainer were working. They were in a small building separate from the house. Remington had put it in for training when she was home, which was usually before every fight. There were bars of varied heights and poles, and various weight and workout equipment. There wasn't a machine in sight, however. When Remington trained, it was all manual work. She stood back so she wouldn't distract Remington. She looked Kai over; the woman was solid muscle, but still not even as tall as Remington. Remington had told her that this woman was the best though. Wynter began to see it as she put Remington through her paces. She had her doing body lifts from a sitting position, then laying down, then she moved Remington to the bars, having her lift her body, bend from the waist to one side, then straighten and then to the other. Remington's entire body was shaking as she moved, but to Wynter's complete amazement, Remington did everything she was told without fail.

That night, Remington was paying for the ultra-hard work out. She could barely move without wincing. Wynter ran her a bath, doing as Kai had told her and putting Epsom salts into the water.

"What the hell was I thinking?" Remington muttered as she slid into the tub.

"You were thinking that defending my honor would be easy?" Wynter suggested.

"Everything hurts…" Remington said.

Wynter grimaced. "I'm sorry babe…" she said, wishing she could do more.

There was a knock on the bedroom door then and Wynter went to answer it. It was one of Remington's cousins, Semina.

"Hi," Wynter said smiling at the girl who was just about her age.

"Hello," Semina said, smiling, "I heard that Remington is training again." She held up a basket. "I brought this for her, it should help with the soreness."

"Oh you are just in time." Wynter said, smiling brightly.

"Give her a kiss for me and tell her to take it easy," Semina said, hugging Wynter.

"Thank you, I will," Wynter said.

"Who was that?" Remington asked from the tub.

"Your savior," Wynter said, as she walked back into the bathroom with the basket. "Semina brought some essential oils over."

Remington sighed. "I do love her," she said, smiling.

Wynter looked through the basket and at the handy labels on the bottles. She opened one and smelled it, closing her eyes.

"Okay, this one is for soaking so..." Wynter said, putting the amount of drops into the water as the label instructed. "It says it's wintergreen and peppermint oils."

Remington leaned back, closing her eyes and sinking lower in the tub, inhaling deeply through her nose.

"Mmmm..." she murmured.

"Is that helping?" Wynter asked, moving to sit on the floor next to the tub, still looking at the items in the basket.

"Feels like it." Remington said her voice languorous.

"Oh, she loves you," Wynter said, grinning. "There's a body wash, a lotion and there's even a massage oil, oh and a salve too. It says it's for tougher spots."

"Yeah, is there enough for my entire body? 'Cause that's what I need right now..." Remington said, grinning.

Wynter laughed softly. "Well, no, but I'm sure we can request more."

After twenty minutes, Remington moved to sit forward, stretching her back. She gasped as she rolled her right shoulder.

"Uh-oh," Wynter said. "That's the bad one isn't it?"

"Yeah," Remington said, nodding.

"Okay, give me your arm," Wynter said, holding out her hand.

Remington looked back at her questioningly.

"Come on, Kai showed me a couple of things, plus I have this stuff," she said holding up a jar from the basket.

Remington moved her arm carefully, lifting it out of the water and toward Wynter. Wynter slid her hand on Remington's arm, feeling for the knot in her muscles and finding more than one.

"Oh babe…" Wynter said, grimacing, as she opened the jar with one hand.

She got some of the salve on her hand, rubbed her hands together and then slid her hand over Remington's bicep, moving her other hand at the same time over her shoulder. Remington hissed a couple of times in pain, but Wynter could feel the muscles relaxing under her hands.

"Just hold on babe…" Wynter encouraged. "I can feel things easing up… just hold on…"

A few minutes later, Remington relaxed again, sighing.

"Where'd you learn that?" she asked.

"Well, Kai showed me a couple of things; she knew you were going to be hating life tonight. But I also looked at some stuff on online."

Remington laughed softly, shaking her head. "Never stop learning things, do you?"

"Well, this whole training thing is new for me, so…" Wynter said, smiling.

"But you're not doing the training," Remington said.

"No, but the woman I love is, so I'm going to know what she's doing so I know how to help when she needs it," Wynter said, her tone matter of fact.

Remington smiled warmly. "Byen oke Lè sa a," she said.

"Meaning…" Wynter asked, her tone leading.

"Well okay then," Remington said, smiling.

An hour later, Remington was sitting up on the bed. She was icing her shoulder and her knee that had started aching wildly. Wynter had gone downstairs to retrieve some dinner for her and went back with two unexpected visitors.

"There she is…" Quinn said, grinning as she walked into the room.

"What're you doing here?" Remington asked, as she started to stand when she saw Xandy walk in behind Quinn.

"No, no, no!" Xandy said, putting her hands out at Remington to halt her movement. "You stay down, Wynter told us how hard you trained today."

Wynter sat on the bed handing Remington the plate she'd brought up. "All protein, no carbs, as promised," she said, winking at Remington.

"God, I'm gonna miss carbs for the next month," Remington said, shaking her head ruefully.

"After you beat Akasha's ass, I'll buy you the biggest plate of pasta you've ever seen," Wynter said, smiling.

"What if I lose?" Remington asked, as she cut up the fish Wynter had brought.

"Not gonna happen," Wynter said, her look sure.

"No it's not," Quinn said with a narrowed look.

"Nope, no way," Xandy said, smiling.

Remington looked at the three of them, shaking her head. "My own personal cheering section."

"Oh you ain't seen nothin'," Quinn said, grinning. "Everyone is gonna be there."

"Everyone?" Remington queried, even as Wynter tapped a nail on the plate, reminding Remington to eat.

"Yeah, even the attorney general herself," Quinn said, grinning. "Apparently her body guard, Kana Sorbinno, is a huge fan of yours."

Remington chewed her food, looking surprised.

"BJ is even chartering a larger plane so he can get more people to New York," Xandy said, grinning.

"You've got some of the heaviest hitters in the music industry coming to this fight," Quinn said.

"I heard Allexxiss is even pulling in fans from the movie business."

"Good God…" Remington said, shaking her head. "I better not lose."

"Stop that!" Wynter said, giving Remington a narrowed look. "You aren't going to lose. You're going to beat the living shit out of Akasha 'Veruca' Salt."

"And to do my part," Quinn said, "I know that Kai is going to be traveling with us, but I'm happy to spar with you too, if you need me to."

"Yeah, I'd really appreciate that, I need different fighting styles to respond to," Remington said, nodding. "Yours is very street, and that's Akasha's too, so yeah, that would be fantastic."

"You got it," Quinn said, nodding, "but we'll need to agree to pull punches," she said, grinning. "Or we both might be out of commission and useless to our girls here."

"I won't let this fight get in the way of protecting our girls," Remington said, smiling over at Wynter.

"Didn't think ya would," Quinn said, grinning.

Before long, they were back in New York and it was the night before the fight. The press had been all over Remington for days asking her how she was feeling about the fight. Her responses had been simply that she was ready. Wynter had been interviewed too, and her responses were much more vehement, since Akasha had stepped up her trash talk, and Wynter had been referred to a few times.

When asked what she thought of Akasha's assertions that Remington couldn't keep her, Wynter had replied, "Well, I'm in love with her, so I'm thinking Akasha Salt doesn't know a damned thing about women. Maybe that's why her own girlfriend tried to get to Remi before."

"Are you referring to Sage Baker?" the reporter had asked.

"Yes, I am," Wynter had said, her blue eyes sparkling as she looked at the camera. "No matter what she told Akasha, Remi would never come onto another woman's girl, that's not her style, and anyone that knows her, knows that for a fact."

"You're saying that Sage Baker lied about Remington attacking her?" the reporter had asked then, looking excited to be getting the juicy scoop.

"Remington LaRoché has more class in one pinkie finger than either of those women could even hope to have, she doesn't have to attack women. So, yes, I'm saying she was lying, and she needs to shut the fuck up. She also needs to stop calling Remi every five minutes, like she has for the last week."

"Well there you have it," the reporter had said, smiling from ear to ear.

"Did you really have to say all of that?" Remington had asked Wynter later that day.

"Yes," Wynter said, "I'm tired of Akasha talking about you like that. No one is telling her to shut up. So I did."

Wynter was not the only one to go on the record. After Wynter's interview, all of Remington's friends and even some of her previous opponents in the ring reported that Remington LaRoché was indeed one of the classiest people they knew and that she had integrity in spades. It only spurred ticket sales further. Within three hours of the tickets going on sale, they sold out.

The night before the fight, Remington and Wynter were cajoled into going out to a club. Remington was stunned by the amount of people there, and it seemed most of them were part of BJ's group. She received accolades from people that she'd never met, but whose music she'd listened to or whose movies she'd watched over the years. It was a surreal experience. At one point, she just needed to escape the insanity. She walked out the back door of the club and lit a cigarette, then stood in the back alley, smoking.

She wasn't completely surprised when Akasha walked out of the door she had. It was obvious she'd followed her. Remington was standing with her back to the wall, one booted foot up on the wall behind her. She looked over at Akasha, her eyes registering absolutely no emotion.

"So you ready for a beat down tomorrow night?" Akasha asked full of bravado and ego.

Remington looked back at her, chewing the gum in her mouth pointedly. "There aren't any cameras out here Veruca, so you really don't need to perform."

"Don't fucking call me that!" Akasha snapped.

Remington eyes flickered with amusement at how easily she'd gotten to the other woman.

"You know all those fancy friends of yours aren't going to help you in the ring tomorrow," Akasha said derisively.

Once again, Remington looked back at her impassively. "Good thing I can actually back up my talk."

"I'm gonna put you down hard," Akasha said, her tone all street.

"You're going to try," Remington replied mildly.

"You wait and see, Remi, you better be ready for your first defeat!" Akasha snapped.

Remington leaned her head back against the wall, her gesture dismissive.

"Don't fucking blow me off bitch!" Akasha snapped, striding over to get into Remington's face.

Fast as lightning, Remington tossed aside her cigarette and straightened from the wall, her stance at the ready.

"Remi?" Wynter queried from her right side. She'd come out of another door farther down the alley and had seen Akasha talking to her and then going at her.

Wynter walked up and put her hand on Remington's arm, looking back at Akasha with barely veiled disgust. Remington turned her head slightly, glancing down at Wynter, keeping Akasha in her peripheral vision.

"What's up, babe?" she asked.

"Quinn was looking for you," Wynter said, sliding her hand down Remington's arm to take her hand, wanting to pull her away from Akasha.

Remington's hand in hers was soft, but when Wynter took a step backward, Remington didn't move, her hand squeezing Wynter's gently. Remington turned then to face Akasha, keeping her hand in Wynter's.

"So, what is it your ego needs right now, Akasha?" Remington asked derisively. "Because I'm here with my girl, and I really don't feel like playing with you right now."

Akasha took a step forward. Remington's hand tightened in Wynter's as she pulled Wynter behind her, even though she gave no outward sign of noticing that Akasha was attempting to be threatening.

"Maybe we should just settle this now in front of your girl, that way I can take care of her after…" Akasha said, winking at Wynter.

"You can't even take care of your cage whores, Akasha, let alone a woman the quality of Wynter," Remington said mildly.

"Let's just see about that!" Akasha said, taking another step forward.

Remington extended her arm behind her, keeping Wynter back, even as she dropped one booted foot behind her in a fighter's stance.

"Come try," Remington said, her voice low and threatening, her look deadly serious.

Akasha noted the tone and the look and thought better of her actions.

"Nah," she said, waving her hand dismissively, "I'd rather put you down in front of all your friends, bitch."

Remington straightened, inclining her head cordially. "As you wish."

"What the fuck…" came an Irish voice from behind Remington and Wynter.

Akasha turned and went back through the door she'd come through.

"What the hell was that?" Quinn asked, walking up.

"Akasha just being Akasha," Remington said. "What's up?"

"Our little sound engineer wants to play somethin' for ya," Quinn said, grinning.

"Memphis?" Wynter asked, smiling.

"None other," Quinn said, grinning. "They got her guest spinnin' right now, so get yer ass in there."

"Well, let's go," Remington said, turning to lead the way back to the door.

Inside, Remington was hailed with applause and cheers. Memphis, the sound engineer for the tour was at the DJ's table, and pointing at Remington, her headphones half on and half off her ear. She leaned over to the microphone and said, "I've been lucky enough to be around Remington for this tour, and I gotta say, she's got some serious style… I put this together for you, Remi, hope you like it!"

The song started off with a techno back beat, that was more rock themed, then Linkin Park's "Hit the Floor" lyrics spoke over the music and said, "There are just too many times that people have tried to look inside of me, wondering what I think of you well I protect you out of courtesy. Too many things that you've said about me when I'm not around, You think having the upper hand means you gotta keep putting me down, but I've had too many standoffs with you it's about as much as I could stand, So I wait till the upper hand is mine!"

A number of people cheered as the song continued. Remington grinned at Memphis, appreciating that the girl had taken into account her taste in music. They'd had a few conversations about it during the tour.

The techno music took on a darker tone and Breaking Benjamin's lyrics to "Follow" were played over it. The lyrics "You know my head, you know my gaze, you'd know my heart if you knew your place!" caused more people to yell, "Yeah!"

The music morphed again into a hard driving beat, and Disturbed's "The Vengeful One" lyrics played over it. "So sleep soundly in your beds tonight, For judgement falls upon you at first light. I'm the hand of God, I'm the dark messiah, I'm the vengeful one." Memphis pointed at Quinn at that point, since it was a song that had once been attributed to the her. Quinn pointed right back at Memphis, smiling broadly.

The music moved to a guitar melody, and the lyrics to Queensrÿche's "Hand On Heart" played. "Hand on heart, A promise, a word and a voice. Hand on heart, A rhythm of hope and a vision of choice. Hand on heart, Promising, I'll never go, Hand on heart." Remington pulled Wynter back to her, her arms hugging her from behind, kissing her temple.

The music changed one last time, to the chorus of David Guetta's "Titanium" featuring Sia. The lyrics saying, "I'm bulletproof, nothing to lose, Fire away, fire away, Ricochet, you take your aim, Fire away, fire away, You shoot me down but I won't fall, I am titanium, You shoot me down but I won't fall, I am titanium."

It was definitely a statement on who Remington LaRoché was, and it had everyone clapping and cheering when the song ended. Remington and Wynter walked over to the DJ booth and Remington extended her hand to Memphis. Memphis, tiny compared to Remington, reached across to shake the other woman's hand.

"That was great," Remington said. "I'd love a copy of that."

Memphis smiled, happy that Remington had liked it. She'd been working on it since the Thanksgiving break when she'd heard that Remington had finally accepted Akasha's challenge. Grinning she pulled out a CD and handed it to Remington.

"I was hopin' you'd like it," she said with a broad smile by way of explanation.

Remington took the CD and slid it into her jacket pocket. "Thank you," she said, her face reflecting the gratitude she had for the younger woman's hard work.

"Catch me after this," Memphis said. "I'd like to buy you a drink."

"I'll buy you one," Remington said, smiling.

"Deal!" Memphis said, laughing.

A half an hour later, Memphis, Remington, and Wynter had a drink together. BJ walked up, leaning over to kiss Wynter's cheek, and extending his hand to Remington. He reached over mussing Memphis' hair with a fond look.

"Nice work," he told Memphis, "we gotta talk." Then he turned to Remington. "So you need anything before the fight?" he asked her.

Remington shook her head. "I'm good," she said.

"Hand that bitch her lungs," BJ said, his tone low.

Remington grinned, inclining her head.

BJ strolled off then. Remington and Wynter looked at each other, grinning. It was an interesting night.

Later they lay in Remington's apartment staring at the lights of the city. Wynter lay in front of Remington on the bed in the master suite. Remington held her from behind, her head above Wynter's on the pillow.

"Remi?" Wynter queried softly, unsure if Remington was asleep, because she'd been quiet for the last ten minutes.

"Hmm?" Remington answered, her mind having been on the fight.

Wynter turned over to look at her. "Have you made a decision yet about Los Angeles?" she asked, her look searching.

Remington blinked a couple of times, having to drag her mind back to the present. She took a deep breath and nodded.

"What did you decide?" Wynter asked, feeling her stomach tie into a knot.

Things with them had been good, but they hadn't had sex in a couple of weeks. Remington said that she needed to save all her energy and tension for the fight. Wynter believed her, because Remington didn't lie about things, but she also felt like they had lost a little bit of their connection because of it. Remington had been really distracted over the last couple of weeks too. Wynter knew it was to be expected, but she just worried that it wasn't just the pending fight.

"I'm not selling this apartment," Remington said, shocking Wynter who drew in a sharp breath in response. "Wait," Remington said, putting her hand to Wynter's cheek. "Let me finish babe. I'm not selling this apartment, because I want us to have a place to come when we're here in New York where we won't be bothered, okay?"

"When we come to New York?" Wynter asked.

"Yes, *we*," Remington said. "And as for the house in Los Angeles, I will move in there with you, but," she said, putting her finger to Wynter's lips, "I will be the one buying Lauren out, not you."

"Remi, that's a lot…" Wynter said.

"I've got it," Remington told her, "and I want to. If we're going to live there, it's going to be ours."

Wynter smiled tightly, with tears in her eyes. "Okay." She said.

"Okay," Remington said, smiling, then she leaned down to kiss Wynter's lips.

Wynter wrapped her arms around Remington's neck, kissing her back and pressing closer. Remington groaned against her lips.

"I can't babe…" Remington said remorsefully. "Not yet… I need all this tension for tomorrow night."

Wynter blew her breath out, nodding. "I know, I know, I'm sorry, it's just been so long…" she said, her voice full of longing.

"I know, I'm sorry," Remington said, "but trust me, it'll give me the edge I need."

Wynter drew in a deep breath, nodding again. "Okay."

The night of the fight finally came and Wynter could see that Remington was extremely focused. She became more and more quiet as the time for the fight drew closer. The entry into the Garden was, as always, theatrical. Remington had requested to use the compilation Memphis had done for her, both because she liked it, and she felt it was doing Memphis a favor getting it played for the crowd and everyone on Pay Per View. Remington also made sure it was announced as a compilation put together by Memphis McQueen. The cameras panned to locate Memphis McQueen who was sitting with Xandy Blue near the ring with the hood of her jacket up over her head. As she noticed the camera pointing at her, she pulled the hood down further.

"I hear a hit single here…" BJ muttered to Allexxiss, who laughed.

"You need to cut her in on the profits," Allexxiss said.

"As I will," BJ said, nodding.

Remington made her way to the ring, as Akasha came in to Rhianna's, "Bitch Better Have My Money."

Wynter and Quinn stood with Remington.

"Classy girl…" Wynter muttered as Akasha came in and threw up both middle fingers to the people booing her.

"Always," Remington said, grinning.

When Remington and Akasha were called into the ring, Remington kissed Wynter's lips, then looked into her eyes. "I love you," she said softly.

"I love you," Wynter replied, giving her a pointed look that drove her words home to Remington's heart.

The cameras clicked away, capturing every moment. Remington climbed into the ring and stood in her corner, her look like stone. Akasha was busy showboating for the crowd, making a show of her muscles and throwing her hands above her head, moving her head from side to side, hood-style. Remington simply looked on, a slightly sardonic grin on her lips.

When Remington was introduced to the crowd as the five-time bantamweight champion, she simply put her hands together in front of her chest, prayer-style and bowed her head to the crowd's thunderous applause.

When Akasha was introduced as the challenger, and it was made clear that this was not a title fight, Akasha screamed that it was because Remington was afraid she'd lose it. It was then explained by the announcer that it was not an MMA sanctioned fight. Remington just stood, moving her neck to stretch it, her look serious. Akasha of course did a victory lap and made a show of getting into Remington's face. Remington didn't seem to notice, staring straight ahead and breathing slowly.

"She's centering herself," Quinn said, standing next to Wynter.

"She can do this, right?" Wynter asked, voicing the slightest doubt for the first time.

"With both hands tied behind her back, love," Quinn said, grinning.

Wynter nodded, appreciating Quinn's bravado, but she was still terrified. Her dream had haunted her for weeks; it still came to mind every time she thought of the fight. Now she was about to watch Remington fight and she was doing her very best to be supportive and not put any of her fears on Remington.

Quinn glanced at Wynter, seeing the way her hand was shaking when she reached up to touch her forehead. Quinn took Wynter's hand in hers and gave it a reassuring squeeze.

Remington and Akasha went to the center of the ring for instructions, then went back to their corners. Remington winked at Wynter as she walked back over. Then she turned around, shifted her neck a couple of times, and then grew still. When the referee gave them the signal to start, Akasha immediately moved in. Remington let Akasha come to her, side stepping the first couple of swings, and shifting around Akasha slowly, her eyes watching Akasha's every move.

For a while Akasha made some half attempts to punch Remington. Remington simply moved her head to avoid them. Akasha bounced on the balls of her feet and then suddenly did a roundhouse kick to try and catch Remington in the head. Remington avoided the kick, but shocked everyone by stepping in, so that when Akasha followed up with a jab, it actually caught Remington in the face.

"What the fuck…" Quinn muttered.

"What?" Wynter asked worriedly as she saw Remington shift back out of Akasha's reach.

"She knows that's Akasha's big move… why did she step in…" Quinn said, shaking her head.

Wynter turned her head back to the ring, seeing that Remington's cheek was bleeding. She had to force herself to breathe as she continued to watch. Akasha's confidence grew, and she threw a series of punches, one of which would have struck home, but Remington put up a gloved hand at the last second.

Akasha did a round of the ring, acting like she'd already won the fight. Remington glanced over at Quinn and saw the perplexed look on the woman's face. She winked at her.

"Son of a..." Quinn said, as she started to grin.

"What?" Wynter asked, worried sick at the moment.

"Just watch," Quinn said, her eyes glowing with excitement.

Akasha made a move toward Remington again, this time going for a jab, and when she missed, she went in for a side kick. Fast as lightning, Remington grabbed Akasha's foot before it could connect, yanking the shorter, heavier woman forward, and took her down to the mat. Akasha hit the mat and tried to roll away but Remington was faster. She reached out a gloved hand and grabbed the other woman's shoulder, shoving her back to the mat on her back. Remington's fist lashed out, punching Akasha in the face twice. She got up then, and waited for Akasha to climb to her feet.

"What is she doing?" Wynter asked, thinking that Remington should have just kept Akasha down.

"Kicking her ass..." Quinn said.

Akasha, mad that she now had two solid hits against her, charged Remington. Remington braced and didn't move out of Akasha's path. She shifted so that Akasha's head missed her midsection, and wrapping her arms around Akasha's neck. Kicking out, Remington dropped to the mat, taking Akasha down with her. Once again, moving with the speed she was known for, Remington shifted and moved to kneel over Akasha's back, grabbing her from behind in a choke hold. She lifted Akasha's head off the matt and held it. Akasha tried to struggle to throw off the hold, but Remington simply increased the pressure on her windpipe, showing that she was more than happy to cause her to pass out.

"She's gonna tap…" Quinn said excitedly.

"She's gonna what?" Wynter asked.

As the crowd cheered and screamed for Remington, Akasha slowly put out her hand, finally tapping out on the mat. Remington held the hold for an extra second to prove a point, then got to her feet. The crowd went crazy.

"Wait, what just happened?" Wynter asked.

"She just won," Quinn told Wynter.

"And that, folks," said the announcer, "is what happens when lightning strikes!"

Epilogue

"So, let me get this straight," Wynter said, looking up at Remington as they danced at the victory party. "You let her hit you on purpose?"

Remington grinned, nodding. "I let her think she was actually scoring hits, yes."

"Why?" Wynter asked.

"Because it gave her the confidence to try something stupid," Remington said.

"Which she did by trying to kick you," Wynter said.

"Yes," Remington said.

Wynter shook her head. "Quinn thought you were crazy."

"I know," Remington said, grinning. "I saw her look."

"That's why you winked at her," Wynter said.

"Yep," Remington said.

Wynter shook her head again. "I wish I would have known. I was freaking out."

"Well, it wasn't an actual plan or anything," Remington said. "I could see she was hesitating, and unsure about her ability, I just used that to my advantage."

"Pretty smart there LaRoché," Wynter said, smiling.

"Mèsi renmen m ʼ," Remington said.

Wynter narrowed her eyes, putting her hand to Remington's lips when she started to translate. "I know this one… I think… you said thank you, love."

"Trey byen, babe, close. I said, 'thank you my love,'" Remington said, smiling down at her.

"Oh, that's the 'm " isn't it? My?"

Remington nodded, smiling.

"I'll get this yet," Wynter said, grinning.

"Here's a new one for you… Jwaye Nwel," she said, leaning down to kiss Wynter's lips softly.

"You got me," Wynter said, shaking her head.

"Merry Christmas," Remington said, smiling down at her.

Wynter glanced at the clock on the wall behind them. It was after midnight, therefore Christmas day officially.

"Jwaye Nwel," Wynter said, smiling up at Remington.

"Trey byen," Remington said, nodding.

"Since it's officially Christmas," Wynter said, smiling as she stepped over to the table where her purse lay. "I have something for you."

She pulled a small rectangular box out of her purse and handed it to Remington.

"What is this?" Remington asked, giving her a narrowed look.

"It's called a Christmas present, Remington, I'm sure you've heard of them," Wynter said, grinning.

"Komik… funny," Remington said, as she opened the box. She stared down at the item nestled inside in shock and awe. "Bondye…"

she murmured. "Wynter this is beautiful…" she said, her tone as awed as her look.

A pendant was nestled in the box, but not just any pendant, it was a highly stylized multi-layered fleur-de-lis with a gothic-looking cross running through it. The pendant was made out of some kind of metal colored in blue, silver, and dark gray. It hung on a thickly linked chain that was also multi-colored with lines of blue, silver, and the same dark gray.

"What metals are these?" Remington asked, touching the pendant reverently.

"Platinum, titanium, and blue tungsten," Wynter said, smiling.

"I've never seen anything like this before…" Remington said, shaking her head.

"That's because no one ever has," Wynter said. "It's custom."

"It's fantastic," Remington breathed. "Put it on me," she said, handing Wynter the box.

Wynter smiled, thrilled that Remington liked the pendant. She took it out of the box and put in on. Remington leaned down kissing her lips deeply.

"Thank you," she said, when she pulled back.

"Well, there's a little more to this," Wynter said, "but only if it's okay with you."

"What?" Remington asked.

"Well, I worked with a designer on it," she said, indicating the pendant, "and well, I talked to Tribal Hollywood. They have a line of MMA jewelry, right now just for guys, but they are really interested in a line representing you."

Remington's eyes widened. "Me? Why?"

"Uh, 'cause you're like awesome," Wynter said, smiling.

Remington blinked a couple of times, looking surprised. "What would I need to do?"

"Basically do what I did and work with the designer to come up with stuff that's exclusively you."

"I don't have any artistic talent whatsoever," Remington said.

"Well, I don't think that's true," Wynter said. "But I'm really happy to help. I was already thinking of something representing Satan."

Remington smiled, loving the idea. "Then we'd have to call it something that's both of us, not just me."

"Like what?" Wynter asked.

Remington look thoughtful for a moment, then started to grin. "What about Lightning Strykes, the strikes with a Y instead of an I like your name."

"I love it…" Wynter said, smiling.

"And I love you," Remington said, smiling.

"I love you," Wynter said, pulling Remington's head down to kiss her lips.

"So I guess since you gave me my Christmas present already, I can give you yours," she said, reaching into her jacket pocket and pulling out a small square box.

"Ah-ha," Wynter said, grinning. "We both had the same idea, apparently."

"I would say so," Remington said, smiling.

Wynter opened the box and almost stopped breathing. It was an incredibly beautiful ring set with sapphires and diamonds. She was further stunned when Remington went down to one knee and looked up at her.

"What are you doing?" Wynter asked, as everyone at the party stopped to look over at them. Even the music stopped.

"Well, I'm hoping you'll say you'll marry me," Remington said, smiling.

"Are you asking?" Wynter asked.

"I am," Remington said. "Ou pral marye avè m', Wynter, will you marry me?"

"Oh my God, yes!" Wynter said with tears spilling over. Remington stood up to kiss her lips as she did.

Everyone clapped and cheered. Wynter and Remington looked at each other, and then Wynter looked at the ring again.

"Oh Remi…" she breathed. "This is so beautiful… It looks vintage… Is it?" she asked, looking up at Remington with wide eyes.

"I was told it's a circa 1930s Art Deco piece," Remington said.

"Oh my God, it's so beautiful," Wynter said.

"They called it a 'mask shape,' it's French," Remington said, smiling. "And that's platinum that it's set in… I figured since you really liked that dress you got, and you said it was Art Deco…" Remington's voice trailed off as she grinned.

Wynter shook her head. "How did you have time to get this?" she asked. "You've been working and training non-stop since Thanksgiving."

"I had help," Remington said, grinning as Xandy and Quinn approached them.

Xandy smiled. "I helped her research a bit but she picked it out."

"You did an amazing job," Wynter said, grinning up at Remington.

"I'm glad you like it," Remington said.

"I love it!" Wynter said.

"Congrats," Quinn said, clapping Remington on the shoulder.

"Thanks," Remington said, smiling.

"This bodyguard thing is hazardous to one's single life," Quinn said, winking at Xandy.

"Oh, I dunno," Remington said, grinning, "it's not so bad." She smiled at Wynter.

"Not too bad," Wynter answered, smiling back at her.

"I love you," Remington said.

"Just remember that," Wynter said, winking at her.

"Bon Bondye…" Remington said. Good God.

Wynter simply laughed, nodding her head.

****

Back in Los Angeles, Memphis McQueen had just gotten home from New York. As she walked up the stairs, she glanced in the mirror. Her white-blond Mohawk still had touches of the red she'd had on the tips lately. *Need to make a change before I got back to the tour*, she thought to herself. Going into her room, she dropped her bags, and kicked off her black leather tennis shoes, pulling off her jean jacket and tossing it on the bed. She took off the multiple long silver chains she wore and hung them on her door. Wearing just her black skinny jeans and white tank top, she walked out into the hallway. She heard her roommate and best friend Oliver on the computer in the office.

"Hey," Memphis said, sticking her head into the office.

Oliver looked up, his brown eyes crinkling as he smiled.

"I saw the fight, it was fuckin' awesome! How was it being there?" he asked.

"Fuckin' awesome," Memphis said, grinning. "Did you hear my track?"

"Yeah, you're gonna get laid so much now," he told her, his grin wide.

"Yeah, 'cause that's my big goal in life," Memphis said, rolling her blue eyes.

"Hold on…" he said, looking back at the computer. "Damn it!" he exclaimed.

"What's the problem?" Memphis asked, walking into the room and looking at the screen. Oliver was chatting in some online forum.

"I can't get this chick to notice me," Oliver complained. "I've tried like a million times, she never even acknowledges my existence."

"That's 'cause you're ugly," Memphis said, grinning.

"Thanks, you're a big help," Oliver said, bumping his head against her arm. "Come on, what do you girls look for in a guy?"

"I wouldn't know," Memphis said, "I only look for girls."

"Okay, but what kind of thing catches your eye?" Oliver asked.

"A sense of humor," Memphis said.

"I've tried being funny," Oliver said, shaking his head.

"Yeah, but you're not funny," Memphis said. "Unless you count funny looking."

"Help me out, what do I say here?" Oliver asked.

"What's so great about this chick?" Memphis asked, moving to perch on the desk next to the computer.

Oliver clicked on the girl's profile, her ID was Kiery22, and brought up her picture. Memphis saw exactly what was great about her; she was beautiful. She had long light brown hair that was pulled to the side in one long braid, and the biggest most beautiful cornflower blue eyes Memphis had ever seen.

"Wow…" Memphis said, blinking a couple of times. "Hell, ask her if she's bi for me."

"Fuck you!" Oliver said, laughing.

"Never gonna happen," Memphis said, grinning. "We already had that conversation over a year ago."

"Well, I got dibs on this one," Oliver said.

"Yeah, if you can get her to pay attention to you," Memphis said, grinning.

"Help a brutha out!" Oliver whined.

"Oh holy Christ, fine!" Memphis said, looking at the words scrolling by in the forum.

After a few minutes, she said. "Okay, type this, 'and they say chivalry is dead.'"

"What? Wait!" Oliver said, trying to type what she said.

"Too late, ya gotta be faster," Memphis said, shaking her head.

"I can't type that fast, and read everything too!" Oliver said.

"Jesus, move," Memphis said, shoving him off the office chair and sitting down. She watched the screen, reading what was going on.

One guy was talking about how all the women in the room must be fat and ugly, because why else would they be there in the first place. Memphis narrowed her eyes, and began to type the words coming from Oliver's ID as Oh-Liver23.

Oh-Liver23 - Maybe they're here to talk to sweet talkers like you, Chad82

Chad82 – Butt out Oh-Liver!

Oh-Liver23 – But Chad you're so cute… come over here big boy…

Kiery22 – OMG Oh L too funny!

Chad82 – shut the fuck up Liver boy!

Oh-Liver23 – But Chad… you said you loved me…

Kiery22 – Oh, Chad, you cad! Shame on you!

Oh-Liver23 – Chad you've broken my poor heart… I'll never love again!

Breck-Good – Chad how could you hurt poor Ollie over there? He loves you so!

Chad82 – I'm no faggot!

Oh-Liver23 – Neither am I! I'm a gay man in a straight man's body!

Kiery22 – Poor Ollie, he's so confused!

Oh-Liver23 – Only you really understand me Kiery... marry me and we'll run away

together!

Kiery22 – Oh Ollie!

Oh-Liver23 – Oh Kiery! <cue music!>

Kiery22 – LOL Ollie you're brilliant!

Breck-Good – Chad seems to have grown rather quiet suddenly.

Oh-Liver23 – Chad? Honey? Babycakes? Sweetie pie????

Kiery22 – Does anyone hear crickets suddenly?

Oh-Liver23 - <listens carefully> I think that's the sound of an arsehole dying...

Kiery22 – Too right Ollie!

Moments later a private chat screen popped up.

Kiery22 – That was brilliant! I believe he's having a paddy as we speak!

Oh-Liver23 – Glad you liked it, What's a paddy?

Kiery22 – Where are you from?

Oh-Liver23 – California, Hollywood actually.

Kiery22 – Brilliant! I believe you American's call it a tantrum.

Oh-Liver23 – Well, babies do what they do.

Kiery22 – Indeed! I loved it, he was all mouth and no trousers anyway.

Oh-Liver23 – Good God, what is that? A man with no pants online, so shocking!

Kiery22 – LOL I know, so true! It means all talk and no walk or action.

Oh-Liver23 – That makes perfect sense now. Hey, BRB, okay?

Kiery22 – Come right back!

Oh-Liver23 – Of course, just for you.

With that, Memphis pushed away from the computer.

"She's all yours, I'm going to bed," she said, and walked out of the room.

You can find more information about the author and other books in the *WeHo* series here:

   www.sherrylhancock.com

   www.facebook.com/SherrylDHancock

   www.vulpine-press.com/we-ho

Also by Sherryl D. Hancock:

The *MidKnight Blue* series. Dive into the world of Midnight Chevalier and as we follow her transformation from gang leader to cop from the very beginning. *Building Empires* and *Empires Fall* available on Amazon now!

The *Wild Irish Silence* series. Escape into the world of BJ Sparks and discover how he went from the small-town boy to the world-famous rock star. *Sparks* available on Amazon now!

Printed in Poland
by Amazon Fulfillment
Poland Sp. z o.o., Wrocław